reasonable doubt

reasonable doubt

Marcia Argueta Mickelson

Bonneville Books
Springville, Utah

© 2007 Marcia Argueta Mickelson

All rights reserved.

The views expressed within this work are the sole responsibility of the author and do not necessarily reflect the position of Cedar Fort, Inc., or any other entity.

This is a work of fiction. The characters, names, incidents, places, and dialogue are products of the author's imagination, and are not to be construed as real.

No part of this book may be reproduced in any form whatsoever, whether by graphic, visual, electronic, film, microfilm, tape recording, or any other means, without prior written permission of the publisher, except in the case of brief passages embodied in critical reviews and articles.

ISBN 13: 978-1-59955-093-0

Published by Bonneville Books, an imprint of Cedar Fort, Inc., 2373 W. 700 S., Springville, UT, 84663
Distributed by Cedar Fort, Inc., www.cedarfort.com

LIBRARY OF CONGRESS CATALOGING-IN-PUBLICATION DATA

Mickelson, Marcia Argueta.
 Reasonable doubt / Marcia Argueta Mickelson.
  p. cm.
 ISBN 978-1-59955-093-0
 1. Women basketball players—Fiction. 2. Murder—Fiction. I. Title.

PS3613.I354R43 2007
813'.6—dc22

2007031547

Cover design by Nicole Williams
Cover design © 2007 by Lyle Mortimer
Edited and typeset by Annaliese B. Cox

Printed in the United States of America

10 9 8 7 6 5 4 3 2 1

Printed on acid-free paper

Para Jose y Cory Argueta—
Gracias por todo el amor y sacrificio

chapter one

The sound of thunder pierced the room, and Julia bolted upright in bed. She pressed her hands to her ears, bracing for the next jarring sound, but it didn't come. She looked around the room, and all was still. A glance at the clock told her she should still be asleep; it was only five o'clock. She edged her way to the window beside her bed and peered out into the looming darkness. There was no rain; the ground was dry and the dark sky was without a cloud. There had been no thunderstorm, only the one that lived in her head and made its way out at unexpected times to remind her she had no peace.

She lay back down and pulled up the comforter in an attempt to regain the sleep that was so elusive at times like this. It didn't come. She tried to shut out the memories that always came after the imagined thunderstorms, but the memories remained and taunted her. She threw back the covers in defeat. A long shower would lighten the tone of this gloomy morning.

After lingering in the hot shower, she drove to Brachman's to pick up a bagel with extra cream cheese to eat at work. Being at her office gave her a sense of order and purpose. She needed to escape the suffocating nightmare and the paralyzing feeling it created.

She licked a mouthful of cream cheese off the toasted bagel as she read the front page of the *Salt Lake Tribune*. She tried to start off each morning with a perusal of the paper and a few minutes of the early morning news on the small TV in her office. She discarded the paper as the local news on the television caught her attention.

"More details are coming to light about last week's murder on the University of Utah campus. The body of the Lady Utes' basketball player Avery Thomas was found last Monday afternoon in the women's locker room. The starting forward for the men's basketball team, Mick Webber, was arraigned yesterday for the murder. Webber and Thomas were engaged to be married, and many are finding this heinous crime hard to believe."

The news package transitioned to a personal interview with the victim's aunt. The woman held a hand to her forehead, steadying her shaking face. Her curly brown hair was in disarray, making her look older than her forty-odd years. Her face was dry of tears, but bloodshot eyes showed she'd been crying since the day she heard about her niece.

"My brother is destroyed. His little girl—she was all he had left. He's been raising her by himself since her mother died. And now she's gone." The woman paused, shaking her head. "We all trusted him, but look what he's done. He killed our Avery."

Julia tossed what was left of her bagel back into the small paper bag. Another gruesome crime committed against women by violent men. As a criminal law attorney, Julia had seen too many cases of men murdering their wives or girlfriends.

She hazarded another glance at the television, only to catch an image of the accused. He was so clean-cut, making it difficult for most people to believe he had committed the crime. *Oh, yeah,* she thought, *he's exactly the type.* She'd seen enough wolves in sheep's clothing to know a murderer didn't always look like one. True, a person was considered innocent until proven guilty. Julia knew that. It was how she made her living, but in cases like this it was almost impossible for her to keep that perspective. She had seen too many women hurt by men to believe Mick was innocent just because he said so.

Julia glanced at her watch; it was time to turn the TV off. Why did she watch the news anyway? It was so depressing. Not any more depressing than some of her cases, she thought as she scoured her desk for the two files she absolutely had to work on that day. She sifted through the contents on her desk but couldn't locate the files. She remembered placing the files on her desk the previous day right before she left, but they didn't seem to be anywhere. She didn't usually misplace things, especially something as important as client files. Julia looked around her office for a few more minutes, checking her bookshelves and file cabinet.

She sighed and looked at her watch again. She would have to wait an hour before Sandra came in. Then she could ask her if she knew where the files were. Eight o'clock was not early enough for the office to start operating. The receptionist really should be there earlier in case she was needed. Julia sighed again, this time more audibly. The kind of exaggerated sigh meant to let someone know you're annoyed. Only there was no one around to hear.

She dropped back into her leather swivel chair, allowing the comfort it provided to dispel her frustration a little. She'd recently done away with the cheap, standard chair Arthur had issued her and had splurged on the soft, luxurious leather office chair. Reasoning that she spent so many hours seated at her desk, she had paid for it herself. The old chair was relegated to a dusty corner of her office.

She spent the next hour checking email and researching a few old cases that were similar to the Santiago case, one of the files she couldn't locate. Teresa Santiago was a twenty-one-year-old woman Julia was defending against charges of accessory to armed robbery. Teresa had unknowingly waited outside a 7-Eleven while her boyfriend had held up the cashier. Julia's entire case was based on the fact that Teresa had no prior knowledge of the crime, but was simply waiting outside as the crime was taking place.

It was Julia's forte. Defending women was her self-appointed calling. Many of the women had allowed themselves to be lured into crime by placing their trust in untrustworthy men. Julia had built up a reputation for it and was now regularly recommended. Helping women was what kept her going, what made her so focused on her career. Defending men was also part of her job, and she did it successfully when called upon, but Arthur had come to know that when a case involved a woman, Julia would throw her heart into it. She spent the remainder of the time looking at one of her pro bono cases. She volunteered once a week at a women's shelter, giving legal advice to the women who couldn't afford attorney fees.

When she heard Sandra bustling at her desk in the outer office, Julia buzzed her. "Sandra, have you seen the Anderson and Santiago files anywhere? I could swear I left them on my desk yesterday."

The soft-spoken secretary cleared her throat before answering. "Mr. Stanley asked me to give the Anderson file to Mr. Kramer and the Santiago file to Mr. Turner."

"What? Why?" Julia pounded a fist on her desk. How could Arthur just take her cases away from her? She had already begun to do preliminary work on both of them.

"I'm sorry, Miss Harris. I don't know why."

"Well, what did he say?"

"He just asked me to give them the files. He didn't say why."

"Surely he said something. Try to remember."

Sandra paused. "He didn't say why."

"Okay," Julia said as she punched the speakerphone off. She pushed her chair back as she stood up, not caring that it hit against the wall. Arthur wasn't in yet; she knew that. Recent health problems had changed his working hours, and now Julia hardly ever saw him before ten o'clock.

Julia had worked for Arthur Stanley for five years now. He had been in solo practice for the thirty-five years he had practiced law in Salt Lake. When he had started having health problems

reasonable doubt

five years before, he'd hired Julia, who was fresh out of Harvard Law School, and later hired two additional attorneys.

She walked down the hall toward Adam's office. Of course, he wasn't in either. She spent several minutes looking on his desk, but it garnered her nothing. She opened a few of his drawers, but the Santiago file was nowhere.

"What are you doing?" came a voice from the open doorway.

Julia gasped. "You startled me," she said. "What does it look like I'm doing? I'm looking for my Santiago file. Why did Arthur give it to you?"

Adam smiled and sauntered in. He was in his early thirties and what most women would consider exceptionally handsome. With short blond hair typical of the "California look," Adam was of a formidable stature that would be intimidating to most. She had seen so many men like him at Harvard. He leaned against his desk and faced her. "I guess Arthur figured you couldn't handle that case. I think he's beginning to see my potential and realize you're not all there is around here anymore."

Julia dug her fingernails into her palms. She looked him in the eyes and managed a fake smile. "More like you couldn't handle any other case. A simple armed robbery, not brain surgery. Maybe Arthur couldn't find anything easy enough that you wouldn't screw up."

"I like your new suit, Julia. Calvin Klein?"

"Save it."

Adam got up from his perched position on his desk and placed his briefcase on it. "Isn't your biological clock ticking? I think Arthur figures you'll eventually trade your briefcase in for a diaper bag. He sees where the real talent is, and that's why he gave the case to me."

"Give me the file," Julia demanded. His demeaning comments didn't deserve a response.

Adam pulled a file out of his open briefcase. "Arthur gave it to me. If you've got a problem with that, go talk to him."

Julia turned around and slammed his door as she walked

toward her office. It was obvious he wanted to be the top dog in the firm, and the fact that a woman held more seniority than he did kept Julia in very low esteem. She tried to be indifferent to his deprecation of her; after all, he wasn't the first man to deride her because of her intelligence. But it was hard not to be hurt by his disparaging remarks. Adam was single, and Julia doubted he would ever find a woman who would measure up to his high standards.

She went into Arthur's office and waited for him. She sat in his chair and stared at the disorderly mound of files on his desk until she knew the tableaux so precisely, she could draw it from memory. She couldn't do any work. Her anger was not likely to dissipate until she had some answers.

Adam's hurtful words permeated her thoughts, and she couldn't make them go away. Perhaps it was because she had always been competitive with Bob Kramer and Adam Turner in the law firm. She worried about having the good cases given to the other attorneys and often resented the fact that Arthur went golfing with Bob and Adam. Although she still had a certain level of seniority over them, having been with the firm a full three years more than either of the two men, she still had to keep her guard up.

Having worked with Bob for two years, she didn't mind him so much; she could even tolerate his dry sense of humor. Julia had met his wife, Denise, a few times and even liked her. In his mid-forties and with more than his share of a receding hairline, she didn't find Bob threatening. He was amicable and had even tried to befriend Julia at first. He would ask her about her day, even seemed to care sometimes, but Julia had quickly put up a wall, indicating she was not interested in casual conversation with him. But still, she didn't mind Bob. Adam, however, was deplorable.

Somewhere around ten thirty, she heard Arthur whistling down the hallway. As he walked in, she stood up and crossed her arms. The stout gray-haired man walked in and greeted her.

Julia put her hands on her hips. "Arthur, why did you take my cases?"

Arthur moved toward his desk and took off his overcoat. She moved over to let him sit in his chair. He sat down and adjusted his glasses. "Julia, have a seat for a minute," he said, pointing to the chair opposite from his.

Julia crossed her arms in front of her chest and hesitated. She expelled a breath and then relented and sat down. "Why did you take my cases?"

Arthur frowned. She was close to crossing the line. Arthur was never overbearing or demanding. He was a kind boss, but he wouldn't accept disrespect. Julia's scowl dissolved as she waited for his answer.

"Those are easy cases. Bob and Adam can handle them. I have something for you that is perhaps the biggest case that has come across my desk. I have absolute faith in you and need your undivided attention on this case. Mick Webber. It's not only an immense case, but it also has personal significance. Mick is the nephew of one of my closest friends, someone I went to college with. I need you to take the case. You are familiar with it?"

Julia nodded, still in shock. Yes, she was familiar with the case. In fact, it had come close to ruining her almost perfect morning ritual. "I didn't know our firm was handling that case."

"We weren't. Mick's father originally hired McNeill, Baron, and Eaves, but he fired them yesterday when he got the impression they weren't convinced of his son's innocence."

Julia laughed. She knew McNeill, Baron, and Eaves's reputation. They were a high-scale law firm with top-paying clients, but the idea that they would believe in the innocence of their clients was laughable. They didn't care whether their clients were guilty or innocent, as long as they were paid top dollar. "So, do you believe he's innocent?"

Arthur nodded. "When his Uncle Clark called me yesterday and explained the situation, I was unsure. Clark and I go back a long ways. We were roommates our freshman year at the U and have remained good friends. He was the best man at my wedding. Anyway, I felt I owed it to him to at least meet Mick and consider helping him. I met Mick this morning, and my gut tells me he didn't do it."

"But the state thinks they have a very good case. I mean, they've charged him with capital murder."

Arthur shook his head. "All circumstantial evidence. We can get around it. You," he said, pointing at her, "can get around it. I know you can. I'm putting this case in your capable hands." Arthur pulled out a thick file from his briefcase and handed it to her.

Julia wasn't sure she wanted to get around it. Sure, she'd defended guilty clients in the past. She believed every person was entitled to a defense; that was why she'd chosen law as a career. But taking this case would mean potentially setting free a man who had murdered a woman in cold blood.

She took the file and opened it, not really focusing on it. Her mind was still reeling. Could she defend him? She looked up at Arthur. It didn't matter. What was important was that Arthur trusted her with such a monumental case. He didn't give it to Bob or Adam; he gave it to her, and she had to prove he'd made the right choice. "I'll start on it right away."

"I want you to go meet Mick tomorrow. I think you'll feel the same way I do. He's an innocent young man. We have to get him off."

Julia nodded as she stood up. She didn't know about the innocent part, but she would give him the best defense possible. "I'll give it everything I have." How could she have doubted Arthur? He believed in her, knew of her potential, and had just handed over the biggest case his firm had ever seen.

Julia spent the next two hours reviewing the facts of the case. Mick Webber was a twenty-three-year-old junior at the University of Utah. He was a returned missionary and active in the Church. He was the starting power forward for the Utes, who apparently were having an outstanding year, being ranked seventh in the nation.

According to friends, Mick had been dating Avery Thomas for about a year, and the two were planning to get married in the summer. Avery also played for the University of Utah as the

Lady Utes' starting point guard, having recently transferred from Weber State University. On February 20, after the Lady Utes finished a practice, Jennifer Jensen, a fellow teammate, entered the women's locker room and found Mick bent over Avery's dead body, the knife in his hand. Mick had stated he found Avery's body lying on the floor and, after checking her pulse, had instinctively pulled the knife out of her prone body. The coroner had stated that Avery died almost immediately after receiving ten stab wounds in her chest and abdomen. Mick pled not guilty, maintaining that he had not killed Avery, but had only found her lifeless body.

Some people in the community, including his father, were convinced of his innocence. Mick's father, James Webber, owned a small chain of sporting goods stores along the Wasatch Front. He was a wealthy man who had vowed to prove his son's innocence. The Webbers were highly active in the Church, and many people in their ward also stood behind Mick. However, the Salt Lake population at large, including Avery's family, wanted Mick convicted of murder.

Julia read an article in the *Salt Lake Tribune* that recounted Avery's background. She was the only daughter of Cal Thomas, a self-employed electrician. His wife had died of breast cancer when Avery was nine years old. He currently resided in Logan, Utah. According to the article, Cal would make the hour-long trips to Ogden to watch Avery play basketball when she was at Weber State. When she transferred to the University of Utah, he continued to make the trips, which were over two hours each way. He'd never missed any of her home games and had made long road trips to many of her away games. Julia was able to put a name to his sister, who she'd seen on the news broadcast that morning. Isabelle was her name, and she was quoted again saying that "Avery was all he had." What a sacrifice he had made to be at all her games. He'd probably turned down jobs in order to take the time to be at her games. And now what was there to show for it? Avery was dead, and Julia was defending her killer, or alleged killer, which was the proper term.

After reviewing the entire file, Julia closed it slowly and leaned back in her chair to think. There was some pretty overwhelming evidence—Jennifer finding Mick in the women's locker room, his fingerprints on the murder weapon. Those would be hard to explain, but as far as Julia could see, there was no motive. It certainly was a case she could argue, but it would all come down to meeting Mick. What would he be like? Arthur had been impressed with him, and Julia valued his opinion. But there was still her initial reaction to seeing his picture on the news. Avery's family was convinced he'd killed her. They knew him, and despite having favorable feelings toward him at some point, they now accused him.

Later that afternoon, Julia worked on a list of preliminary questions she would ask Mick tomorrow. After thinking about her new case for a while longer, she shut down her computer. Surrendering the comfort of her chair, she stood up. She picked up her leather briefcase and swung the strap over her shoulder. Pulling on her wool coat, she waved to Sandra as she walked out into the cool evening.

Julia drove to the YMCA for her weekly judo class. She'd been taking various self-defense classes since college, had already mastered Krav Maja, and had recently turned her focus to judo. Julia enjoyed her new instructor and felt that her moves were improving. As she followed the instructor's lead, doing each exercise carefully, Julia thought about the Mick Webber case.

She'd defended clients in the past who she believed to be guilty. That was part of her job, a key ingredient of the American justice system. The attorney's opinion of guilt or innocence was irrelevant. What made Mick Webber's father think that his son deserved an attorney who believed in his innocence? That arrogance only compounded what Julia was beginning to believe. Maybe it was her gut feeling upon seeing Mick's picture. Julia had come to rely on her gut and always paid heed to it. Or perhaps it was Aunt Isabelle's eyes, pleading for justice. He was Julia's client and she hadn't met him yet, but she was certain he had killed Avery.

The case was hers, and if she was successful, it could make

her career. She could become partner of the law firm. That was what was important now. Any lingering thoughts of Cal Thomas or Aunt Isabelle would have to be put aside.

After the hour-long class was over, Julia called in an order to China Moon. Her favorite restaurant's number was programmed on her cell phone. Sue, the owner, already knew Julia would be ordering beef and broccoli and pork fried rice. She drove the half-mile to China Moon, where her order was waiting for her. After paying for the take-out, Julia headed for her two-bedroom condo near Foothill Boulevard.

Julia ate in front of her computer like most nights. After checking and answering her email, she paid a few of her bills online. Then she logged on to the help forum website where she read and posted messages every few nights. Her particular interest lay in the rape help forum where rape victims posted messages, telling their stories, asking for help, or reaching out to other victims. The women who wrote were from all over the world. Julia had been posting regularly on the website for several years. For the most part, she offered advice, sometimes legal advice to rape victims who didn't have anywhere else to turn. Other times, she simply posted her story so other victims could find solace in knowing they were not alone. It was therapeutic for Julia to read others' messages of having survived rape, of feeling hope, and of finding love despite the hurt. She only hoped some of her messages helped the others as well.

As she read over the new postings, Julia realized it had been over two weeks since she'd last read or posted any messages. There were more than twenty new messages that had been posted over that period of time, with numerous replies for each one. She had been so focused on her cases the last few weeks that she hadn't taken the time to log on to the forum.

Some of the messages were posted by women she had previously chatted with, many like her, years beyond their horrible experience. A few of the messages had been written by new women who had never previously posted on the website.

Someone calling herself TLE99 had written: "I was raped,

and my attacker's trial begins soon. I'm petrified of testifying. It's like I have to relive it all over again in front of a bunch of people. He'll be in the room, looking at me. I really don't know if I can go through with it. Please help!"

Julia immediately empathized with the woman and wanted to reach out to help. She typed a message with words of encouragement, advice from a legal standpoint, and praise for the woman's courage to bring her rapist to trial.

The next message Julia read really struck her. REE22 wrote, "I can't believe I'm writing this down, but until I write it down or say it out loud, it's almost as if it didn't happen. I was raped by someone I know almost a month ago. I haven't told anybody. I can't tell anybody. This friend started showing interest in me several months ago, but I just ignored it. Now that he raped me, I'm so scared. Why would he do this? He says he has huge love for me. But how can you hurt someone you love? I've already waited too long and no one will believe me. What should I do?"

Julia's heart was pounding as she repeated in her mind one phrase: "I can't tell anybody." That had been Julia's motto for so long. That was perhaps why she still had incessant thoughts about that dark night more than eleven years ago when she had been raped. As her mind suddenly returned to that horrible day, she began typing, in hope of helping a woman who she had once been.

Her fingers moved furiously on the keyboard as she began her story. "I was a sophomore at Harvard when I was raped. Matthew was the smartest guy in my class, the picture of the all-American boy, and someone I thought I could trust. After he raped me, I felt the same way you do. I couldn't tell anyone. Who would believe me? He was so admired and well liked. I kept the ugly secret to myself and never sought help. To this day, I have not told a soul, not anyone in my family, not any friends. The only ones that know my story are the women of this forum who know me simply as IVYLG. I also didn't think anyone would believe me. After all, it was someone I knew, a man I even dated, not someone lurking in the bushes. I still regret that decision to stay quiet. I should have told someone, sought help a lot sooner, and worked through my feelings. I encourage you to tell someone. Anyone. Tell your mother, a relative, a friend, anybody. You shouldn't keep it bottled up inside you. You can't get over it by yourself. You have to rely on others. This is advice I never took, and I am still facing the consequences. The night it happened there was a thunderstorm going on, and to this day, I can't hear thunder without reliving that awful day. I know it's hard to trust others right now, after what happened to you, but please tell somebody. And if you want to, it's not too late to press charges. The longer you wait, the harder it will be. I am a lawyer and am willing to give you legal advice if you want it. Please let me know what else I can do to help."

After Julia finished typing her message, she took a moment to recover from the onslaught of memories that rushed back as she relived her harrowing experience once again. It was cathartic for her to share her experience, but it always took a while to recuperate from thinking about that traumatic day.

After typing a few more messages to women who had written asking for help, Julia logged off the website and curled up on the couch. As she thought about the women who had recently undergone the trauma of a rape, she wished she could do more. Julia wanted to reach out to them and help them, but beyond typing words of encouragement, there was little else she could do.

chapter two

The next morning, Julia indulged in a longer-than-usual shower. She dried her long, dark hair and then dressed in a tan pantsuit and dark brown ankle boots. Her dark wool coat was a necessity today. She walked out to her Acura and, after letting it warm up for a few minutes, edged her way onto I-80 toward downtown, along with what seemed like the rest of the world.

She arrived at her usual hour and remembered the time when Arthur used to be the first one there. Not so anymore. He had certainly changed in the five years she'd known him. When she had first met him, he was career-driven and spent long hours at the office preparing for his cases. Since he'd started having heart problems, he had reprioritized his life and spent much more time at home. For the past two years, it felt like Arthur was more of a figurehead, handling very little of the legal work in the office. He kept shorter office hours and delegated most of the cases to Julia, Bob, and Adam. He deserved it, she supposed. His years of hard work had built Arthur a reputation in Salt Lake, and thus his practice was still thriving. Now he was enjoying the fruits of his labor without having to labor as much.

Julia spent the next hour in her office. She logged on to the Internet and read several newspaper articles about Mick. She also read a short editorial about Avery's family. There were a few quotes from Aunt Isabelle, recounting how Avery had suffered a seemingly career-ending knee injury in high school. Despite doctors' claims that she would never play again, Avery had spent numerous hours in rehab and proved them wrong. Aunt Isabelle's brown eyes haunted Julia; the mere mention of her name brought an image of those bloodshot eyes to her mind. No matter how hard she tried, Julia couldn't push away the persistent image of Aunt Isabelle pleading for justice. It was as if the woman was in front of Julia, begging for her help, chiding her for agreeing to defend Avery's murderer. She tried to force the thoughts away, into the deep recesses of her mind where she kept unwanted emotions and feelings.

Her appointment to meet Mick Webber at the county jail was scheduled for nine thirty, and she wanted to be well prepared. Arthur buzzed her a little after nine, just as she was getting ready to leave. She walked into his office, where Arthur and another man stood up as she entered.

"I want you to meet Pablo Torres," Arthur said, signaling toward the man across from his desk. He was a Hispanic man, close to her age with an olive complexion and dark wavy hair that was neatly trimmed and combed. He wore a navy blue suit, which suited his tall frame.

She took a step toward the man and held out her hand. "Nice to meet you, Mr. Torres. I'm Julia."

Pablo shook her hand firmly. "Good to meet you, Julia."

"Why don't we all have a seat?" Arthur asked in a pleasant, relaxed voice.

Both men waited for her to take a seat first. "Actually, Arthur, I was just leaving. My appointment is at nine thirty," she said.

Arthur waved away her argument as he took a seat behind his grand mahogany desk. "I know, I know, but this will only take a minute, and it needs to be done before you leave."

Julia looked curiously at Pablo Torres and sighed as she took a seat. After she was seated, Pablo sat in the leather armchair next to her.

Arthur smiled graciously. "I've just hired Pablo as our newest associate. Our caseloads have increased over the last few months, and I plan on cutting back my time at the office a little more, so we need some more manpower."

Julia felt like rolling her eyes. Great! Another man being added to the already over-manned boys' club. Just what she needed. It was hard enough dealing with Bob and Adam. Now there was one more man to pit against her. "Okay," she said, not wanting to say what was really on her mind. "Was there anything else before I leave?"

"Julia, Pablo will be working with you on the Mick Webber case. He's going to second chair the case."

Julia nearly jumped out of her seat. "I don't need someone to second chair my case. I can handle it."

"This is not a request. It is an overwhelming case, and I know you can handle it, but I call the shots around here. We can't lose this case. Now, I don't doubt your ability, but the more help you can get, the better."

"But, Arthur—"

"Listen to me," Arthur said, putting up a hand to cut off further comments. "I gave my word to an old friend. I can't give it my personal attention like I used to. My doctor keeps telling me to retire. I need you to understand that I have to do all I can to ensure we win this case. Pablo is here to help you. You put him to work. I want him to go with you to meet Mick."

Julia wanted to argue, but she knew there was no use. Arthur had spoken, and she had come to know when she could get away with putting in her final word. This was not one of those times. She came quickly to her feet and walked toward the door. "I'm driving," she said.

Pablo stood up behind her and said a few words to Arthur before he followed her out the door. Julia quickened her pace and was already seated in her Acura with the engine running when Pablo opened the passenger door. She knew he was receiving a cold welcome to the firm, but she didn't care. It wasn't Pablo she was angry with. It was Arthur. He was so dense that he failed to recognize when he was overexerting his power.

She shifted the gears aggressively as she drove up State Street. In no mood for conversation, she concentrated on the drive. She was thankful that Pablo abided by her imposed silence, but it only lasted for a short while.

Pablo cleared his throat when she stopped at a red light. "Pez?"

Julia narrowed her eyes and turned toward him. "What?"

He held out a Superman Pez dispenser. "Have one. It always helps me when I'm stressed."

Julia shook her head. "I'm not stressed."

"So you're always like this?"

"Like what?"

"I'm sorry you're mad about working with me, but you shouldn't be. I was in the top of my class. I have a lot to offer, and I can help you on your case. I'll help you with whatever you decide: research, depositions, interviews."

Julia shifted into first as the light turned green. "It's not you; it's just Arthur. He would never do this to Bob or Adam. I'm always his dumping ground. I've been here longer than either of those guys, but he still treats me differently."

Pablo withdrew a few Pez and popped them in his mouth. "Well, I apologize that you perceive I'm being dumped on you, but this is my case too. This job is important to me. You're not the only one who has something to prove."

Julia shrugged as she stopped for another red light.

"So, Arthur tells me you went to Harvard," Pablo said.

Julia nodded.

"Undergrad or law school?"

"Both," Julia said, turning to look at him for an instant before she shifted to proceed through the intersection. "What about you?"

"ASU for undergrad and BYU for law school."

Julia didn't comment as she pulled into the county jail parking lot. "So did Arthur fill you in on the details of the case?"

Pablo nodded. "He told me the basics. I've also been following it in the news."

Julia grabbed her briefcase out of the car and led the way toward the jail. Pablo followed behind her as they were cleared through security and led into a small visiting room. A bright fluorescent light illuminated the deep scratches that had been etched over time in the small table below. Boredom or frustration had driven the previous occupants to engrave the table with permanent imprints of their stifling time spent in that room. Several minutes later, a guard led Mick Webber into the room. Mick's eyes went from Julia to Pablo before he proceeded into the room and sat across from them.

Mick Webber wasn't what Julia had expected. From the articles she had read, he was a campus superstar, the highest scoring member of his team. She had expected an arrogant, confident man to saunter toward them with his shoulders held high. Instead, the man who dragged his feet to the table was a tall, gaunt, sallow-eyed individual who didn't have the least air about him. His face was thinner than in the pictures she had seen, with hollow features that made him appear older than his twenty-three years. His dark brown hair was longer than it had been in the pictures. And wearing the county jail issue, Mick Webber seemed far from the handsome young man she remembered glimpsing on the news.

Julia introduced herself and Pablo to Mick, who politely greeted them. "Mick, you are aware your father retained Arthur Stanley's firm as your new counsel?"

"Yes, ma'am."

"And you're okay with that?"

Mick shrugged. "I think so. If that's what my father thinks is best."

Julia smiled. "Okay, then. I will be representing you, and Pablo will be working as my co-counsel."

Mick only nodded. He sat across from her, his arms crossed on the table. His eyes were glassy and downcast, and Julia could sense that he was only a fragment away from breaking down.

"We are both here to help you. Our main objective is to get you released. I want you to trust me, but I also have to know that I can trust you. I need you to be completely truthful about everything. Don't hold back anything, even if you think it won't matter. Okay?"

Mick nodded.

"I want you to start from the beginning, when you found Avery, and tell us everything. I know you've already done this several times, but I need to hear it from you."

"Okay," Mick said, straightening up in his chair.

"Is it okay if I tape record what you say so we can refer back to it?"

Mick nodded as Julia pulled out a small tape recorder from her briefcase. She noticed that Pablo took out a small notebook, which he placed on the table. She pressed the record button and then urged him to start. "So you were supposed to meet Avery outside the arena?"

"I waited for almost twenty minutes, and then I went to look for her. The arena was empty by then, and I had seen almost all her teammates leave, so I thought it was strange that she hadn't come out yet. When I got to the locker room, I called her name a few times, but when she didn't answer, I went in."

"About what time was that?" Julia asked.

"It was a little past five, but not quite five thirty."

Julia jotted down a few notes. "Did you see anyone when you first entered?"

He shook his head. "And I didn't see her at first, but as I went in further—" Mick grasped a hand to his face, covering it almost entirely with his big hand.

Julia looked away; she couldn't watch the large basketball player sob openly. She shifted in her chair. It was probably made of the hardest wood she'd ever felt. After several minutes of self-imposed silence, Mick wiped his tears and looked up again.

"I saw Avery lying on the floor. There was blood on her shirt. I ran to her and felt her neck, checking for a pulse, but she was gone." Mick looked down at the table, his hand covering his eyes.

"Go on," Julia said.

"A knife was stuck in her chest, and I pulled it out."

Julia shivered. It hadn't seemed that cold when she'd first entered the room. "Why did you pull it out?"

"Instinct, I guess. I know it sounds stupid, but I wasn't thinking. You don't think about fingerprints when your fiancée has a knife in her chest."

"How long were you in there before Jennifer Jensen came in?"

"About a minute."

Julia saw that Pablo was writing in his notebook, but his hand blocked her view. She turned back to Mick. "What time was it when Jennifer came in?"

"I don't know. I wasn't paying attention to the time."

"What was Avery wearing?" she asked.

"I don't know. I don't remember."

"Was it her uniform?"

Mick closed his eyes for a moment and then shook his head. "I don't know."

Julia leaned forward in her chair. "What did Jennifer say? What did she do?"

"She screamed, and I think it sort of brought me back into reality. I realized what it looked like and dropped the knife, but she was already out the door. The police came shortly after, and I guess you know the rest from there."

Julia nodded.

"It still seems like a nightmare to me," Mick said.

"Do you have any idea who would do this?" Pablo asked, speaking for the first time.

Mick shook his head. "No. Everyone loved Avery. She was so good; I can't imagine anyone not liking her. In a sense, she was the leader of her team. They all looked up to her. She played the point, so everyone always seemed to turn to her, and not just on the court. There's not a single girl on that team who didn't love Avery."

"You said you saw the other girls leave the practice while you were waiting for Avery?" Julia asked.

"Yes."

Julia wrote a few notes on her legal pad. "So they must have seen you too?"

"Yeah."

"Well, we'll be sure to get their statements and compare the time they saw you with the time of death," Pablo said, almost reading Julia's mind. "It's as close to an alibi as we can get."

Julia and Pablo spent another ten minutes asking Mick questions, taking notes as he answered. As Mick related the events of the past week, Julia wondered if he was capable of killing a girl he said he loved so much.

As they walked toward the car, the chill of the morning still hadn't succumbed to the sunlight beginning to peer over the mountain, and Julia shivered slightly. In the car, she turned the heater on high and waited for the car to warm up before going.

"So, what do you think? Do you think he did this?" Pablo asked, interrupting her thoughts.

"It doesn't matter whether I think he did it."

"I think he's innocent," Pablo said.

"What? You think he didn't do it just because he said so?"

"No, I just don't get the impression that he did it."

Julia laughed as she backed out of the parking spot. "So you can tell if a person is guilty or not by what? Just looking at them?"

"No, but—"

"Listen, Pablo. Let me give you a word of advice. Most of the clients you will represent are guilty. It's a rarity, albeit a pleasant one, when you can defend an innocent person. Every defendant has the right to counsel, but not necessarily the right to have their counsel believe in their innocence. You can't be so naïve as to believe that your client is always innocent."

"I'm not being naïve because I don't believe Mick did this. I can have an opinion in this matter, right?"

"I guess so, but I still say you have a lot to learn."

The rest of the drive back to the office was done in relative silence as Julia mulled over different ideas about how to approach

Mick's defense. Arthur's earlier statement came back to her. Mick's father had sought a new attorney because the first hadn't believed that Mick was innocent. Although both Arthur and Pablo believed Mick had not committed the crime, what would his father say if he knew that she still believed he was guilty?

Once they were back in her office, they worked on a list of people to interview. They would be receiving statements from various witnesses the next day, which would answer some of their questions, but Julia wanted to have a tentative list ready. She then put on her headphones and listened to portions of Mick's statement, trying to catch key details that needed to be probed further. How long had Mick been in the locker room before Jennifer Jensen walked in? Was it possible for someone to be naïve enough to touch a murder weapon? Or was it his way of covering up the fact that his fingerprints were all over the murder weapon? She listened to Mick Webber's voice, wondering if it was the voice of a heartless killer. She glanced at Pablo, who was reading over his notes. She wondered what he had perceived to be important, but she didn't want to ask.

chapter three

Pablo watched Julia as she wrote furiously on her legal pad. She was deep in thought and was absolutely dedicated to her task at hand. He'd noticed her before. A few days prior, when he came to discuss the job offer with Arthur, Pablo caught a glimpse of Julia in her office. She didn't see him, but he watched her for a minute as he walked down the hall. He was initially drawn by her long, black hair. It was what most attracted him to a woman. She was beautiful; that was not in question. Even her unfriendly demeanor did not detract from her beauty. But what was it that brought about her surly deportment?

She made no effort to disguise her displeasure in working with him. He felt like an intruder, but that was just the way it was going to have to be. This was his case too, and he had to delve in.

As he used Julia's computer to browse the Utes' website, he looked at the bios and pictures of Avery and her teammates. All of her team members would have to be questioned thoroughly. He began writing some of the names down and then decided it would be easier if he could get his hands on a media guide. Pablo was always more visual, and if he had a media guide with all the information he needed, it would be easier to formulate thoughts and questions. He looked up for a moment and noticed Julia watching him.

Julia chewed on the tip of her pen. "What did Mick mean when he said Avery played the point?"

"She was the point guard. You know, she brings the ball down court, passes to the others, initiates plays, does most of the ball handling."

Julia nodded. "So do you think the other players were jealous of her?"

"Not really; maybe the second string point guard."

"Second string?"

Pablo laughed. "Do you know anything about basketball?"

She shook her head. "Nothing."

"Well, the second string point guard comes off the bench. She doesn't start, but comes in when the coach takes Avery out of the game."

"So, who was the second string?" Julia asked.

Pablo turned back to the website. "Lexy Andrews."

"We'll have to question her," Julia said as she pulled the pen out of her mouth and jotted something down on her legal pad.

"I agree," Pablo said, turning in Julia's swivel chair to face her. "Have you ever been to a basketball game?"

"Not that I can recall," she said, not looking up from her legal pad.

"You've never seen Mick Webber play?"

"I've never even heard of Mick Webber until after Avery's murder."

"Well, I saw him a couple of times when the Utes came down to Provo to play the Cougars. He's phenomenal."

Julia continued scribbling.

"I think you should go to a basketball game. If you can learn to understand the game, you'll understand Mick. Basketball is a way of life for him; it has to be so devastating to sit in that jail cell and not be able to play with his team."

Julia shrugged. "Maybe I'll try to go to a game sometime."

"The regular season's over, but the Mountain West Tournament is starting next week. I think we should go and see Mick's team play. You might get some insight into him."

Julia considered it for a moment. "Okay. Why don't you take care of the tickets and give Sandra the receipt? She'll reimburse you for them."

"Okay," Pablo said, turning back to the Internet to find out the site of the tournament. Luckily, it was being held at the Energy Solutions Arena in Salt Lake City this year, so at least they wouldn't have to travel anywhere to see it.

Arthur walked in a few moments later as Pablo and Julia were discussing the list of people they wanted to interview. They filled him in on their meeting with Mick and talked about a few of the facts.

Sandra buzzed in to tell Arthur he had a phone call, which he picked up on Julia's extension. After a brief conversation, Arthur turned to Pablo.

"Pablo, do you play golf?"

Pablo smiled. "I live to play."

"Good. Adam and I had a two o'clock tee time, but he's in court and the judge called a recess. They readjourn at two thirty, so he won't be able to make it. Why don't you come with me instead? I hate to golf alone."

Pablo could never turn down a golf game. Asking him not to golf was like asking him not to breathe.

"We can rent a set of golf clubs for you at my club."

"Well, actually, I carry my clubs and shoes in my trunk. I never know when I'm going to get the urge to go hit a bucket of balls. It's sort of a stress reliever for me."

Arthur laughed. "A man after my own heart. And to think I didn't even know you played before I hired you. It was like fate."

Pablo considered the offer. It was one he'd normally accept in a hurry, but stress lines around Julia's eyes made him rethink his haste to accept. "Are you sure I should take time away from this case right now?"

"It's just for a few hours," Arthur said. "So, how did you get so interested in golf?"

"My father was the head groundskeeper for a country club in Phoenix. I used to go help him sometimes, especially Saturday mornings. I also caddied all through high school and played on the ASU team for a couple of years."

"They have an excellent program. I'm impressed. ASU is perhaps one of the best in the nation."

Pablo nodded. "I really learned a lot playing for ASU."

"I see I have a pretty good game on my hands. That's good. Adam and Bob are no competition for me. Sometimes I get bored playing with them. I like being able to play with someone who can compete with me," he said, nodding. "I'm really looking forward to this game. Why don't we leave at twelve thirty and grab some lunch at the club before our game?"

Pablo agreed, feeling a little overwhelmed by Arthur's friendliness. It didn't seem right to have the boss take him to lunch and a game of golf on his first day. More than that, the lines around Julia's eyes intensified and she vacillated between pursing her lips and biting them. She didn't say anything throughout their conversation, but as she chewed on her bottom lip, Pablo wondered if he should rethink it. Too late. Arthur left, and Pablo was alone with an angry woman.

He attempted to steer the conversation with Julia back to the case, but she was fired up. It was after Pablo asked her a second question regarding one of the witnesses that she threw her pen on the desk, missing his hand by only an inch.

She pulled herself up, grabbed her coat and briefcase, and walked toward the door. "I'm going to lunch."

Pablo shook his head at the slammed door. Just when things started to go a little more smoothly between them, the golf game had ruined what was the beginning of a working relationship. He turned back to the computer and continued the research he'd begun. At least he could get some work done in the hour before he had to go with Arthur. He would worry about damage control with Julia after golf.

reasonable doubt

* * *

Julia slammed the Acura door closed as she took her keys out of her coat pocket. Starting the car, she pulled out into traffic and worked her way up State Street to Mi Ranchito. Their chicken enchiladas always made Julia feel better. It was only eleven thirty, so the lunch crowd hadn't made it in yet. Julia sat in a quiet corner booth, waiting for the waitress to bring chips and salsa. After she was served, she ate silently, thinking about what it was that really bothered her.

Arthur had slighted her yet again in favor of the new guy. Golf. It was the one thing that set her apart from the other attorneys. She didn't know how to play, but Arthur didn't even know that because he'd never asked. The law firm that had once run so smoothly with she and Arthur working case after case in unison had now become a regular old boys' club. Recently, golf and Jazz games had become more important to Arthur than winning cases. There didn't seem to be a time when Arthur wasn't inviting Adam and Bob to go to a Bees or Jazz game, to play golf, go hunting, or over to his house to watch the Super Bowl. She was completely left out. Not that the simple fact of being left out bothered her. It went deeper than that.

Arthur had hinted he was thinking of taking on a partner so he could cut back even more. She wanted to be named partner, but it didn't help that she was constantly being left out of everything. She didn't know what they talked about during their boys' club outings, but Julia felt certain it was about work. They probably mulled over cases, with Bob and Adam swaying Arthur to give them the better cases. Being left out of those golf meetings precluded her from learning Arthur's more personal thoughts about the law firm. And now Pablo had been welcomed in with open arms, further isolating Julia.

As Julia savored the tasty chicken enchiladas, she became determined that she would be named partner when the time came. She would prove, through her efforts in managing cases and her performance in the courtroom, that she was the best attorney in the firm, thus deserving to be Arthur's partner. STANLEY AND HARRIS. That is what the sign over their office would read.

Julia lingered at her table, watching the lunch mob crowd in and then thin out. She was in no hurry to get back to the office. There was no way she would risk running into Pablo before he left with Arthur. She could still see Pablo's smug face as Arthur raved about Pablo's love of golf. His look of self-satisfaction had instantly incensed her. He had one up on her, but it would only be temporary.

As she went up to pay, she watched a woman helping a baby out of a high chair. Julia recognized her from Smith's grocery store. She was a cashier, and Julia had once overheard the woman saying to another coworker that her husband had "left for good this time." There were two little boys seated at the table with her, and Julia wondered how the woman managed with three children. As the man behind the counter rung up Julia's check, she kept her eye on the woman as she prepared to go, coaxing her boys into their coats.

"I'd like to pay for her check as well."

The man looked to where Julia pointed. "For her? Were you with her?"

"No, but I'd still like to pay."

He shrugged and rang up both checks. Julia wrote him a check and slipped out the door just as the woman and her children approached the counter.

That evening after dinner, Julia sat in front of the computer. She wanted to check the new postings in the help forum. Julia was eager to see if the women she had responded to had posted anything new. She was particularly worried about the woman who had recently been raped and hadn't told anyone. Julia had lived through that nightmare and knew that the woman needed to reach out for help. She hadn't replied, and Julia only hoped that at least the woman had read her message. She once again posted another message for the woman, encouraging her to seek help.

Julia also took a moment to read a post from the woman

reasonable doubt

whose trial had begun. It seemed that opening statements had gone well, and the woman felt hopeful about the ensuing trial. Once again, Julia typed a message of optimism and support. She read and posted a couple more messages before shutting down the computer and retiring to her bedroom.

After a day filled with disappointment in her job and discouragement with her new case in which she could possibly be defending a murderer, Julia needed comfort. Turning to the scriptures was always the answer at times such as this. Julia fingered the worn leather of her scriptures, thankful for the solace they had brought her during times of desperate loneliness.

She read Hebrews chapter 11. By faith, the children of Israel passed through the Red Sea, and by faith, the walls of Jericho fell. Faith brought about mighty miracles. Having faith could bring her the peace she craved, if she just endured. After letting the soothing words comfort her needy soul, she said a prayer, expressing all the pain and hurt she felt in her heart. She gave thanks for all of her blessings and asked for the fortitude to deal with the obstacles she would continue to face in her life.

The next morning, the radiance of the sunlight that filtered through her sheer curtains gave Julia a sense of renewal. She was ready to face the day, prepared for whatever challenges she would meet. After a shower, Julia dressed in black suit pants, a freshly starched white blouse, and a tailored black jacket that matched her pants.

The parking lot wasn't empty when she arrived at the office. An old Volkswagen Jetta was parked in one of the stalls in front of the office. Julia looked around to see if the owner was nearby, but it wasn't completely out of place for a vehicle to be parked there. Once in a while, friends of the tenants that lived in an apartment complex behind the office parked their cars there. Oftentimes on Mondays, she would find the lot almost full of the apartment dwellers' guests, who had spent the weekend partying there. Usually by the time the office opened for business, most of the vehicles had left.

Julia slid her key into the keyhole and pulled on the handle, but it was already unlocked. Why would the office be unlocked when Sandra's car wasn't there yet? She usually came in a little later. Fear crept into Julia as she turned around to eye the unfamiliar Jetta. Could the owner of the car be in the office? And how did he get in? Should she get back in her car and drive away? Should she call the police? Or should she go inside and face whatever or whoever awaited her? Thoughts of helplessness so many years ago collided in her mind as she decided to venture inside. Although fear had left her paralyzed many times since her rape, she was not going to allow it to overcome her ever again.

Julia quietly pushed the door open and surveyed the front lobby. Nothing seemed out of place, so she continued farther into the office. The light was on in her office at the far end of the hall, and she slowly approached it. Silently, she peered through the open doorway and saw Pablo seated behind her desk. Arthur had mentioned that she was to share her office with Pablo until they could find him his own office space, but where did he get off just taking over her desk? And didn't he look comfortable in her leather chair?

She walked briskly into her office and placed her briefcase down beside the reports that Pablo had been reading. "I see you made yourself comfortable in *my* chair."

He looked up. "Good morning to you too."

Julia shook her head as she pulled off her coat and threw it on an empty chair. "What are you doing here so early?"

"I wanted to get a jump-start on the day."

"So Arthur gave you a key? Well, when you sneak in here in the mornings, you really should lock the door behind you. You about gave me a heart attack when I saw the unlocked door. If there is no one in the lobby, lock the door. Someone could just waltz right in here and you wouldn't know it."

Pablo sighed. "All right. I didn't realize we were in such grave danger of having people waltz into the office."

Julia ignored his sarcastic remark. "So that's your old Volkswagen out there?"

Pablo nodded. "What? Did I take your parking spot too?"

"No. I just wanted to know."

"Can we get past the trite remarks and get to work?"

"Okay, but that's my chair. You can have this one." Julia pulled her old chair from the corner and placed it next to her leather swivel chair. "Here," she said.

After he vacated her chair, she sat down to read through Mick's initial police statement. She wanted to compare it to what he'd said to her the day before.

Later that morning, the law firm of McNeill, Baron, and Eaves sent over its entire file on Mick Webber via messenger. Julia and Pablo spent the next two hours combing through the arrest and police reports, witness statements, arraignment transcripts, and the autopsy report.

A little after noon, Adam sauntered into her office. His boisterous voice shattered the quiet of the room. Without even a glance at Julia, he walked toward her desk and introduced himself to Pablo, who was seated next to her. Pablo rose to greet him.

Adam shook Pablo's hand. "I'm Adam Turner. It's nice to meet you. I apologize that I didn't get a chance to meet you until now. I've been a bit overwhelmed with my cases, as well as a couple I had to take over from Julia."

Julia continued reading through her file, pretending his statement didn't affect her.

"Nice to meet you," Pablo said in return.

"Arthur tells me you're a pro on the golf course. We should get together to play sometime. I'm always up for a challenge."

"Sure. I never turn down a game."

Julia wished Adam would finish with his pretense at civility and leave her office. Much to her disappointment, Adam took a seat across from her desk and continued his conversation with Pablo. She persisted in ignoring him and tried to concentrate on the file she was reading.

"I came by to see if you wanted to join me for lunch. I'm meeting Bob downtown. He's also been wanting to meet you."

"Sure, I think we both could use a break." He looked at Julia, who glanced up at that moment. She quickly looked back down.

The last thing she wanted to do was have lunch with the three of them.

She could feel Adam's eyes on her as he talked. "She never wants to come with us. She'd rather stay holed up in here and eat in front of her computer."

Again, Julia let Adam's remark slide. There was no way she was going to let him have the satisfaction of knowing she was bothered by what he had to say. Not getting the reaction he sought, Adam rose to his feet.

"Well, Pablo, I'll probably leave within ten minutes. I'll drive if that's okay. I just got a new sound system installed in my 'vette. You have to check it out."

"Uh, okay. Sounds great."

"Good. Well, I'm glad Arthur hired you. Julia's going to need a lot of help with this case he just gave her."

Julia slammed her file down and looked up. "I don't need help. I can win my cases by myself."

Adam smirked and settled his hands into his pockets. "Well, I'm just surprised Arthur would give this case to such a man-hater. You'll probably botch the case on purpose just to put another man behind bars. That's where you think we all belong, right?" he said with a smile.

"Some more than others. Now leave. A few of us are actually trying to work around here."

Adam winked at her. He waved and then turned around to walk out. She watched Adam leave her office and then refused to meet Pablo's gaze. He probably had a cocky grin waiting for her. Men always stuck together.

"I take it you two don't get along," he observed.

Julia sighed and glanced over at Pablo's perplexed look. He wasn't grinning at all. "What do you think? How could anyone possibly get along with a man as egotistical as that?"

"I'm sorry. He shouldn't talk to you like that. If you don't want me to have lunch with him, I won't."

Julia was shocked. Did she hear him right? Did he actually care what she preferred? "What do I care? This whole office is a boys' club. You now have your exclusive invitation to join, so don't decline on my account."

Pablo shook his head and got up. He grabbed his suit jacket and left her office, closing the door behind him. Julia threw her pen at the closed door. To add insult to injury, Adam had now maligned her in front of Pablo. For some reason, being disgraced in Pablo's presence intensified the humiliation. Being harassed by Adam was recoverable. Having Pablo witness her embarrassment was like being scolded by her mother in front of her friends. But Pablo was not her friend, and she shouldn't care. But she did.

chapter four

On Thursday, Julia and Pablo were still knee-deep in research. Julia was baffled at how easily they had indicted Mick. All of the evidence was circumstantial, not one shred of motive or intent. Of course, they had the prints on the murder weapon, and then there was Jennifer Jensen, Avery's teammate. She could be considered an eyewitness, but Jennifer didn't actually see Mick stab Avery. Jennifer came in after the fact and saw Mick standing over Avery's body, but that alone couldn't implicate Mick. There were still so many extenuating circumstances. Several of Avery's teammates had seen Mick standing outside the arena, minutes before the estimated time of death.

Pablo had compiled a list of all the people Mick remembered seeing as he waited for Avery. Julia and Pablo would be personally interviewing each of those people, hoping someone would substantiate Mick's presence near the estimated time of death. Mick needed an alibi.

Julia was also planning to interview Mick again. She needed to get a feel for his relationship with Avery. Did they argue? How well did they get along? If there was any known contention between the two of them, the prosecution could attempt to use it as motive. Julia also needed to get character witnesses who would vouch for Mick. There was so much to do and so little time to do it. The presiding judge, Judge Walters, was pushing for an early trial date, and the prosecutor wasn't fighting it.

As Julia sifted through the witness reports at her desk, Pablo sat across from her, reading through the autopsy report, taking numerous notes. For the first time, Julia was thankful she had his help. The chore of reading through the entire file was monumental, and the trial promised to be overwhelming. He had been a great help, and for the first time, Julia had to admit it to herself, although she wouldn't vocalize it.

Pablo looked up from his notes just in time to catch Julia watching him. She turned away, flipping through the pages of the report she'd been reading. Julia could feel his gaze on her, but she didn't want to look up.

Pablo cleared his throat. "So, are you still planning on the tournament tonight?"

Julia nodded. "Yeah. If you just give me my ticket, I'll meet you there."

"It's going to be an emotional game. Without Mick, the Utes are going to have a hard time of it. I almost feel sorry for them. Their hearts won't be in it."

"So, how does this tournament work?" Julia asked, unable to hide her ignorance of basketball. She'd never been interested in sports. Sports were a barbaric means for males to exhibit their macho and chauvinistic tendencies.

"Utah plays Air Force tonight. If Utah wins, then they play Colorado State, which already beat UNLV. If they win that game, then they go on to play in the championship game on Saturday."

"Sounds awfully complicated. Do you think Utah has a chance?"

Pablo shrugged. "They can probably pull off a win tonight, but the rest of the tournament will be difficult without Mick. And there's not much of a chance for them in the NCAA tournament."

"NCAA tournament?"

Pablo laughed. "You really don't know anything about basketball."

Julia shook her head, not entirely amused by the fact.

"The tournament that Utah is playing in right now is only for their conference: the Mountain West Conference, which is composed of schools in their immediate region. Then there's the national tournament that includes the best teams in the nation, basically. Utah will get into the tournament because they're ranked number one in their conference, but the chances of them advancing very far, like to the Elite Eight or even Final Four, are slim without Mick."

Julia couldn't keep the terminology straight and figured it really didn't matter. Mick Webber was in the county jail; he wasn't going to be playing basketball anytime soon. And if he was ever going to play anywhere other than the prison courtyard, she had to focus on his case. She had agreed to attend tonight's game and, on some level, felt like it was something she needed to do. If she was going to begin to understand the team dynamics, she had to see them in action. She wanted to see Mick's teammates in their element, wanted to envision Mick Webber playing basketball. If she had any hope of understanding exactly what happened to Avery and how it all came to rest on Mick Webber's shoulders, Julia needed to experience basketball. Basketball had been at the core of Mick and Avery's relationship.

After work, Julia went home to have dinner and change. She warmed up leftovers from Chinese take-out she'd picked up the night before. She spent only a few moments checking her personal email and the help forum, and she was disappointed there was still no response from some of the women she had replied to previously. It always worried her when one of the women in the rape forum dropped off with no further communication. The women who continually posted messages seemed to receive some solace from the encouragement and advice they received. However, the women who posted only once or twice and were never heard from again were possibly not receiving any other form of therapy or aid. Julia knew what it was like to be one of those women, and for someone whose trauma had been recent, it was not an easy thing to deal with without help from someone.

Feeling depressed at the fact that there was little she could do to help those women, Julia resigned herself to think about something else. Currently, her main focus had to be Mick Webber. His life was in her hands, and she needed to keep his trial as her focal point.

She changed into jeans and a blue turtleneck sweater, pulled on her wool coat, and went outside. It was only a half hour before game time, but Julia hadn't expected traffic to be this terrible. The cars moved slowly up 300 West as they edged toward the Energy Solutions Arena. Pablo had told her the Utes usually played in the Huntsman Center by the University, but because this was the MWC tournament, it was being held in the Energy Solutions Arena. She entered one of the adjacent parking lots and paid the parking fee as she followed the cars in front of her toward an empty parking spot. Julia then followed the crowds that headed toward the arena.

Apparently other games had been going on during the day, but most of Salt Lake was turning up to watch their beloved Utes take on Air Force. Julia climbed the steps toward her seat and spotted Pablo. She felt uneasy about coming to the game with him, but she figured since it was work related and was absolutely not a date, it would be okay. It was more like research for their case. Surely he saw it the same way.

She hadn't been on a date since college—since Matthew. Her trust in men had been destroyed, and she wasn't certain if it could ever be renewed. Currently, she was content to focus her life on her career. Julia was helping people and at present, that was all that mattered.

She finally reached her designated seat and sat down next to Pablo.

"Hi," he said as she sat down. "Ready for your first basketball game?" The eagerness in his eyes was almost childlike.

"I guess."

He showed her the program he'd bought and went over some

of the general facts of the game. He pointed out some of Mick's teammates and his coach, all people they would want to interview.

Although she'd never sat through an entire basketball game, she understood the basic rules and asked Pablo only a few questions when the referee blew the whistle.

It was quite a physical game. There was a lot more body contact than she'd imagined. She could see what Pablo meant about it being an emotional game.

Pablo shook his head. "The heart of their team is sitting in a county jail."

"It must be difficult for them to focus on the game."

"I wonder how difficult it would be for Mick if he was here right now. How hard would it be for him to sit on the bench and watch his team play? No doubt he would cheer his team on, but not being able to help them would be devastating for him."

Julia's thoughts turned to Avery. She had loved the game too. The women were also competing in a similar tournament, and the Lady Utes were playing without their starting point guard. How difficult was it for them to play without Avery? Their loss had been altogether more upsetting. Their teammate was dead—had been murdered in a most vicious manner—and yet they had to proceed in playing without her.

Pablo interrupted her thoughts. "Jason Gullege, the shooting guard, is one of Mick's best friends." Pablo pointed him out. "That's Jason. He's their second highest scorer, but he's missing a lot of his shots."

She could tell his game was off. He kept losing control of the ball.

"And that is Brian McKay, taking the ball out," Pablo said, pointing out another player. "He took over as the starting power forward after Mick was arrested. He's in foul trouble right now. If he gets five fouls, he will foul out and have to leave the game."

"He's a friend of Mick's, right? I think I remember reading a brief statement he made," Julia said.

"Yeah, he'd be a good one to talk to also."

reasonable doubt

Despite the low shooting percentage and foul trouble, the Utes led at half time. Pablo made some notes in the program and then held out a tub of popcorn he'd bought during half time. "Would you like some?" he asked.

Julia nodded. "Thanks," she said as she grabbed a handful.

Pablo let out a small laugh as he tossed a piece of popcorn in his mouth.

"What?"

"Nothing," he said. "It's just nice to see a woman with a hearty appetite. A lot of women would say no."

"I like to eat. There's nothing wrong with that."

"I know. That's fine. It's just that most women would—"

"Don't stereotype women."

Pablo shook his head and ate another piece of popcorn. "I'm not saying anything bad, really. I think it's good that you like to eat."

Julia sighed and turned her attention back to the game, rubbing her buttery hand on her jeans. Brian McKay grabbed the ball away from a player on the other team, knocking him down to the ground. The referee blew his whistle, and Brian went to sit on the bench.

"Did he foul out?" Julia asked.

"No, the coach is just benching him, trying to save him for later. We should also talk to the coach, Dick Hayes. Maybe we can try after the game. He's one of Mick's supporters. He's given the media several statements defending Mick."

Julia agreed. "He would be a great asset as a character witness."

During the second half, Julia felt as though she knew more about what was going on in the game. The Utes regained their composure and defeated Air Force. The crowd erupted in jubilant cheers and thunderous applause. Julia and Pablo descended the steps down to the floor. Although they were not allowed onto the court, they were able to get Coach Hayes's attention after he had completed several media interviews.

The tall, thin man approached Julia and Pablo, who stood

behind the first row of seats directly behind the Ute bench. Coach Hayes was wearing a dark blue suit and shoes that were not from a department store. The silver streaks in his brown hair enhanced his long face and brought out his cobalt eyes. A closer look at his eyes showed he'd not been sleeping well.

Pablo congratulated Coach Hayes on the outcome of the game and told him they were from Arthur Stanley's firm, representing Mick Webber.

Julia introduced herself, half-shouting above the noise that surrounded them. "We would like to meet with you when your schedule allows. I really feel your testimony might help Mick's case."

Coach Hayes nodded. "I'll do anything to help Mick. I think very highly of him, and I know he didn't kill Avery." He reached into his suit jacket pocket and pulled out a business card. After scribbling a phone number on it, he handed it to Julia. "Call me on Monday and we can set something up."

Julia agreed and then Coach Hayes excused himself to attend a press conference. She then followed Pablo up the stairs toward the exit. They joined the crowd filing out of the arena and went outside.

"Where are you parked?" Pablo asked. "I'll walk you to your car."

Julia looked around, orienting herself. She remembered she had parked in the lot just south of the arena. "I parked in that lot, but you don't have to walk with me. I'll be fine."

"I parked in that general direction too, so I'll just walk with you."

Julia agreed and walked toward the intersection. For some reason, Pablo walking her to the car made Julia more nervous than having to walk alone. She had no reason to feel threatened by Pablo, but even such a general closeness to a man made her uneasy. It had been years since her attack, but the walls always came up when she was in such proximity to a man. She had vowed, years ago, to never let herself be vulnerable. It was a code by which she lived, the only way she could guarantee something like that would never happen again.

Julia looked around the parking lot. It was filled with people walking toward their cars. Her uneasiness wore off as she approached her car. She thanked Pablo for walking her to the car and then got in, quickly locking the doors before she started the engine.

The next day, Julia had a meeting with Vince St. Peters, the lead investigator in Mick Webber's case. She'd dealt with him in prior cases and had always considered him a hardworking, fair man. She hoped his astute manner would be of some benefit to her case. On the phone, Vince had said he didn't have much time, but he would give her ten minutes at the courthouse while he waited to testify in an unrelated case. Julia walked down the hall toward the courtroom he had indicated, the clicking of her heels quickening as she hurried to find him. She wanted to have plenty of time with him before he was called into the courtroom to testify.

Vince St. Peters was standing just outside the courtroom, talking on his cell phone. Julia caught her breath as she slowed her pace, wanting to give him time to finish his call. The seasoned detective wore his job experience on his face; the years of investigating crimes had taken their toll. His graying hair had begun to infiltrate his goatee, and the wrinkles around his eyes were indicative of too many late nights. Detective St. Peters's tall frame made him a formidable opponent. He saw her approaching, acknowledged her, and finished his phone call.

"Hi, Miss Harris," he said, extending his hand.

Julia took his hand. "Thank you for making time to meet me."

"So this is about Mick Webber," Detective St. Peters said, not wasting any time.

"Yes," Julia said. "I need to know if you have any other leads you're looking into."

Detective St. Peters tucked his phone into his coat pocket and shook his head. "There are no other leads, and the investigation is currently closed."

"Closed?" Julia asked.

"We have our guy, Miss Harris. Why would we waste more of our manpower when the man who killed Avery Thomas is sitting in a jail cell?"

"What if he didn't do it?"

The detective laughed. "As far as I'm concerned, he did."

Julia bit her lip, trying to contain her frustration. "Certainly there were other leads you looked into. You couldn't have just arrested my client without ruling out any other culprits."

Detective St. Peters pulled his ringing cell phone out of his pocket and looked at the caller ID. Replacing it in his coat pocket, he looked at Julia. "We did our job, Miss Harris. We arrested the man who we believe committed the crime. He was found at the scene of the crime, murder weapon in hand. Why would we look anywhere else? Our part is done; the rest is up to the D.A. I believe he's guilty; whether he is declared guilty or not is up to you."

Julia frowned. Clearly, this was a waste of time. He had no inclination to help. He'd washed his hands of it. "I guess that's it, then?"

"There isn't anything else I can do."

"Well, thank you for your time. I'll probably be in touch."

Detective St. Peters shrugged as he pulled out his ringing cell phone. The police department was convinced Mick had done it, and nothing short of an acquittal would get them to continue the investigation. Julia could understand. She wasn't so sure Mick was innocent either, but as his attorney she had to try everything.

chapter five

Pablo woke up on Saturday feeling aimless. After a long, laborious week, he felt disoriented. There were no phone calls to make, no witnesses to meet. There was only a long, empty day filled with no appointments. He wasn't used to that. After allowing himself the rare luxury of sleeping in until nine, he ate breakfast while reading *Newsweek*.

Ordinarily, Saturday was the crowning day of his week, the day he rewarded himself with leisure and the pleasant company of Christina. Christina. That was what was missing in the equation. While he was in law school, he had worked unceasingly throughout the week, communicating with Christina via phone calls, email, and an occasional lunch together. She had also been in school, so their schedules hadn't allowed for much time together. On Saturday, they would spend most waking moments with each other, either studying or playing. They would spend a larger portion of the morning at the Harold B. Lee Library and then rewarded themselves with a racquetball game at the RB, a picnic at Kiwanis Park, or a lunch at a Mexican restaurant. On Sundays, they would go to church together, make dinner together, and hold hands seemingly the entire day.

That had all changed about a month prior to his accepting Arthur's offer and moving to Salt Lake. Up until that moment, his life was all mapped out. He and Christina would get married a few months after he started his new job. Within a year, they'd start a family. But that wasn't the way it had played out. The fairy tale ending had an alternate conclusion, one he still couldn't understand.

Pablo had not recovered from that fateful Saturday in which his plans had been altered. He remembered thinking that morning that he was ready for their relationship to progress. They'd met in their BYU ward and dated exclusively almost from the start. Although they hadn't talked about it, he had envisioned them getting married. He hadn't proposed yet, but he figured that as soon as he did, they wouldn't wait long before starting a family.

Christina had other plans, however. That day, she had proudly announced her intentions of applying for medical school. He couldn't see waiting that long to have children. He wanted to start a family right away. She wanted to wait several years to get married and to postpone having children. After trying to work through their differences, they'd both concluded that it wasn't right. They didn't have the same goals. She wanted to be a surgeon, but how would that fit into the life he had envisioned?

Thinking back on that day, Pablo wondered if he could have done anything differently. Could there have been a way to work it out? It was doubtful. They wanted different things. As Pablo moped around the house, he wondered how his favorite day had become his worst. Saturdays were meaningless now, without Christina. But was it specifically Christina he missed, or was it something else?

* * *

On Saturday, Julia called the main Webber Sporting Goods store on Foothill Boulevard and found out that Mick's father was working all morning. She decided to pay him a visit. She hadn't met him yet and was anxious to talk to him. When she looked in the phone book, she was surprised to see there were five of the stores in the Salt Lake area, and she remembered Arthur had mentioned that the Webbers also owned two stores in Provo and one in Ogden.

Webber Sporting Goods was nearly empty for a Saturday. She had expected to find the store busy with customers renting skis for the last of the season. There was only a handful of cars in the parking lot, and inside the store, Julia counted more employees than customers. She explained who she was to an employee, who then led her back to Mr. Webber's office.

Mr. Webber stood up as she walked in. He had a slight resemblance to Mick, with the same tall frame.

"Hi, Mr. Webber. My name is Julia Harris. I'm with Arthur Stanley's firm, representing your son."

Mr. Webber nodded and extended his hand. "Your firm came highly recommended by my brother. I wasn't so sure at first since your firm isn't proven in this type of case, but I've also seen that a higher-end firm isn't what I want either. Clark was so sure about Arthur. I decided to give it a chance. I hope you don't disappoint me."

The fact that she still believed Mick was guilty could be disappointing to him, but it was enough that Arthur and Pablo believed in his innocence. "I assure you, Mr. Webber. We're on this case 100 percent."

He indicated a chair for her to sit in. "Glad to hear it. I was a little worried at first when Clark told me Arthur couldn't represent Mick himself. I guess with his health problems, he can't really take the case on right now."

Julia took a seat in the black leather office chair. She'd been questioned before as an attorney because of her gender and age. She wasn't sure which was the case this time. "I am quite capable of handling this case."

Mr. Webber sat back in his chair and crossed his arms. "I don't doubt your capability, but my son didn't do this. I know that. Do you?"

Belief in a client's innocence had to be earned. It wasn't included in her legal fees. "I only met him a few days ago. I'm still trying to find out more about the case."

"I understand. I'd be happy to answer any questions. I know my son better than anyone. I'm convinced he didn't do this. What else do you need to know?"

"I need to know a little more about his relationship with Avery. I know the prosecution will try to argue they had a volatile relationship or that maybe there was a lot of contention."

"There wasn't a lot of contention."

Julia nodded. "I'm glad to hear that. The prosecution will look for every possible angle to distort the picture of the perfect couple. They'll dig up some eyewitness who swears they had an argument in public or someone who saw Mick yell at Avery. The prosecution is usually pretty good about turning up stuff that isn't even there."

"I really don't think there's anything they can find on Mick. I'm not saying he's perfect, but there's one thing I know. He would never ever hurt Avery."

"Good. So he has no history of violence whatsoever? No fights in high school the prosecution will dig up? No problems in his youth?"

Mr. Webber looked at Julia with tired eyes. He fought back tears. "Mick is a good athlete. Yes, he's aggressive. Yes, he's a little rough, but he gets the job done. Some people call him the king of flagrant fouls, and it's true to some degree. He's a very physical player, but he keeps it on the court. He would never do this to anyone, especially not someone he loves."

"Okay, well thank you for the information." Julia disagreed with Mr. Webber's belief that aggression was permissible in getting the job done. She couldn't appreciate basketball if it meant that being rough was acceptable.

Mr. Webber stood up and extended his hand, which she shook. "You have to get my son off, Miss Harris. He didn't do this, and our entire family is suffering for it. Mick is destroyed. My wife is having a breakdown, and my business is really getting hit. People don't want to buy from a father of a man accused of murder. It's your job to change that. I'm counting on you to exonerate him."

"We are doing all we can," Julia said as she walked toward the door.

Mr. Webber nodded. "I expect you won't let me down then?"

"It's my only case. I'm giving it all my time," Julia said. "Good day, Mr. Webber."

It was her only case, and she was giving it all of her time, but something in her interaction with Mr. Webber left her feeling uneasy. He expected her to believe Mick was innocent; it was a requirement in hiring her as an attorney. But she didn't think Mick was innocent. Aunt Isabelle's eyes haunted her every time she entertained the belief. The picture of the beautiful young woman who was murdered prevented her from believing Mick was innocent of any wrongdoing. However, the Mick Webber case was hers, and she needed it to clinch the partnership. Getting Mick acquitted would be the evil means to the end that would make her career. So she would give Mick Webber all of her time, but she would not give him her faith.

On Monday morning, Julia made it a point to get to the office earlier than usual. She didn't want Pablo outdoing her again. She was also feeling overwhelmed with Mick's case. There were so many thoughts and questions going through her mind. She was going to visit Mick again today and would also be seeing Jennifer Jensen, Avery's teammate who found Mick with Avery's dead body. Although she'd read Jennifer's preliminary statement, there were so many questions she wanted to ask her.

Julia was caught up in her thoughts and didn't hear Pablo walk into her office. She looked up just as he crossed the office and came to sit by her in the chair she had designated as his. She went right into the agenda for the day. After spending an hour going over a few notes and brainstorming questions and ideas, Julia offered to drive. She didn't feel comfortable going into someone's car that she didn't know well, and driving her own car made her feel more in control.

Twenty minutes after they arrived the guard finally ushered Mick into the visiting room. After some small talk and inquiring whether Mick was being treated well, Julia delved into her questions.

"Mick, I need you to tell me everything about your relationship with Avery. Don't leave out any small detail, even if you don't think it's important. Everything is important. The prosecution is going to ask you intimate details. I'm sorry to say that your life will be an open book."

Mick sighed.

"You've already told us how you met, but I need to know more details about your relationship. Don't take this the wrong way. Believe me, the prosecution will ask you far worse." She paused before continuing. "How well did you two get along? Did you argue?"

"No!" Mick said, quickly getting defensive. "We were just like any other couple. Of course we had our disagreements, but it's not like we fought all the time."

"Mick," Pablo said gently. "This is just what Julia is talking about. The prosecution is going to try to paint a bad picture of you. They'll ask you questions a hundred times worse than that. You can't lose your cool or give the jury any reason to doubt you."

"I'm sorry," Mick said. "Avery and I loved each other very much. We weren't the perfect couple, but then, who is? We disagreed about small stuff, but the important issues, we felt the same about."

Julia nodded. "I know the two of you were active in the Church. I hate to ask this, but I promise you the prosecution will ask. Were the two of you intimate?"

Mick looked away before answering. "We were going to get married in the temple, Julia. What do you think?"

"I'm sorry. I had to ask. Believe me, Mick. This is no easier for me than it is for you; the interview, I mean." Julia looked down at her notebook and attempted to formulate her thoughts.

"Mick, we're not accusing you of anything. We just really need to understand your relationship so we can best defend you," Pablo said.

Mick nodded.

Julia looked up from her notes. "From my estimation, we are

looking at a few possibilities. The killer had some fascination or obsession with the women's basketball team. Maybe he watched the practice and waited for it to end. He waited until almost all the players left and then attacked Avery once she was alone. Who knows if he singled her out or it happened by chance that she was the last one to leave. Was she always the last one to leave?"

Mick shook his head. "No, not really. I don't think so, but then again, I didn't always meet her afterward."

"Let's check with her teammates," Julia said, signaling to Pablo, who made a note. "Another scenario would be that the killer is someone Avery knows, someone who had specifically targeted her and found the chance when she was alone. Are you sure you can't think of anyone who disliked her?"

Mick traced his finger on a pen mark that had been etched in the table. "No one that I know of. She didn't have any enemies."

"Did you know all her friends?" Pablo asked.

"I think so. I knew all the people she talked to or told me about." Mick looked down and continued to rub his index finger on the pen mark.

Julia pondered his statement for a minute. "Is there any reason to believe she was hiding anything from you? Anything at all?"

He shot his head up. "No. We didn't keep secrets." He relaxed a bit and then continued. "But I did get the feeling something was bothering her the last few days before she was killed."

"Something like what?" Julia asked.

Mick shrugged. "I don't know. Just a feeling I had. I asked her a few times, but she said it was nothing. I think she was just nervous about the end of the season and our upcoming wedding."

Julia sighed. "The only other explanation I can think of is that it was somebody on the team who was jealous of Avery. Is there anyone that stands out to you, Mick?"

"No, not at all. I can't imagine any of her teammates doing this to her. Everybody loved her, and that's not an exaggeration."

Obviously, someone didn't love her—that's why she was dead. "Well, our objective is to get you acquitted. Right now, we really don't have much to go on. Character witnesses will be our best bet. We'll be interviewing the players on both the men's and women's teams, as well as your coach. Anyone else that could help our case?"

Mick shrugged. "I really don't know."

"Well, at this point what we're going to focus on is reasonable doubt. The prosecution has to prove beyond a reasonable doubt that you're guilty. What that means is that in order for the jury to convict you, they cannot have any doubt in their mind that you are the one who killed Avery. It's our job to put reasonable doubt in the minds of the jurors. Character witnesses will help, and so will showing the prosecution's lack of evidence and your lack of motive. They really have no motive. We will bombard them with doubts. It's your job to keep thinking of things that will help build your defense. Anything that you can think of, call me day or night. I need to feel that I can trust you, Mick. Don't keep anything from me. Okay?"

Mick nodded without looking at her.

Later that morning, they had an appointment with Jennifer Jensen at the law firm. Julia greeted the tall, thin brunette. Jennifer forced a smile and took the chair that Julia offered her. She looked around the room, avoiding eye contact.

Taking her seat behind her desk, next to Pablo, Julia introduced herself and thanked Jennifer for coming in. "We've read through your statement, Jennifer. You stated that you initially left the locker room at twenty after five and then came back at approximately five thirty. What was the reason for your return?"

Jennifer patted her skirt with both hands and then crossed her legs. "I had forgotten my hairbrush, so I went back to get it."

Julia made a note. "And at precisely what time did you see Mick?"

"When I first left the locker room, I saw him in the hallway that leads to it. He was walking in the direction of the locker room. I think it was about five twenty or so. I talked to him for just a minute. He asked me if I'd seen Avery, and I told him she was still in the locker room."

Julia wrote furiously as she listened to Jennifer. "So you left the building and then came back at five thirty, you said?"

Jennifer nodded. "Yeah, it only took me a few minutes to realize I'd left my brush, so I went back. I would say it was five thirty."

"I know you've already done this, but can you please describe what you saw?" Julia asked.

Jennifer bit her lip and looked away. "I saw Avery on the floor covered in blood, and Mick was sort of kneeling next to her. He was holding the knife in his hand."

Julia sympathized with the girl who'd just lost a friend, but she needed to get some answers. "What were your immediate thoughts?"

"I thought, 'He killed her. I can't believe he killed her.'"

Pablo leaned forward and held Jennifer's gaze. "Did you really think he killed her?"

"That's what it looked like," she said, turning away.

"Before that day, would you have imagined Mick Webber could kill Avery?" Julia asked.

"No, not at all. I would never think that, but then I walked in on him and the look on his face—" Jennifer put a hand to her mouth and stifled a sob. "I keep seeing the look on his face. I can't describe it, other than to say it was horrible. The whole thing was horrible."

"Okay." Julia sighed. She wasn't getting anywhere with Jennifer. "How would you describe their relationship? Did they get along well or argue a lot?"

"As far as I could tell, they got along well. I never saw them fight. Avery and I used to hang out a lot, and she would tell me about what they did together. She didn't really complain about him or anything. I know she seemed preoccupied the last few days. I asked her what it was. I think she was nervous. She said she felt a little pressured by Mick. He wanted to make all these wedding plans, maybe even move up the date. I know they were meeting with their bishop that night. She was probably nervous about that."

Julia thought for a minute before asking the next question. "Do you know if she was seeing anybody else?"

"No." Jennifer shook her head. "Mick was the only guy for her. She never even looked at another guy."

"Was she getting cold feet about the wedding? Maybe reconsidering?" Julia asked.

"I don't think so. She wanted to marry Mick, but she just felt overwhelmed. The wedding was planned for June, and she didn't want to start making plans until after the tournament. I think she was feeling like she was being pulled in so many different directions."

"Can you think of anyone who would want to kill Avery? Is there someone who could have done this?" Pablo asked.

"Mick did it. He's the one who killed Avery."

Julia looked at Pablo, a frown across his face. "What possible reason could Mick have to kill his fiancée?" Julia asked.

Jennifer shrugged. "I really don't know what was going through his head. Maybe he just cracked. He was under a lot of pressure too. All the experts were predicting that Utah would be in the Final Four, probably a contender for the national championship. I guess he just couldn't handle it. I don't know. Why don't you ask him?"

Julia frowned. After a few more futile questions, she led Jennifer out of the office. When she returned Pablo was writing a few notes. Julia slumped down into her chair with an exasperated sigh.

"Doesn't look good, does it?" Pablo asked.

She shook her head. "She's pretty convinced. The impact of walking in on them has obviously left her traumatized."

Pablo pulled the Superman Pez dispenser out of his jacket pocket and popped two in his mouth. He offered some to her.

She took it from him and examined it. It was fully stocked with yellow candy. "She'll be a convincing witness too. I don't know what we're going to do about her."

"Well, what she thinks is inadmissible. You'll just have to keep the questions strictly factual."

"I know." She closed the Pez dispenser without taking a piece and shot her hand toward him in returning it. "I know how to cross-examine a witness."

"Look, we're working on this together. Don't bite my head off for giving you a suggestion."

Ignoring his statement, she turned back to her notes. "We have to talk to Mick's teammates. His closest friends were Brian McKay and Jason Gullege. I'll take Brian if you want to talk to Jason. We have to get something. We have nothing!" Julia rose and slammed her notebook down on her desk. "I can't lose this case," she said walking around to the other side of her desk.

"We'll get him off, Julia. We just have to turn over every rock and talk to everyone out there. Something will turn up."

"I can't lose this case," she repeated, not having heard a word Pablo said. "Arthur has hinted that he wants to name a partner. If I lose this case, he'll never choose me. I can't let Adam or Bob win. I can't." She looked at Pablo. "Or you. He'll probably choose you just because you're the best golfer. That's all he cares about anymore. If he picks you as his partner, then you'll spend the whole day playing golf while the rest of us work ourselves weary." Julia shook her head. "You're in, you know. You're in the boys' club. And I'm out. I'm always out of everything. I can't lose this case."

"Will you shut up?" Pablo said. "There are things more important than your career, you know. Like Mick's life. Why don't we concentrate on that?" Pablo wrote a few notes in his planner and then grabbed his briefcase. "I'm going to find Jason. I'll see you later."

Julia shook her head as she watched his retreating figure walking down the hall. What was the matter with him? Why was he so touchy all of the sudden? She sat back down in her chair and looked over her notes. It just didn't look good for her or Mick. If she didn't completely throw herself into the case, Mick wouldn't get acquitted and she wouldn't get her promotion.

chapter six

Pablo tried to calm his anger as he drove to Jason's house in Bountiful. Julia had upset him, focusing on her career rather than on Mick's case. Wanting to be partner surpassed her desire to help Mick. Was she really that self-centered?

Pablo pulled into the circular driveway of the Gullege home and parked behind a black BMW. The house was a two-story stucco, with an arched entryway. Jason was the starting shooting guard on the Utes, and from what Mick had told him, one of his closest friends. Pablo remembered Jason's awful night on the court at the MWC tournament. He could guess Jason was not having an easy time with his friend's situation.

Pablo rang the doorbell and waited several moments for it to be answered. A tall young man answered the door. His blond hair fell across his forehead, and Pablo recognized him from the media guides he'd read. "Jason, hi. I'm Pablo Torres, representing Mick Webber. I wonder if I could talk to you for a few minutes."

"Hi," Jason said, extending his hand. "Come in."

Pablo entered the house and followed the barefoot Jason into the sprawling living room. "Thanks for your time. I just wanted to ask you a few questions about Mick."

Jason sat down on a leather loveseat and motioned for Pablo to sit across from him in an armchair. "Anything. I'll do anything to help Mick."

"He mentioned you've been friends for several years?"

Jason swept his long bangs off his forehead. "We both started at the U the same year. We were red-shirted our freshman years, and then we both went on our missions at the same time. We've been playing together now for three years."

"And how well did you know Avery?"

He sat up on the edge of the loveseat, his elbows leaning on his lanky jean-clad legs. "I only knew her through Mick. We'd all hang out together sometimes.

"How well did they get along?"

"Really well, I guess. They didn't argue much or anything. They're both so easy-going. He loved her so much, and Avery would do almost anything he asked her to."

"Can you think of any reason why anyone would do this?"

Jason sighed loudly and shook his head. "No. I can't think of why anyone would do this to her. Probably just some crazy guy that sneaked into the locker room."

"If we called you as a character witness for Mick, what could you say about him?"

"He's my best friend. He's the kind of guy you can really count on. He'd do just about anything for his friends. You could call him in the middle of the night and ask him for a favor. He'd do it." Jason paused for a minute and looked away. He sighed and then shook his head. "I know he didn't do this. He's not capable of it. The man worshipped Avery. He would do anything for her. Someone who loves a person as much as he loved Avery couldn't kill her. It's just not in him. I don't know how, Mr. Torres, but you have to get him off. He just didn't do it."

Pablo nodded. "We're going to do everything we can. It's not looking very good for Mick, but with a couple of character witnesses like you and the state's lack of motive, we have a chance. Let me just ask one more question. Does Mick have a bad temper?"

"Sometimes, maybe."

"When the prosecution cross-examines you on the stand, be sure they're going to ask you that. Can you think of any instances that Mick lost his temper?"

"Only on the court. He was a very physical player. He's gotten his share of technical fouls, even been ejected a few times. Some call him the king of flagrants. Then, there was the incident with the chair."

"The incident with the chair?"

Jason nodded. "Last year, he fouled out on a terrible call, and he picked up a chair from the other team's side and threw it onto the court." He shook his head. "He got a lot of heat for that, but his temper was mostly on the court. Off court, I can't see him being violent."

"Well, please call me if you can think of anything that will help," Pablo said, standing up. He gave Jason a business card and then departed.

Mick's temper on the court could present a real problem. Was it possible Mick restricted violent outbursts to the basketball court? Could there have been a time his temper followed him off the court? What if he'd felt provoked just as he had during the basketball game? Could Avery have done something to incite that type of rage?

Pablo was certain the prosecution would use isolated events such as the "chair incident" to portray Mick in a negative light. How many spectators witnessed that incident, knew Mick's temper roused him to aggression, and would link the episode to violence against Avery? The media would likely exaggerate the incident as well, probably dredge out similar occurrences and make Mick out to be a monster.

* * *

As Julia drove to meet with Brian McKay, she thought about what Pablo had said. He had been way out of line. How dare he accuse her of not caring about Mick's case? Self-preservation was not a bad thing. She had to look out for herself, worry about her future. Mick's case was her means of achieving her career potential. If she won such an immense case, one that had personal meaning to Arthur, then how could he deny her the partnership? It wasn't fair for Pablo to judge her for wanting to attain success. Pablo's judgmental words followed her, and she wondered why she cared so much about what he thought.

Julia met Brian at the appointed place. He was sitting in a corner booth of the Pie Pizzeria just off campus. His blond hair looked as if it had been buzzed recently. He was drinking a 7-Up and having a couple slices of pepperoni pizza. He asked her if she wanted something. Julia declined.

"How long have you known Mick?"

"We just met this year when I made the team."

"So, you and Mick are close friends?"

Brian nodded. "Yeah. I hate to see him go through this. I know he didn't do it."

"You don't believe he's capable of violence?"

Brian looked down at his drink. "He's a guy. All guys are capable of violence."

Julia studied his face. Not exactly the answer she was expecting. She took a few notes in her Franklin planner. "How would you categorize his relationship with Avery? Did they ever argue?"

"Sometimes, I think."

"Did he say to you whether they had any problems?"

Brian shrugged. "I don't know, maybe."

Julia knew that "maybe" equaled "yes." "Maybe they had problems?"

"Everyone's got problems."

Julia leaned forward in her chair, trying to meet Brian's eyes. He looked down at his plate. "What kind of problems?"

"She was always worried about what he wanted, what he needed."

"He told you that?"

Brian shoved his plate away, the last of his pizza crusts abandoned. "No, she did. She went out of her way to please him, like making him something on his birthday, and I don't think he really appreciated it."

"So Avery felt he took her for granted?"

Brian looked away. A noise in the kitchen caught his attention. "Hey, I know he's my friend, but that doesn't change the fact that he's a bit self-centered." Brian shook his head. "Like on the court, he's such a ball hog. I don't know if I've ever seen him pass the ball. That's how it was with Avery. He always wanted her to pass the ball, but he never wanted to pass it to her."

Julia assumed he was speaking metaphorically. "So their relationship was one-sided?"

"Yeah. If Mick didn't want to do it, they didn't do it. Would you like to sit around all night and watch Mick play video games?"

"Is that what they did?"

"A lot of times. We just hung out at Mick's place. Jason and I would take turns getting beat by Mick, and Avery would just read a book or something. Then we'd all watch *SportsCenter*. She used to try to get him to go a play or a concert, but he never wanted to."

"And have you ever seen Mick lose his temper?"

Brian took a drink. "Sometimes, I guess. I wouldn't want to be on the receiving end of one of his right hooks."

"Has he ever been violent off the court?"

"You know, just the usual."

Actually, she didn't know what the usual was. "What do you mean?"

"You know, a little shoving if someone gets up in his face."

"What would be an example?"

Brian shrugged. "Like at dance clubs or pick-up games."

"Pick-up games?"

"When we hang out at the park, we might join some guys playing basketball. Sometimes football."

"But you've never seen him hit someone?"

He shook his head and threw his balled up napkin on his plate.

"How do you feel about possibly testifying on Mick's behalf? You would be a character witness."

"I don't know. I guess I could. Isn't there someone who's known him longer?"

"We're considering Coach Hayes and Jason Gullege. We would just like to keep our options open."

"Okay. I'll think about it."

"Good. I know Mick would really appreciate your help."

"I'll do what I can," Brian said, looking at his watch. "My next class is starting soon. I have to go."

Julia handed him her card. "Here's my office phone number and my cell number. Call me if you can think of anything else that will help."

"I will," he said as he got up. He shook Julia's hand and then drank the rest of his soda.

On the way back to the office, Julia stopped at Jim Franco's office. It was time to call in extra help. Jim was a private detective that Arthur's firm used on occasion when they needed to delve into a case. They were sparing no expense on Mick Webber's case.

Jim was in. He came out to greet her and ushered her into his office. She'd worked on and off with Jim since she started at Arthur's firm, and he had really come through for them in the past. He'd gained Julia's perpetual allegiance the time he had found an eyewitness who exonerated one of her clients. She still didn't know where he'd found the eyewitness. That was his strength—finding something when it seemed that there was nothing to find.

Jim was in his late forties, about Julia's height but a little overweight. His black curly hair was peppered with gray, and his olive complexion indicated his Italian background.

"I'm sure you've heard we're working on the Mick Webber case."

"I figured I'd be hearing from you," Jim said, swiveling in

his chair. He drummed his fingers on his desk. "So, what do you want me to look into?"

"I don't even know, Jim. I'm not sure about this one. Part of me thinks he did it, not that it matters. But I feel like there's something out there we have to find. I doubt the police investigated other suspects and scenarios beyond Mick. They fingered Mick right away, and I don't know if they followed up on any other leads."

"We can start by looking at the backgrounds of some of the people who knew her. Give me a list of friends, teammates, ex-boyfriends."

Julia nodded as she wrote in her Franklin. "Okay, I'll send that to you later today. What else?"

"No alibi, huh?"

"Several people saw him outside the Huntsman Center as they were leaving, but technically he still could have had enough time to kill her."

"I'll dig around to see what else I can find."

"Thanks, Jim. You're a great help. I just don't know where else to look right now."

"We'll come up with something," he said tapping his pen on his desk. Julia was used to Jim's nervous habit of fidgeting. He always had to be moving or tapping something. He couldn't sit still very long.

Julia thanked Jim and drove back to the office. Although she still didn't have much, she felt better. Jim would turn something up, she knew it. When she reached the office, Sandra told her Arthur wanted to see her. She peeked her head in his office and found him talking to Pablo and another gentleman.

Arthur saw Julia and beckoned her into his office. He introduced Mick's uncle, Clark. He was about Arthur's age, but several inches taller and leaner. He was well-dressed; Julia guessed Armani. He rose to shake Julia's hand firmly.

"We were just updating Clark on the case. Pablo told me he met with one of Mick's friends. Did you have any luck with his other friend?" Arthur asked.

reasonable doubt

"I met with Brian McKay, one of his teammates. He is considering acting as a character witness." Julia hesitated bringing up Brian's view of Mick and Avery's relationship. Uncle Clark might jump right in and defend Mick, and Julia didn't really want his biased opinion. "I stopped by Jim Franco's office, and he's going to start doing some digging. I'm sure he'll turn something up by the end of the week."

Arthur turned to Clark and explained their relationship with Jim Franco. He touted Jim's talent in private investigation and swore if there were something to find out, he would find it. Although there wasn't any good news regarding Mick's case, Clark was satisfied to know a private investigator had been hired.

Julia felt grateful she had stopped by Jim's office. At least they had some positive progress to tout.

Soon the conversation turned to sports, as in any room with a majority of men. Clark lamented that Utah was defeated by Colorado State in the MWC tournament. He was certain that if Mick had been allowed to play, Utah would have been tournament champs. They also talked about Utah being matched up with Monmouth College in the NCAA tournament. Apparently the brackets had come out on Sunday, and everyone was eager for the games to begin on Thursday.

Julia felt left out of the conversation, as was often the case when men talked about sports. She didn't have anything to contribute, but she knew the conversation did have a direct link to Mick. They all knew that without Mick, Utah was doomed. It was just a game, she thought. It didn't really matter. What mattered was that Mick was still sitting in jail, and no amount of lamenting over basketball would do him any good. Instead, she let them indulge in their sorrow regarding the state of University of Utah basketball.

On Wednesday morning, she and Pablo drove to Coach Hayes's office on campus. He was leaving in a few hours for Houston, where the team would play against Monmouth College in the NCAA tournament. He had made time for their meeting despite his busy schedule.

The coach's office was small but filled with character. His walls were covered in team photographs of past years. Several newspaper articles were framed and mounted on the wall as well. One photo showed the coach in his twenties, dressed in a basketball uniform, spinning a ball on his index finger. A large dry erase board depicted the tournament bracket that Pablo had shown her earlier in the week. The word *Utah* had been written in several times, and it showed the team winning each of its ensuing games with their name scribbled in big red letters at the very center. Coach Hayes was accustomed to winning.

Julia thanked him for the meeting, and she and Pablo sat down across from him. Coach Hayes sat up straight in his chair, arms crossed in front of his broad chest. He nodded his head and motioned for her to speak.

"Please tell us any information that will help Mick. What kind of person is he? Did you have any discipline problems with him? That sort of thing." Julia pulled out her Franklin planner and prepared to make notes.

Coach Hayes leaned back in his chair and rubbed his chin thoughtfully. "What can I say about Mick? He's an excellent young man. He's a leader on the court and not just because of his basketball skills. Yes, he's the best player on this team, the reason our team is ranked where it is, but that's not all. He's an example in loyalty. I trust him implicitly. I know for a fact he could never do what they're accusing him of."

"Can you remember any outbursts or displays of violence?" Julia asked.

The coach sighed. "He's a physical player, but he's not violent. Not in this sense." He paused for a moment and then sighed again. "He was well known for his aggression on court. I'm sure they won't hesitate to bring that up."

Pablo leaned in as he spoke. "True, but if we can prove that his outbursts were contained on the court, then it might put him in a better light. As long as there aren't any instances of violence off the court, no fights or anything like that, we should be okay. If there is no history of violence, it will be difficult for the

reasonable doubt

prosecution to prove that Mick is capable of such a crime. It won't exonerate him, but it will present him in a better light."

Julia nodded. "We plan on presenting several character witnesses to testify that Mick is an upstanding person. Would you consider being one of those?"

"Absolutely. I'll do anything I can to help. I love that young man like a son, and what he is going through is unbearable. I can't understand how anyone believes he did this."

"Well, we appreciate your willingness to testify. You're a very respected member of this community, and I think your support will really help," Pablo said.

"Who are some other character witnesses you have in mind?" the coach asked.

Julia turned a few pages in her planner. "We've talked to a couple of his teammates. We're going to ask Jason Gullege and Brian McKay. We're hoping they would make good character witnesses."

The coach frowned. "Jason, yes, but I don't think that Mick and Brian got along very well."

"I got the impression they were close friends," Julia said.

Coach Hayes shrugged. "I guess I don't really know who was friends with whom off court. I don't get involved in that aspect, but as far as playing goes, Brian often complains that he doesn't get enough playing time. I always got the impression that he wanted to go in for Mick more often, but I guess that's just the competitor in him."

Julia made a note of it and then thanked the coach once again for his time.

Coach Hayes leaned forward and covered his face with his large hand. "I've gone to see him a few times. It's been so hard for me, but I wanted to let him know that I support him. The last time I saw him, he was so different from the Mick I know. He seemed so defeated, so absolutely hopeless. He hasn't quite given up, but he's close."

"We're doing everything we can," Julia said.

Pablo stood up. "I guess we'd better let you go. I know your time is limited, but we appreciate you taking the time to meet with us. We'll be in touch in a few weeks, once your schedule has opened up more."

Coach Hayes stood up and shook both their hands. "Thank you for what you're doing for Mick. I'll do whatever I can."

Julia put her Franklin in her briefcase and closed it. She stood up and followed Pablo to the door.

"Good luck tomorrow, Coach," Pablo said.

Coach Hayes sighed. "It's ridiculous to be thinking about basketball while Mick is wasting away in a jail cell. It almost doesn't seem right to be playing, but I guess we just have to keep going."

"It's what Mick would want. Win for him," Pablo said.

"Thank you. We'll give it everything we've got."

Pablo initiated the conversation in the car. "It must be difficult for Coach Hayes to continue coaching a team without Mick. I'll bet it wasn't easy after Mick's arrest."

"He looks like he can handle it."

"I know, but just think how devastated the players must be by their friend's arrest and absence, and Coach has to put up a brave front for them."

"I guess that's why he gets paid the big bucks."

"And he's publicly supporting Mick and has to face national scrutiny. The national media will be talking about the murder, about Mick being accused, not about their athletic merits. The Utes will forever be tarnished by this event. From now on anytime they play a nationally broadcast game, it will be brought up. I don't envy this team."

Julia slammed her hand against the steering wheel. "It's just basketball. It's really quite trivial, compared to what the real world has to offer. A woman is dead, and you're worried about basketball."

Pablo shook his head. "Do you think there will ever be a time when we'll agree on something?"

"I guess we agree that we want to win this case."

"I know that I do, but you're still convinced that Mick did this."

"But I still want to win. I need this win."

"Your promotion? Your career? Isn't that a little trivial when you think about what the real world has to offer? A man's life is at stake here."

Julia brushed aside his comment and didn't respond. There was no point. Yes, Mick was probably guilty, but she needed this win. She needed that promotion, and negative talk from her co-counsel was not going to discourage her.

chapter seven

On Friday morning, Julia worked on several briefs while Pablo researched jury consultants. Mick's father had approved the costs associated with a jury consultant, and Arthur had directed Pablo to find the one who would be best suited for their case.

Julia enjoyed the silence that settled over her office as they both worked diligently. The quietude that had accompanied their simultaneous labors was disrupted when Bob and Adam came in without knocking.

"Princeton just upset Kentucky. Who'd you have Pablo?" Bob asked, walking toward their desk, his NCAA bracket in hand.

The day before, March Madness, as they called it, had descended on the office and infected the four men as they'd furiously filled out their brackets, each choosing different teams to win the final. As the day had progressed, an endless series of interruptions occurred when each team that advanced was announced, along with commentary on the subsequent match-up. She couldn't believe how many games had been played the previous day. In past years, she had been spared the annoyance of the tournament as conversation and speculation regarding the games had been kept in the other men's offices. This year, since Pablo was sharing her office, the chaos had migrated into her office, and she was tired of it.

Pablo pulled out his bracket and scanned it. "I had Kentucky winning that game. I have them going to the Elite Eight. That's going to hurt me."

Adam moved closer and stood next to Pablo, eyeing his sheet. "I picked that upset. I thought Princeton could pull it off. I can't believe you had Kentucky going so far. They're not that good this year."

Julia watched as the men lamented about this team or that one. It was amazing how much energy and attention they gave to a meaningless succession of games. The only game she had given any interest to was the Utah game. They had lost to Monmouth College.

Adam continued to criticize some of Pablo's picks, and Pablo folded his chart and returned it to his pocket.

"I'm having some guys come over tonight to watch the games on my new high-definition big screen," Adam said. "You should come, Pablo. Bob's going to be there."

"Yeah, you should come too," Bob said.

"I'll probably just watch at home."

Adam gave Pablo a little shove. "You're just mad because I picked BYU to lose. Did you think they had a chance? Come on, it's a miracle they even made it."

"Thanks anyway. I think I'll pass."

"She's rubbing off on you," Adam said, pointing to Julia with his chin. "You're getting to be a bore too."

Julia stiffened up at the mention of her name. "Adam, get out of here. Does Arthur know he's paying you to spend your day filling out those stupid sheets?"

Adam winked at her. "He's the one that gave it to me, Julia."

Bob turned to walk out. "Sorry we interrupted. We'll get going." He poked Adam with his elbow, which didn't move him an inch. Adam was so much taller and more stubborn; it wasn't easy to move him against his will.

"Bye, Julia." Adam smiled and winked again before departing.

Julia reacted in her usual way when Adam infuriated her. As she launched her pen against the closed door, she wondered how many unsuspecting pens had left their marks on that door.

Pablo looked at her and laughed.

Her wrath had made her forget that he was still seated next to her. "He's a jerk, you know?"

He nodded. "Yeah, I know. I'm sorry."

"It's not your fault. He just likes to infuriate me. It's what he does best around here."

"Well, you shouldn't let him get to you," Pablo said.

She sighed and stretched her arms over her head. "I can't help it. I try to ignore him, but he knows exactly what buttons to push."

"So you throw pens at him?"

"At the door. I don't throw the pen at him; I throw it at the door after he's left. It lets out my aggression a little, I guess."

Pablo smiled. "Well, if it works, then I guess keep doing it. I won't tell."

Julia couldn't help but smile in return. She wasn't used to having men elicit smiles from her, but Pablo's understanding helped to lighten her mood.

* * *

Friday evening was depressing for Pablo as he began to unwind from his busy week. Although Adam had invited him to join his March Madness viewing party, he didn't feel like going. He wasn't much in the mood for company. Besides, Adam wasn't a member of the Church, so he figured there would be drinking at his place. He also didn't care for the way Adam treated Julia. He was so unkind and disrespectful. Pablo hadn't said anything so far, but if Adam continued the disdainful treatment, he'd soon be hearing what Pablo thought of him.

Work had kept him going all week long. He'd had little time

to think about Christina, but now that he was home, she was all he could think about. What was she doing? Was she thinking of him too? As he recalled the breakup, he felt disoriented about his future.

There wasn't one overriding quality that he was going to miss. Perhaps he was more in love with the idea of being in love and getting married than he was in love with her. He had felt so ready to move forward in his life. When he was offered his first real job, he had wanted to take the next step. Marriage was what he truly wanted. He wanted to come home to someone each day. He wanted a family, children to greet him as he walked in the door each afternoon. All of those dreams had been possible with Christina.

Christina symbolized the prospects of a happy future, and that's what he'd lost. Christina wasn't meant for him. She was out of his life, and now he had to continue in search of the true happiness that he knew was meant for him. Feeling more at peace, he turned in for the night. He didn't want to feel alone tomorrow, thinking about how Saturdays used to have such meaning. He thought about calling Leonard, his old BYU roommate, to see what his plans were.

* * *

On Saturday morning, Julia drove down to American Fork. She was determined to learn to play golf. The golf pro at the public golf course had guaranteed she could learn in only a few lessons. She didn't want to try any of the Salt Lake courses; she knew too many people. If she ran into anybody on the golf course as she was learning how to play, it would be embarrassing. American Fork was far enough away that she most likely wouldn't run into anybody she knew.

Julia walked toward the shop. Behind it lay the course and a sprawling view of the Wasatch Mountains. The course was nestled in a valley of large trees. Golf carts and their occupants dotted the expanse of lush green grass.

Lyle, the golf instructor, was exactly what she had pictured after she talked to him on the phone. He was in his late thirties, attired in knee-length shorts and a short-sleeved light green shirt with a collar. He was very tanned from overexposure to the sun. He discussed the classes, and she paid him. He picked up a bag of golf clubs, handed her one of them, and told her to follow him. Julia followed behind Lyle, whose swift pace kept him a few steps in front of her. She heard him say, over his shoulder, something about her grip on the golf club.

"Hold it no more tightly than you would hold a bird," he said as he reached the designated area.

Hold a bird? Julia didn't know exactly what he meant by that, but she figured it meant she shouldn't strangle the thing, which is precisely what she was doing. Julia relaxed her hold on the golf club and directed her attention to Lyle. He said something about a ten-finger grip and then held out his club to show her how to hold it. Julia tried to mimic his grip on the golf club.

Lyle moved toward her and rearranged her hands on the club. "If your hands are rotated too far to the right, it will make the ball curve to the left. If your grip is wrong, it will throw off your whole game. Make sure you can see at least two knuckles of your left hand."

Lyle explained the proper stance, helping her position her feet about shoulder width apart. He then pushed her back slightly, bending her forward, telling Julia that her spine should be straight, from her head to her tailbone. He moved her hands into position and slowly pushed her head down. Julia held on tightly to the golf club, not wanting to let go for fear that she would mess up the grip he had carefully explained. Lyle tapped her legs with his golf club, explaining that she should bend forward from her hips, not her knees.

It was so much information at once, and Lyle talked quickly, almost as if he wanted to get through the lesson. He talked about proper aim and alignment, much of which Julia missed as she was trying to maintain her correct grip on the club and her feet in the proper position. Lyle said she should pick a target and aim toward it. "Your target should be something in the distance in the line you want your ball to go. Pick an immediate target, about four feet in front of the ball, and then draw an imaginary line from the ball to your distant target."

Julia looked out past the ball and tried to do what he suggested. He urged her to take a few practice swings and explained the proper form to do so. As Julia awkwardly swung the club, he critiqued her form and pointed out what she was doing wrong.

Just as she was going to take another practice swing, an older couple approached, and Lyle told them to play through. As Lyle pulled Julia over to the side, he explained that it was proper etiquette to allow other golfers who perhaps played faster to play through. Since it would take Julia a while to get her swing down, they could let the couple proceed.

Julia watched as the man and woman each took their swing, making it look so easy. Julia's lesson went on as Lyle went back to correcting her swing. He placed a ball on the tee and demonstrated the proper swing. Julia tried to emulate his swing as she practiced several times. He finally let her hit the ball, which didn't travel nearly as far as the balls hit by the older couple.

As they moved through the course, Lyle explained the different golf clubs and their purposes. He took what he termed the driver from her hands and placed it back into the bag. Lyle quickly named off the other clubs in the bag; Julia only caught a few of the names—3-wood, 4-iron, 5-iron. She took her second shot, which traveled farther. As they walked toward the ball, Lyle explained that it was a three-par hole and, ideally, she should make it in three shots or fewer.

Lyle continued spewing golf terminology as they approached the third hole. Her swing improved, but her grip was still uncomfortable. Lyle helped her into position and told her to keep her head down as she prepared to swing. He stopped her when he realized that two men were approaching their hole. He suggested they let them play through. Julia agreed. She certainly didn't want anyone watching her as she attempted to swing.

They stepped aside, while Lyle called out to the approaching men that they could play through. Julia looked up and recognized one of the golfers. Pablo. Her heart faltered as he came closer. She wished the ground could swallow her up. She cringed at being found out—and by Pablo, of all people.

He didn't immediately recognize her as he approached the tee. His companion stepped up first and Pablo stood behind, catching her eye as he went to thank her and Lyle for letting them play through.

"Julia! I didn't know you played golf," he said.

Julia forced a smile, but inside she was dying. How could this be happening? "You don't know everything about me."

Pablo gave her an amused grin and stepped up to the tee. He placed the ball down and expertly took his position. Julia watched as he swung his club perfectly, hitting the ball high in the air. The men watched with baited breath as the ball soared almost past their vantage point.

Pablo's partner whooped suddenly and punched the air. "Hole in one, man! How'd you do that?"

"Watch and learn, Leonard," he said. Pablo smiled and then turned around to grin at Julia.

How could he be so conceited? Lyle was impressed as he enthused about Pablo's perfect swing and follow-through. He congratulated Pablo on his hole in one and seemed forever changed by witnessing such a feat.

For the rest of the lesson, Julia heard little else than Lyle rant and rave about what an amazing swing that Spanish guy had. Julia wasn't sure what annoyed her more: Lyle's touting of Pablo or his cultural insensitivity. She wanted to tell Lyle that Pablo wasn't from Spain, and a more correct term would be Hispanic. She didn't say anything. Instead, she just endured an hour of Lyle criticizing her every attempt at a swing.

After the lesson was over, Julia regretted having made an attempt. What was she thinking? She couldn't learn how to play golf in one day. As she gingerly fingered the blisters on her hands, she scolded herself for having gone to the golf course. It was so humiliating to see Pablo and his smugness at being so superior in golf. She would never be good enough to compete with Pablo or Arthur. Besides that, Arthur would never even want to play with her. He was a guy's guy. Sometimes she wondered why he'd even hired her to work at the firm. It was obvious he got along better with all the men.

It was ridiculous to have even attempted to learn golf. She vowed to never set foot on a golf course again. She dreaded Monday and the comments Pablo would make about her lame attempt to learn. He would probably make fun of her and even tell the other attorneys. She could picture them laughing at her.

When Monday morning came, she braced herself for the onslaught of ridicule, but there was none. Pablo didn't even mention golf.

"Did you read the newspaper this morning?" Pablo asked as he took the seat next to hers.

"No," she said, taking the paper from him. She scanned the front page and noticed a picture of Mick's father, James, standing outside one of his stores.

"People have been boycotting Webber Sporting Goods. There were over a hundred protesters at his downtown store on Saturday. Many were holding signs saying that the store is financing a murderer's defense. Some aggressive protesters were blocking customers' entrance into the stores. Most of the customers just drove away."

Julia shook her head. "I can't believe that."

"They're saying that store probably saw an 80-percent decrease in sales for a Saturday. They interviewed Mr. Webber. He thinks they might have to close some of the stores."

"I guess the public really thinks he did it. That could affect our jury pool."

Pablo turned the page of the newspaper that Julia had spread out on her desk. "The media is painting a bad picture of Mick. They're making him look like some rich, privileged guy who is trying to get away with murder."

"This isn't going to help our case," Julia said.

"And it could ruin the family's business. Mick hasn't gone to trial yet, but in the public's eyes, he's already been convicted."

chapter eight

That evening at home, Julia pulled out her Franklin and looked through the numerous pages of notes she had written while interviewing Avery's teammates and friends. They had spent most of the day tracking down all the women and were able to speak to several of them. Reading through her notes, Julia tried to recall each encounter. Melissa Crews was the team's center. Her stature was misleading because Melissa was a demure, sweet girl who couldn't hurt a fly. Julia wondered how she was able to intimidate her opponents on the basketball court. Melissa had said she'd left practice early, at five minutes to five, to make a doctor's appointment and didn't see Mick at all. She and Avery weren't that close, and she didn't know many intimate details of Avery and Mick's relationship, but she had felt that Avery's game had been a little off just prior to her death.

They'd next met with Natalie Lemmon, a freshman on the team. She had informed them that she didn't play much, but Avery had befriended her right away. Natalie was overcome with emotion as she talked about Avery's friendliness and generosity. Natalie said that she usually walked out of practice with Avery, but on the day in question, Avery had told her to go ahead. Avery was going to take a shower, which she apparently didn't typically do in the locker room. Natalie remembered that Avery had explained she had a meeting with her bishop after practice and didn't have time to go home to shower and change. Natalie also said that she'd seen Mick waiting for Avery outside of the Huntsman Center at a quarter after five and stopped to talk to him for a minute. Pablo had questioned Natalie regarding the time, and she had been quite sure that it was fifteen minutes after five, because she'd checked her watch just prior to leaving Mick.

They'd also questioned Jean Staley, who was a senior on the basketball team. She was, by far, the most mature of the girls. She seemed to be taking Avery's death in stride and was very matter-of-fact in her answers, almost devoid of emotion. She had stated that she'd left the locker room only a few moments after Natalie. Jean had followed Natalie out and noticed when she'd stopped to talk to Mick. Jean didn't look at her watch but figured it wasn't long after five because she always left practice promptly. Jean stated that she wasn't very close to Avery, but they got along fine as far as teammates went.

Jean did remember coming to practice early one day and seeing Avery, who had been alone in the locker room, crying quietly. Avery had quickly wiped her tears away upon noticing Jean and turned her face away. Not wanting to embarrass Avery, Jean didn't question her, but pretended she hadn't seen her crying. Jean couldn't think of any reason Avery would be crying.

Lexy Andrews was the slender back-up point guard who played only when Avery sat on the bench, which apparently had been rare. Although Avery's outstanding ability on the court diminished Lexy's playing time, there seemed to be no jealousy or ill will. She, in fact, was very affected by Avery's death and was now either unwilling or unable to play for long periods of time. She had been at practice on the day in question and remembered Avery had been distracted on the court. Avery had guarded Lexy during scrimmage, and Lexy had scored easily several times, surprising herself. Lexy wasn't sure what to attribute her sudden success to and reasoned that it was Avery's inattentiveness.

Lexy had left precisely at five o'clock and had hurried to make a bus, so she either didn't see Mick waiting for Avery or had left the arena before his arrival. She couldn't remember exactly what time she'd passed the exit doors, but she could verify that she'd taken the five twenty-five shuttle bus.

Alicia Simmons was Avery's roommate as well as her teammate. She played the shooting guard position and was Avery's best friend. She sobbed at various intervals during their interview and cried uncontrollably for minutes at a time. With a quivering voice, she explained that she had not attended practice on the day of the murder. Alicia had been home with the flu and hadn't seen Avery since that morning. Julia had prodded her about Mick and Avery's relationship.

Alicia thought they were perfect for each other. They had much in common and got along well. Mick and Avery seldom argued, mostly because Avery was so accommodating and easygoing. Alicia did confide that Mick was putting pressure on Avery just prior to her death. In the last few weeks, he had taken over the wedding plans. He'd taken the initiative in making many of the arrangements, while Avery procrastinated doing her part. It had seemed odd to Alicia because Avery wasn't the kind of person to put things off. It was just a case of nerves, Alicia had reasoned.

Julia had asked Alicia if she could think of any reason Mick or anyone would want to kill Avery. She couldn't think of any reason. Alicia felt it couldn't have been Mick, but she couldn't be sure. If not Mick, what other explanation could there be? There was more to learn from Alicia, perceptions buried under grief. It would be worthwhile to question her again, when the sorrow had subsided.

After reading the last of her notes, Julia closed her legal pad and tossed it aside. She sighed and massaged her temples, willing her sudden headache to go away. The testimonies they'd gathered that day did little to improve their defense. The statements were solid, with almost no holes for her to magnify. Mick was seen by several people right outside the arena. He had stopped to talk to Natalie Lemmon for several moments. Five minutes later, he'd run into Jennifer Jensen just outside the women's locker room. That gave him ten minutes that were unaccounted for, during which he would technically have had enough time to kill Avery. Mick certainly had enough time to kill Avery before Jennifer came back into the locker room. Jennifer had been adamant that she was gone for a full ten minutes and that when she'd left, Avery was very much alive.

Mick, however, maintained that when he walked into the locker room, Avery was already dead. Julia didn't believe him. There was so little time between when Jennifer had left the locker room and when Mick had entered it. Five minutes at most. How could anyone have sneaked into the room while Mick and Jennifer conversed outside of it and stabbed Avery over ten times before sneaking back out just before Mick entered it? It was impossible.

Any other explanation for Avery's death, besides Mick's direct involvement, was unlikely. Could he have done it? Julia had been quite certain about it from the beginning. As she'd watched the first newscast, she had denounced his innocence. Even after meeting Mick, Julia couldn't believe that he wasn't guilty. She'd spent the last few weeks working tirelessly on his case, trying to find a way to get him acquitted, and yet she was still not convinced of his innocence. Would she ever know for sure?

Even if he hadn't murdered Avery, there was no way to prove it. But Julia had to find a way to do it. Her career depended on it. She carried the daunting thought with her to kickboxing that night. Somehow, taking out her frustration on the boxing bag alleviated her overwhelming stress.

The next morning, she and Pablo reviewed their notes from the previous day. They even toured the locker room, evaluating all the entrances. In addition to the main entrance, there was a back door—an emergency exit that led to the parking lot. That could easily have served as an escape for the killer, if indeed it wasn't Mick. However, a fire alarm would sound when the door was opened. There was no report of an alarm sounding that day, so unless the culprit disabled the alarm in some way, there was little chance of him leaving undetected. Julia made a mental note to investigate the emergency exit.

Pablo and Julia spent the rest of their day going through evidence and statements and doing research. At five o'clock, Julia wasn't ready to go home yet. She was on a roll, finding cases that had previously convicted people solely on circumstantial evidence. Many of them had been overturned years later after when further evidence was found. Julia was trying to build her case on the fact that all they had against Mick was circumstantial evidence. They didn't have a motive or any eyewitnesses. Jennifer had seen Mick after Avery had already been killed. She hadn't actually seen Mick do it. They had very little evidence; not enough to convict Mick on, or at least she hoped not.

So far, Julia had found several cases that could corroborate her strategy. Although her stomach was telling her it was dinnertime, she was eager to stay and continue her research. She looked over at Pablo, who was immersed in the police reports. He was rereading them in an effort to find something that could substantiate Mick's claim that he came into the locker room after Avery was killed. Pablo wasn't in a hurry to go anywhere either.

A half hour passed and she knew it was time to appease her hunger. If she called China Moon now, her order would be ready by the time she got there. She could bring her food back and eat at her desk. She wasn't ready to stop now; she had to keep going while her rhythm was good. A little break wouldn't hurt though.

"I'm going to order some Chinese take-out. Would you care for any?"

Pablo looked up from his files. "I was just realizing how hungry I am. I could go for some Chinese."

Julia pulled out a menu from her top drawer and handed it to Pablo.

"You're prepared," he said, taking the menu. He decided on sweet and sour chicken with pork fried rice.

"I'll call the order in and then go pick it up." Julia dialed

China Moon's number from memory and placed the order.

"I can pick it up," Pablo said.

"That's okay. I'll do it. I could use a little break."

"Are you sure? I don't mind going."

Julia stood up. "That's okay. They know me there. Sue would be very surprised if you picked up my order. She probably wouldn't give it to you."

Pablo laughed. "Sounds like you're a regular. Well, I'll pay." He reached into his back pocket for his wallet and pulled out a twenty-dollar bill.

Julia hesitated to take his money. She certainly didn't want him paying for her meal. He probably felt it was even since she was going to get it, so she took the money. When Pablo went to close his wallet, Julia couldn't help but notice a picture of a beautiful dark-haired woman. Who was she? Ordinarily, Julia kept her inquisitiveness to herself, but today she felt compelled to ask.

"Who's the woman in the picture?" she asked, pointing to his wallet.

He reopened his wallet and looked at the picture for a moment. He laughed to himself. "I'd forgotten that picture was in there. It seems odd, since I open my wallet at least once a day, but I guess her picture has become so commonplace that I didn't even notice it." He thought to himself for a minute, forgetting her question. Looking up, he suddenly remembered Julia was standing right there. "This is Christina," he said, slipping the picture out of its sleeve. "She's my ex-girlfriend. I guess I just forgot to take it out." He looked at the picture once again before letting it fall into the adjacent trash can.

Had he really done that? Thrown the photograph away with little remorse? "I take it you don't care for her anymore," Julia said.

He shrugged. "I don't know, but I'm not going to carry her picture around anymore. We broke up a few weeks ago."

"Sorry." Julia wasn't sure what to say. She didn't make it a habit of prying into other people's personal lives, but she was interested in finding out more about Christina.

"That's okay. It's all for the best." He sighed and looked away.

Julia didn't want him to feel like he had to tell her, but she also didn't want it to appear as though she didn't care. She wasn't sure if she should excuse herself to pick up the food, or just wait. She waited.

Pablo looked back up at her. "We were pretty close. I was contemplating marriage the day we broke up. We just have different goals in life, I guess. I was ready to take the next step. I wanted us to get married and start a family, but she has other things she wants to do with her life right now. She doesn't want what I want, and I can't force her to."

"I'm really sorry."

Pablo sighed. "I didn't mean to bore you with all that. You're probably anxious to get out of here and pick up the food."

"It's okay. I don't mind. Thanks for telling me. I know that must be difficult to talk about."

He nodded. "It is, but it's getting easier. I know it's for the best, so that helps me put it in perspective."

Julia agreed and then left. She wondered how much Pablo had loved Christina. If two people really love each other, shouldn't they work things out no matter what? Who was she to have an opinion? She'd never even met anyone she would think about marrying.

When she came back, they took a break from work and enjoyed their Chinese food. It was the first time in a long time that Julia didn't read a file or search the Internet while she ate. It was nice. They didn't talk about the case or about Christina. It felt good to just make small talk and not discuss anything stressful. Julia needed a break from thinking about the case.

After she'd finished her food, she took a while to get back to work. She drank the rest of her bottled water, and Pablo resumed reading through files. Julia threw out her bottle as she finished and took her seat behind her desk. They worked in silence for several minutes. It was so quiet in the office; the only noise was the turning of pages or the soft clicking on the computer. Julia jumped when she heard the thunder strike. It had caught her completely off guard. She hadn't heard a forecast of thunderstorms. She usually checked the weather in the morning and prepared herself when thunderstorms were predicted. Today, she was not prepared.

Thunder struck again, and she covered her ears. The cacophony of the murderous sounds evoked terrible memories. She hated thunder. The vicious noise took her back to a moment in her life that she prayed every day she could forget. Julia closed her eyes, but the memories came more vividly. As she opened them, she looked around the room, searching for comfort. There was none. There was only Pablo, and he was watching her. She wanted him to leave, to not be there while she was paralyzed with fear. When the thunder came, nothing made sense to her. All she could do was shut down until it went away. She couldn't control the immediate response her body had to the sounds. Turning away from Pablo, she pulled her legs up on her chair and wrapped her arms around her knees, hugging them to herself.

"Are you okay?" Pablo asked.

She nodded, but couldn't speak. Staying in her position, she waited out the thunder. She was glad when, after several minutes, it began to pour, and she couldn't hear the piercing sounds that always made her entire being ache.

Julia noticed that Pablo had found a Jazz music station online and was playing it loudly. He glanced at her every few minutes, and Julia pleaded with herself for composure. He caught her eye, and she looked away.

"I just hate thunder. That's all."

"I understand. I'm the same way with heights."

She nodded and hoped that was the end of the conversation. He'd already witnessed her panicked reaction to the thunder. She didn't want to have to rehash the entire event or answer any questions.

"Always have been," he continued. "For our senior class trip in high school, we went to an amusement park. I almost didn't go. Of course, everyone was excited about the roller coaster. You know how friends are. They pressure you, make you think you should at least try. I wouldn't do it. Anyway, the whole bus trip home, they all made fun of me for not going on the roller coaster. Of course, they didn't understand. When you're scared of something, it's beyond your control. You can't help it."

It's beyond your control. She'd told herself that before, but it did little to assuage the guilt she felt over losing power over emotions and reason. "So after all these years, are you still afraid of heights?"

"Absolutely. I probably always will be. I prefer to keep my feet planted on the ground. Nothing wrong with that, right?"

"Right." It took her a few more minutes to recuperate, and she attempted to get back to work, but other thoughts had assailed her once functioning mind. Attempting to do work was fruitless. When she felt sure that the thunder had passed, she said goodbye to Pablo and hurried home. She needed to feel safe, to be in a place where she could shut herself off from the entire world.

* * *

Pablo read through a forensics report detailing the murder weapon. He couldn't focus on the report; his thoughts kept turning to Julia. Pablo thought about her strange behavior from the day before. She was so terrified of the thunder. He'd wanted to ask her about it, but decided she most likely didn't want to talk about it. Julia was a private person, and he figured there was a lot inside of her that she guarded, not wanting to share it with anybody. He hoped one day they would be friends, and she would trust him with whatever it was that caused her pain.

Turning his thoughts back to the report in front of him, he read through the description of the knife that was used to kill Avery. It was an ordinary Bowie hunting knife, with no distinguishing features. Pablo had seen enough of them during hunting trips with his dad and friends from church. He wondered if there was any way to do a trace of it, to see where such a knife could be purchased, but it would likely do them no good. That type of knife was so common and would certainly be carried by almost any sporting good store in the city. Webber Sporting Goods probably carried such a knife, a fact that the prosecution would be sure to bring up. They would cite Mick's accessibility to the murder weapon as evidence that he could have committed the crime. Pablo sighed as he realized that this case was growing increasingly difficult to defend.

chapter nine

The next day, Julia pulled into the parking lot and took a deep breath of fresh air as she stepped out of her car. Although there was a profound chill in the air, it felt refreshing to breathe it in. She'd spent most of her lunch doing a few errands and had only had time to grab a half sandwich at Subway.

She walked into her office and took a seat behind the desk. Pablo wasn't there, and she wondered where he was. She was feeling flushed from running around and was grateful to finally be able to sit down. She was about to check her messages when Pablo walked in.

"Bad news," he announced as he walked toward her waving a pile of papers. "I just got this discovery faxed over from the prosecutor's office. The owner of McAllister's Pharmacy has signed an affidavit and is willing to testify under oath that Avery came into his pharmacy on February 19 and purchased a pregnancy test."

Julia grabbed the fax from his hands. "What?" As she scanned the fax, it confirmed what Pablo had said. "How can this be? Is he sure?"

"Bart McAllister, the owner of the pharmacy, remembers

reasonable *doubt*

Avery coming in that evening. He's a University of Utah alumni and lifelong fan. A season ticket holder, in fact, so he recognized her immediately. He says she paid with her credit card, and he's even fished out the credit card receipt. The prosecution is going to enter it in as evidence."

Julia shook her head, shocked by the news. "I can't believe it. You know what that means: either Mick is lying to us or the prosecution just got their motive. Either way, it can't be good."

Pablo hung his coat up and then slumped down into his chair. "Do you think Mick knew about this?"

"I don't know. He swears they weren't intimate." Julia reread the fax, disbelieving it. Everyone said Avery was such a good girl, but buying a pregnancy test didn't necessarily mean she wasn't. It only meant the prosecution had the upper hand.

"Maybe she was buying it for a friend," Pablo suggested.

"That's just what I was thinking, but there's no way to prove that. We'll have to talk to all of her friends and teammates again."

Pablo sighed and stood back up. He paced the office and then looked at Julia. "What if she was buying it for herself? What if Mick is telling the truth when he says they weren't intimate? What if she wasn't faithful to him? What if the prosecution tries to argue that Mick found out about this other guy and that's why he killed her?"

Julia shut her eyes, not wanting to think about that possibility. "We have to talk to Mick."

"Let's go," Pablo said, taking his coat off the coat rack. "We need to talk to him now. I can't stay here questioning every possible angle."

"Okay," Julia said. She grabbed her coat and followed Pablo out the door. So much for relaxing in her chair. Pablo offered to drive, and she agreed. The more time she spent with Pablo, the less threatened she felt by him. She followed him to his Volkswagen, where he opened the door for her.

As they drove to the county jail, they speculated about how the pregnancy test would impact the case.

After a ten-minute wait, the guard ushered Mick into the conference room. Dark circles surrounded his eyes, and his haggard features denoted suffering, but Julia wondered if that suffering was due to mourning Avery or living in jail. She already doubted his innocence, and this recent revelation did nothing to detract from her opinion of Mick. Julia wasn't thrilled at the idea of confronting him, but he had some explaining to do.

Julia looked at Pablo before addressing Mick. Instead of the usual inquiries as to how he was doing, she just went right into it. "A local pharmacist has signed an affidavit stating that Avery purchased a pregnancy test the day before she died. Do you know anything about that?"

Mick sighed and looked down, holding his face in his hands. Julia gave him a moment before continuing. "Mick, do you have any idea why Avery would have bought a pregnancy test?"

He finally looked up. "It only happened once."

Julia groaned and looked away. She was angry, not only because her case had just taken a nosedive, but also because Mick had lied to her. "What just happened once?" she asked in a blistering voice.

"We were only together once," Mick replied.

"Together, as in intimate? Intimate, as in I asked you before if you two were intimate and you said no."

"I'm sorry. I lied, but that's the only time I've ever lied to you."

"And I'm supposed to believe you?" Julia asked.

Pablo put a calming hand on Julia's arm. "Look, Mick, you can see why this is upsetting. We really need to trust you. Every detail about your relationship is going to come out. We would prefer to hear those from you, instead of from the prosecution."

"I'm sorry."

Julia took a deep breath and vowed to remain calm. "Okay, let's start from the beginning. Why did you lie to us?"

"We didn't mean for it to happen. We got carried away. Like I said, it only happened once. Of course, we both immediately regretted it. We were going to see the bishop the night she died.

We were going to tell him and talk about getting married right away. We both realized we wouldn't be able to get married in the temple, and we were sorry about it, but we still wanted to get married."

"I thought you were meeting the bishop to get your temple recommends?" Pablo asked.

"That's what the appointment was originally scheduled for, but we were going to tell him everything as soon as we got there."

"Mick, why did you lie to us?"

He shook his head. "I don't want people to think of Avery that way. She wasn't that kind of girl. She was really good, but sometimes good people make mistakes. We made a mistake, and I just don't want to see people judge her for it now that she's dead. I don't care what people think of me, really. They couldn't possibly think any worse of me, but Avery doesn't deserve that. I guess I just thought we could keep it private and nobody would have to know." He paused and wiped a stray tear from his face. "No matter what you think, I wasn't trying to protect myself. I was protecting Avery. Something I couldn't do when she was alive, and I was hoping I might be able to do that for her now, but I guess I can't."

"Mick, when did this happen?" Pablo asked.

"It was a few days before she died."

"A few days before she died?" Julia asked. "How many days?"

"It was a couple days after Valentine's Day. The eighteenth," Mick said.

"The eighteenth? That doesn't make much sense," Julia said. "She bought the test on the nineteenth. A woman doesn't buy a pregnancy test the day after she has sex. A test wouldn't work that fast. Are you sure, Mick?"

"Positive. It only happened once and it was that day. A guy doesn't forget his first time, okay?"

Julia nodded, only out of professional courtesy. She wasn't sure she could believe him. He'd already proven that he wasn't above lying. Why should she believe him that it only happened once? Her doubts, however, were not for him to know. "Maybe she was buying it for a friend. Can you think of any of her friends who might need a pregnancy test?"

Mick shook his head. "I don't know."

"We're planning on asking all of her friends and teammates. Maybe someone will know something," Pablo said.

Julia looked right at Mick. "If she was buying it for herself, Mick, it's not good. That means the prosecution has motive."

"What do you mean motive?"

Pablo walked over to where Mick was sitting. "She means the prosecution will try to make it look like you weren't the only guy she was with. Maybe it had happened before, a few weeks before, perhaps, and that's why she was buying the pregnancy test."

"No way! Avery is not like that," Mick said, standing up.

"We're not saying that," Pablo explained. "We're letting you know what to expect from the prosecution. They're going to say she was unfaithful to you, and that gave you motive."

Mick shook his head. "Even if that's true, which it most certainly is not, I would never kill her for it."

"We're not saying that, Mick. Pablo just wants you to be aware of how it's going to play out. This isn't good. We just have to think of a way to prevent it from completely ruining this case."

Pablo and Julia spent a few more minutes talking to Mick about the possible implications of the pregnancy test. Mick was more dejected than before. He wasn't sure what to think, and any way he looked at it, this wasn't going to get better any time soon. Although she was not pleased to have been the bearer of bad news, she was still disappointed that Mick had lied to her. Could he have done this? His lying gave her more reason not to believe in him.

Julia and Pablo left the county jail, and she knew there was a long road ahead.

"He lied to us!" Julia ranted as Pablo drove away from the county jail.

"Do you think he's lying about more than that?"

reasonable doubt

"Maybe. I don't know. How can we believe anything he says?"

"What he said about wanting to protect Avery makes sense to me. I think he believed he could keep it a secret. Who else knew, but him and Avery? Since Avery's dead, he's the only one that knows. At least, that's what he thought."

"Maybe. But how could he think he could get away with it? This changes everything. Now they have a motive."

Pablo entered the freeway. "I don't think the fact that she bought the pregnancy test will be admissible. There's no way to prove that she was buying it for herself."

"Oh, the prosecution will try to get it admitted."

"But they risk making Avery look bad. No prosecutor ever wants to make the victim look bad."

"They'll risk it just to make Mick look worse," Julia said. "He's the one on trial, so it will make more of an impact on his reputation. He's a clean-cut Mormon boy, returned missionary, but he was having sex with his girlfriend a few months before they were getting married in the temple. Everyone assumed they would be married in the temple. Right?"

"Terrible," Pablo said.

"It gives them motive. They can say he killed her just to cover up the fact that they were intimate. It gives them something. Motive. It was the one thing we had over them. The one thing I was clinging to. They couldn't show motive. But now they can. Urgh! I don't know what we're going to do now." Julia shook her head. It seemed that no matter what they did, they kept getting further and further away from winning their case.

Pablo hastily exited the freeway and drove toward State Street, away from their office.

"Where are you going?" Julia asked, annoyed he was not making efficient use of their time.

"You need to relieve some stress," Pablo answered.

"But where are we going?"

"Whenever I'm feeling stressed, the only way I can get rid of my anxiety is to go hit a bucket of balls."

"A bucket of balls?" Julia asked. The last thing she wanted

89

to do was hit a bucket of balls, whatever that was. Why couldn't he just drive them back to the office, so they could get working on the case?

Pablo pulled up into a parking lot. "This is a driving range. I come here sometimes just to get my aggression out on the balls. Come on, I'll show you."

Julia groaned and reluctantly got out of the car. She watched as Pablo opened the trunk and pulled out his golf clubs. "It's freezing," she said.

"Come with me," he said, taking her hand. Pablo paid for a bucket of balls. He handed Julia the bucket and slung his golf clubs over his shoulder.

She followed silently behind him as they reached a tee. Pablo placed his golf clubs down and pulled out a driver. "There's nothing that helps relieve tension like really letting one of these go." He placed a ball on the tee and drove it almost out of Julia's vantage point. "Here, you try," he said handing her the driver.

Julia rolled her eyes but indulged him. Maybe hitting the ball really hard would help her. She could take her anger out on the ball. It couldn't hurt. Trying to remember what Lyle had taught her, Julia held the driver. Pablo placed a ball on the tee for her. She tried to get the grip right but wasn't sure if she could remember how he had told her to hold it. Taking a few practice swings, she watched her hands. It didn't feel right, but what did it matter?

"Your golf swing is all wrong. That golf instructor doesn't know a thing. I bet he told you to keep your head down. Well, don't listen to him. You're holding your head in a rigidly locked position." Pablo gently lifted Julia's chin up. "There should be some space between your chin and your chest. Your spine rotates in a counterclockwise direction on the follow-through, so your head comes up along with it. So if you try to keep your head down, you won't get a good follow-through."

Julia nodded and held her chin up, still holding onto the golf club.

"He probably also told you to take a slow backswing," Pablo

said, shaking his head. "I was watching him give you instructions. It took all the self-control I had to not go over there and tell him how he was messing your swing up." Pablo stood behind her and covered her hands with his, showing her how to take practice swings. As his arms draped around her, she instinctively wanted to push them away. But it was a gentle, unassuming touch. His arms didn't demand anything; they were soft and wrapped around her like a flannel blanket on a snowy day. They brought her a comfort that was unfathomable in such close proximity to a man. Normally she'd never allow a man to be that close to her, but today the last thing she wanted to do was push him away.

Pablo stepped away and talked her through the rest of the process. Julia swung the driver and connected with the ball, sending it careening into the open range. It felt good to swing as hard as she could, hitting something and letting out her aggression on it. And it was more satisfying than playing on a course, where she had to actually take aim at something. Hitting the ball here was more freeing; she didn't need to have control of it as long as she sent it soaring in the air. She hit a few more balls, in various directions. None of them went far or anywhere near where she was aiming, but it didn't matter. What mattered was that after hitting ten balls, she did feel much better.

Pablo had been watching her swings but didn't say more in the way of correcting her. When she'd had her fill, he just smiled.

Julia couldn't help but smile back. "That does feel good. I can see why you say it helps take away your stress."

Pablo nodded. "Bucket of balls, that's my therapy."

Julia handed him the driver. "Your turn. I don't think I could hit a whole bucket."

"I'll do a few, but then you have to do some more after you've rested. Okay?" Pablo took the driver from her and in a most methodical manner, proceeded to drive the ball far past the three-hundred-yard mark.

Julia stood back and watched Pablo. She put her hands in her coat pockets, trying to warm them. The evening was cold, and she couldn't believe she was out here with him. Although Julia knew very little about golf, she couldn't help but be impressed. It was like watching Liberace play the piano, his hands moving masterfully in a task it seemed he was born to do. After Pablo nearly emptied the bucket, he returned the driver to Julia and let her finish the balls off.

"You're pretty good," he said just as she hit the last one.

"Yeah, right. You're just being nice."

"I'm not. You are good. When the weather gets nicer, we can play a few holes."

Julia shook her head. "I'm not playing with you. You'll just get all holes in one."

Pablo laughed. "No. That was just a lucky shot." He picked up the bucket and carried his clubs back to the car. "Why didn't you tell me you wanted to learn to play golf? I would have given you lessons."

"Yeah right, like I wanted you to know."

"Why not?"

"Never mind," she said, shaking her head.

"So, why do you want to learn to play?"

"It's stupid. I thought if I could learn to play, Arthur might invite me along to one of his boys' club outings. I really want to make partner, and I guess I just figured that playing golf would make the difference. Stupid, I know."

Pablo opened the door for Julia and then popped the trunk to put his clubs away. Coming around to the driver's side, he sat down. "It's not stupid, Julia, but you should know that Arthur isn't dumb. He's not going to pick the best golfer. He wants the best attorney, and that's you. Everyone knows that. Bob and Adam know. I know. Arthur knows. Maybe it's not fair that he doesn't invite you to play, but that's more of a social thing for him than a work thing. Trust me, you're not missing anything. He doesn't even talk about work; all he talks about is his game. I wouldn't worry about it."

Julia shrugged. "I guess you're right. I just get tired of him playing favorites."

"Well, just know that if it's golf Arthur wants, he'll ask Bob or Adam. If he wants someone to try the biggest case of this firm's history, it's you he wants."

Julia looked at him and noted the sincerity with which he spoke. She smiled. "Thanks. I needed to hear that."

"You're welcome," he said as he started the car.

Julia rubbed her hands together to warm them up. "I'm starving. Have you ever eaten at Mi Ranchito?"

"No, is it any good?" he asked.

"The best chicken enchiladas in the world."

Pablo laughed. "Really? Well, this I have to see. Where is it?"

Julia gave him directions, and within minutes they pulled up to the small parking lot. It felt odd walking into the familiar restaurant with someone. She'd always eaten there alone; it was sort of her little sanctuary away from the world, but tonight she would be sharing it with Pablo. Even the waitress who usually seated her was surprised to see Julia with someone.

Pablo looked at the menu. "So, are you sure these are the best chicken enchiladas in the world?"

Julia nodded. "Mmm, yes," she said, almost tasting them.

"I don't know. I'm of the opinion that my mother makes the best chicken enchiladas in the whole world. And, using her recipe, I make the second best chicken enchiladas in the whole world."

"Is that right?" Julia asked. "Well, try them and we'll see."

They both ordered the chicken enchilada platter, and as usual their meals were ready in a very short time. Julia was starving. After only a half of a sub for lunch and exerting all her energy on Mick's case and the golf range, she could eat every bite.

"So, what do you think?" she asked, after Pablo had devoured several bites of enchiladas.

Pablo swallowed and took a drink of water. "Not bad, but I can't say they're the best in the world."

Julia rolled her eyes. "You never agree with me on anything."

"Sorry, but if you tasted my mother's enchiladas, you would understand. I'll have to make them for you sometime. Of course, mine are only the second best."

"Well, for now I'll stick with these," Julia said as she continued to take ravenous bites.

After they finished eating, they lingered at their table, snacking on the remaining chips and salsa. They spoke about the case, wondering how to proceed next. As they shared ideas, Julia realized how nice it was to have a co-counsel on this case. Apart from Arthur, she'd never really worked with another attorney. And it had been years since she'd worked with Arthur. For the past few years, she'd done her own work without anyone else to rely on. Suddenly it didn't feel so bad to have Pablo to work with. He was very intelligent and intuitive, and sharing the Mick Webber case with him was more of a blessing than she had been willing to admit.

The rest of the week was spent talking to all of Avery's friends and teammates again. Avery's purchase of the pregnancy test had made the front page of the *Salt Lake Tribune* the day after Pablo and Julia had been made aware of it. Julia was glad for the foreknowledge because the news had caused a minor commotion in Salt Lake. There was speculation about the matter, which turned the tragedy into a scandal. Ordinarily, such a discovery would not cause so much uproar, but the fact that both Mick and Avery were from families that were active in the Church gave the matter great significance.

Speaking to Avery's friends didn't get them anywhere. None of them were willing to admit they knew anything about a pregnancy test. They all were shocked to hear that she would buy one. Alicia Simmons, Avery's roommate, said she'd never seen Avery with one and couldn't imagine she'd bought one. She'd tried to think back to the date that Avery had allegedly bought the pregnancy test, but she couldn't think of anything specific that had occurred that day. When asked if she could think of anyone for whom Avery had bought the pregnancy test, Alicia couldn't name anyone. Therefore, it became reasonable to assume that Avery had bought the test for herself.

chapter ten

Pablo was reading through Avery's teammates' testimonials when Sandra announced a phone call from the county jail.

"Mr. Torres," the sheriff began, "I want to inform you about an incident involving your client, Mick Webber."

"What happened?"

"Mr. Webber was involved in an altercation with another inmate."

"I can't believe it. What exactly happened?"

"It seems this other inmate verbally provoked Mr. Webber, who in turn threw a punch. I just wanted you to know. The press has gotten wind of it. They've already called several times for comments. I thought I should prepare you. I imagine it will be in the newspaper tomorrow."

Pablo sighed. "Thanks for calling. I'll take care of it." Pablo wasn't sure what he was going to take care of. This wasn't going to help their already overwhelming case.

Their defense hinged on the fact that Mick had no violent history outside the basketball court, no overriding tendency toward violence. Character witnesses were lined up to testify that Mick was incapable of committing a violent act. Their entire defense had now been obliterated with one large blow, courtesy of their own client. Well, Mick had better be prepared to give some answers because Pablo was about to demand them. Pablo stood up, pulled on his suit jacket, and then walked swiftly out to the parking lot. *What could possibly possess Mick to get into a fight?* he thought. How could he put their case, and more importantly his own life, on the line by acting out violently?

When Mick entered the visiting room, Pablo noticed several bruises on his face, along with a swollen lip.

"What happened, Mick?" Pablo asked without waiting for Mick to sit down.

Mick avoided Pablo's eyes and kept his gaze down. "He deserved it."

Pablo waved an angry hand. "Is that all you can say?"

"I'm sorry," Mick said quietly.

"Don't apologize to me. You're the one who will suffer from this. You do realize how this makes you look, right?"

Mick looked up and nodded. "I know it doesn't look good. It was stupid. I shouldn't have done it." Mick paused and then sighed. Emotion overcame him as he continued. "I couldn't let him get away with what he was saying about Avery."

Pablo looked down and nodded slowly. He breathed deeply, allowing his anger to dissipate. He looked up at Mick's solemn face and bloodshot eyes. "I'm sorry, Mick. What was he saying?"

"Oh, you know. That she was running around on me, sleeping with other guys, and that's why I killed her." Mick shook his head. "They can say whatever they want about me. They already do, and I don't care. But I can't sit there and just listen to anyone say something vile against Avery. She was the most decent person I've ever known, and I will not allow anyone to say otherwise."

"I'm really sorry he said those things. I'm sure you felt quite angry, but, Mick, it's not going to do her any good if you lose your temper. Quite the opposite, in fact. If you allow yourself to lose control of your emotions, it can be detrimental to this case and to your future. You have to brace yourself for a continued onslaught of negativity. The prosecution will overwhelm you with statements that you are not going to like, that are, in fact, false. But you have to control your temper. This is only the beginning, Mick. It's not going to get any easier, but you have to be able to deal with it."

Mick nodded mechanically. "I guess I'll have to, but I don't know how I'm supposed to let someone get away with saying something like that about the woman I love."

"You have to," Pablo said. "I didn't know Avery, but from what you've told me about her, I don't think she would want to see you reacting this way. Is it safe to say that she wouldn't want to see anyone getting punched for her sake?"

"I know that. It's just so frustrating. I'm stuck here, and I can't do anything to help find out who really did this. Look, I know what I did was stupid. I promise I'll keep myself in check. I won't do it again. I'm sorry I've made your job harder."

"And I promise you that Julia and I will do everything we can to win this case. It is absolutely the top priority in both our lives. I can assure you of that."

Mick stood up and extended his hand to Pablo. "Thank you for everything. I'm sorry. I hope I didn't screw up too much."

After departing, Pablo felt uncertainty regarding the case. Today's event would hurt their defense. They had to find some piece of crucial evidence—an eyewitness, or the true killer. All of those scenarios seemed improbable, meaning that his and Julia's daunting task had just become impossible.

* * *

Julia picked at what was left of her taco salad. She wasn't much in the mood to eat, which was unusual for her. Mick's violent outburst the week before had ruined their portrayal of him as nonviolent. Now, she was left with little shreds of truth to piece together for the defense of a man who could likely have committed the murder. Julia wrapped up her salad and tossed it into the garbage can adjacent to her desk.

Sandra buzzed in to tell her she had a call from Jim.

"Hi, Jim. I hope you've got good news for me. I need something."

Jim chuckled. "It's not much, but it may help. I just faxed over a formal complaint and restraining order that were issued to Jack Sanderson. He's the Lady Utes' current coach, but ten years ago he coached a junior college in Los Angeles. Apparently, he got involved with one of the girls on his team. They had a romantic relationship. When the girl's parents found out, they contacted the administration. She was of the age of consent, so no criminal charges could be pressed, but he was fired. The parents filed a formal complaint and had the restraining order issued. He coached at one other JC before accepting his current position."

Julia jotted notes as Jim talked. "So, what could this mean?"

"It could mean nothing. In fact, it is probably nothing, but of all the backgrounds you asked me to check out, that's the only one that's turned up with anything negative. Like I said, it's probably nothing, but I just thought I should mention it."

Julia sighed. It did seem like nothing, but she could at least check it out. "Well, thanks. Why don't you check up on this guy some more; maybe you can see if he had an alibi the day of the murder."

"You got it. I'll have a talk with him."

"Thanks. And, please, keep looking, Jim. There's got to be something we're missing."

"I'm still on the lookout, and I have several phone calls that I'm waiting to be returned. So be patient. Something will come up. Sorry it wasn't much."

"That's okay. Thanks, Jim."

Julia hung up the phone with resignation. She had hoped Jim would have come up with something by now. They still had nothing. The prosecution had Mick's prints on the murder weapon and had him at the crime scene.

"Sandra gave me this fax," Pablo said as he walked in and handed it to Julia. "What is it?"

She looked quickly at the five pages that Jim had faxed. "Some dirt Jim dug up on Coach Sanderson. I guess he had an intimate relationship with one of the girls he coached on a team several years ago." Julia scanned the restraining order. She stood up and began to pace the floor.

"So what does that have to do with our case?" Pablo asked.

"Nothing directly. Jim's going to check his alibi, but it could turn out to mean nothing. We could use it to our advantage, though. It says in this restraining order that Coach Sanderson was stalking this girl, and her parents were afraid for her safety. We could use this," she said, stopping suddenly.

"How?"

"Reasonable doubt. We introduce this into evidence and show the jury that there was a potentially dangerous man coaching Avery's team. Just as this other girl feared for her safety, every girl on that Lady Utes team was in danger. Here is a man who preys on the young women he coaches. Avery could have just been another one of his victims. Only this time, he was worried about being caught, so he took steps to prevent that from happening."

Pablo made a face. "You're just speculating."

"That's reasonable doubt. It doesn't have to be the truth; it just has to be enough to create a doubt in the minds of the jurors. So we call Coach Sanderson as a witness and ask him about his past. We don't have to make assumptions. We just let the jury draw its own conclusion. Just enough to acquit Mick."

Pablo took the fax from her hands and took a moment to read through it. "You can't do that. This happened over ten years ago and has nothing to do with this case."

Julia grabbed the fax back from him with one swift motion and sat back down. "Don't be so naïve, Pablo. It's what has to be done sometimes if you want to win a case."

"It's wrong. You would be smearing this man's reputation."

Furious that he was second-guessing her methods, Julia clenched her teeth. "How so?"

"This is ancient history. It's probably something he doesn't want coming back up. You could destroy this man's career by reintroducing the topic. The university might not want further embarrassment. He could lose his job."

"That's not my concern. Mick's case is my concern. I will do whatever it takes to show reasonable doubt. I can't let an opportunity like this pass by. It's all we've got."

Pablo sighed and sat down across the desk from her. "We'll find something, but not this."

"We don't have anything else."

"Julia, this isn't the way to win a case."

"What do you know about how to win a case? You're a novice."

"I may be a novice, but I would never ruin someone else's life just to win a case."

Julia pushed her chair back and stood up. Turning her face from Pablo's judgmental stare, she walked over to the window. She thought about Pablo's words despite her annoyance toward him. Watching the steady stream of cars going up State Street, she tried to imagine Coach Sanderson's surprise when the evidence was brought up in court. It wasn't fair, but was there any other way?

She heard Pablo's movement behind her and soon felt his presence directly next to her.

"I know you want to win this case, Julia, but I don't think this is the way."

Julia sighed softly, her ire subsiding and evolving into sadness. "We don't have anything," she said.

"I know," he said. "We'll find something."

He placed his hand on her shoulder and she immediately shrugged it off. She turned away from him and walked back to her desk. Although he was probably right, she didn't like being told what to do, especially by a man. Ignoring the fact that he was standing there expectantly, she turned to her computer and began typing an email. Julia could feel him watching her. After a minute, he turned around and walked out of the office. She picked up a pen to toss at the door, but stopped herself. Pablo wasn't Adam. He didn't deserve to have a pen launched at him. Pablo wasn't Adam, she repeated to herself. Adam was in an iniquitous category of his own. Pablo wasn't like that. She had worked with him long enough to know that Pablo was different from most men she knew. He was kind and respectful. Honest, by far, was the best word to describe him. Pablo was even becoming someone she thought she could trust.

chapter eleven

Julia and Pablo headed for Ogden in Pablo's Volkswagen. They were interviewing Avery's teammates and coaches from her previous team at Weber State. There wasn't much time left, and they had to dig into Avery's past in hope of finding someone they could connect to the murder.

The forecast on the radio called for a light dusting of snow by nightfall. Julia frowned. Their last interview was scheduled for five o'clock, so if they left by six, they would be home before the snow started falling.

By lunchtime, they'd met with three of Avery's past teammates. The interviews had been quick and uninformative. None of them had added any useful information. They had a fast lunch at a Mexican taco shop on Wall Avenue and then headed toward Harrison Boulevard, where Avery's ex-boyfriend, Todd Nielsen, lived.

Todd shared an untidy apartment with three other Weber State students. Todd was different from what Julia had expected. She had pictured him to be tall with a muscular build, perhaps a little like Mick. But Todd was about Pablo's height and rather thin. He had a full head of dark curls and wore a pair of small rim glasses. Pablo and Julia sat across from Todd at his small kitchen table. Julia hesitated to put her legal pad down on Todd's table, which was splattered with jelly and dusted with bread crumbs. Right in front of her was a sticky spot, perhaps maple syrup that had solidified. She tried not to touch the table and did her best to ignore it as she and Pablo questioned Todd.

Todd gave them a quick scenario of how he'd met Avery and a synopsis of their relationship. They had met in a sociology class, where they'd been in a study group together. After the semester ended, Todd and Avery began seeing each other and had dated exclusively for about six months.

Julia jotted a few notes on the legal pad, now on her lap. "Do you mind if I ask why you broke up?"

"Avery wasn't as committed to the relationship as I was."

"So you broke up with her?" Pablo asked.

Todd hesitated. "It was sort of a mutual decision."

Julia wondered if that was an accurate account or just his perception of it. "Were you and Avery on good terms after the break-up?"

"You could say that."

Not a definitive answer, but it didn't look like he wanted to say anything else regarding the matter. "Had you seen her since the break-up?"

"Only a few times, by accident."

"Here in Ogden?" Pablo asked.

"Once down in Salt Lake, at the mall, and again at the U campus."

Julia leaned in and almost put her elbow on the table. She quickly lifted her arm and placed it on her lap. "What were you doing on campus?"

Todd looked away. Perhaps he had finally noticed the huge pile of dishes in the sink. "I was visiting some friends in Salt Lake."

"Could we get the names of those friends?" Pablo asked.

Todd looked away from the sink and faced Pablo. "Why?"

"We would just like to ask them some questions," he replied.

"They don't live there anymore," Todd said.

Julia wanted to pursue the matter, but she sensed that Todd was getting defensive. "Had you seen Avery lately?"

He shook his head. "Not since she'd started dating that basketball player."

"Can you think of anyone who would want to harm Avery in any way?" Julia asked.

"No, I don't know why anyone would want to kill her. Avery was one of a kind."

After the interview, Todd walked them to the door. When the door had closed behind them, Pablo and Julia looked at each other.

"What do you think?" Pablo asked.

Julia started walking toward the stairwell, and Pablo followed her. "I'm not sure what to think. I still don't get a real sense of why they broke up, but I think it was probably her doing. He just didn't want to admit it."

"Do you really think all of his Salt Lake friends moved? Why wouldn't he want us to talk to them?"

Julia shrugged. "I don't know. I think I'll have Jim look into his background. It's worth looking into. I have a feeling he's about as clean as his apartment."

Pablo laughed as he opened the door for her. Julia made a cell phone call to Jim's office and left the information with his secretary. Pablo drove a few miles up Harrison to Avery's old roommate's apartment.

Sarah Bale had been her roommate for the two years Avery had attended Weber State. They'd maintained a good friendship and had still communicated via email. Sarah was a small-framed blonde woman who looked every bit the part of the college cheerleader. Sarah explained that she and Avery had a lot in common. They'd both enjoyed sports and often went running or played tennis together. She had been saddened when Avery had decided to transfer but was happy for her friend's subsequent success on the better-known basketball team.

"I went down and watched her play a few times. She was awesome. I really missed her, but it felt good to know she was happy. We still got together every once in a while, but we both had busy schedules, and even when we saw each other, it wasn't the same. There's nothing like being roommates, you know?" Sarah smiled despite her eyes brimming with tears. "I just never imagined something like this could happen."

Julia patted Sarah's arm. "I'm really sorry you lost your friend. From everything I've heard, she was a wonderful girl."

Sarah nodded as she attempted to compose herself. "She was. I just can't believed this happened, you know?"

Pablo leaned in to speak. "Can you think of anyone who would want to harm her, Sarah?"

"No. It must have been some crazy guy she'd never met. No person who knew Avery would want to kill her."

"And you've met Mick before?" Julia asked.

"Many times. He'd bring her up to visit once in a while, and I got to know him pretty well. Avery loved him."

"And you don't think he could have done this?" Pablo asked.

"No, I don't think so. Not the Mick I know, but I guess you can never be sure. People can seem like one person, but underneath be a totally different person. I don't know. I guess if the police think he did it, it could be a possibility. I just don't know. I wouldn't want to be on that jury. I don't think I could decide."

Pablo shifted in his chair. "How well do you know Todd Nielsen?"

"I knew him pretty well while he and Avery were dating. I never see him anymore."

"What can you tell us about their relationship?" Pablo asked.

"At first it was good, but then he got very controlling and jealous."

"Like how?" Julia asked.

"He didn't want her going out with her friends. He'd call her every night to see what time she got home. He didn't even like her to go on road trips with the team. He said he didn't know if she was meeting up with other guys in different states."

"How did Avery react to all this?" Julia asked.

"She didn't like it. She tried to reason with him, but it was like he didn't trust her. He thought she was seeing other guys, which she wasn't. She's not like that."

Julia made some quick notes. "Did he ever get violent with her?"

"No, not that I know of. And he wasn't verbally abusive either. It was more like manipulation and guilt. He made her feel guilty about things. Like he would say that she didn't love him as much as he loved her. And why did she hurt him when he loved her so much? He played with her mind, and she bought it most of the time. She felt bad that she couldn't do more for him and that she made him mad so much. But the problem wasn't Avery; it was him."

Julia nodded. "I think I understand. So who broke up with who?"

"Oh, she broke up with him."

Julia and Pablo looked at each other. "Are you sure?" he asked.

Sarah nodded. "She just couldn't take his games anymore. She broke up with him and he went nuts. He'd follow her to class and write her long love letters, telling her how much he loved her. He even serenaded her once outside the apartment." Sarah rolled her eyes. "He would send her, literally, loads of flowers. He'd write her poems. He was crazy in love. We would see him at night, parked out on the street just watching her window. I think he wanted to know if any guys were coming over to see her, but she didn't date anyone else after him. Not until Mick."

"So how long did this go on?" Julia asked.

"He stalked her for the rest of the semester, until she transferred. I think that's part of why she wanted to move, to get away from him. It was also a good opportunity to play for a better school, but he was a big part of it too. I think he used to go down to Salt Lake and look for her."

"Is there any possibility Todd could have killed Avery?" Pablo asked Sarah.

"No, I don't think so. He was obsessed with her, but he loved her. He wouldn't kill her. But then again, I don't know. I can't think of why anyone would kill anyone." She paused and wiped away a few tears. "That was over a year ago. I don't know why he would do that now. Todd's moved on, I think. I heard somewhere that he's engaged."

"Well, if you can think of anything else, please call us." Julia handed her a business card and thanked her for her time. They left Sarah's apartment and headed for North Ogden to meet with Avery's former coach.

"So, what do you make of this Todd Nielsen?" Pablo asked as they drove. "She makes him out a lot different than the guy we met."

"I had a feeling he wasn't being completely truthful. I think he's really worth looking into. I'd be interested to see what Jim turns out, and I think we'll be paying him another visit in the next few weeks."

Pablo agreed. "I think we should probably call some of Avery's friends who we talked to today and ask them what they know about him."

"Good idea. We can do that tomorrow."

Avery's coach offered nothing of substance. He didn't know much about Todd Nielsen, and the only information he could relay was how he had helped to improve Avery's jumpshot. As they left the coach's house in North Ogden, Julia watched the sky and worried about the impending snow. She hoped they would be well on their way to Salt Lake before the flurries began.

Pablo echoed her thoughts. "Snow's about to start soon. Maybe we should skip dinner and head straight home. Or we could go through a drive-thru and eat on the way."

"Drive-thru's fine," Julia said, increasing her pace toward the car.

By the time they reached a nearby KFC, it had started to snow. The snow was falling hard, snowflakes the size of popcorn. It didn't hold any hope of letting up soon. Thankfully, their order was ready quickly, and before Julia finished her chicken wrap,

reasonable doubt

they were already on I-15 and headed home.

The pace on the highway was slow, like Los Angeles at rush hour. Most cars kept their speed at about thirty miles per hour. The snow fell like a waterfall, a constant and infinite stream of flakes, making driving conditions hazardous. The visibility was shot, and the highway was slippery. Pablo had turned the radio to a local station, which was announcing an alarming series of precautions. People were being told not to drive if they didn't have to. Road conditions were bad and only promised to get worse. The forecast called for six to eight inches by nightfall, a big change from this morning when they announced flurries starting around nightfall.

Julia knew that weather could be unpredictable, but if they had known such a treacherous storm was coming, they would have postponed the trip. "I wish I had known how bad the weather was going to be."

"Well. There was no way to know it was going to snow like this. I think it even surprised all the weather guys."

"I guess so. I just hate to be out when the weather's like this."

Pablo took a sip of his drink and then returned both hands to the steering wheel.

Julia sighed. "At this rate, we'll never get home."

"I know, and it doesn't look like it's going to get any better."

A half hour later, they were just getting out of Ogden, and the snow hadn't slowed. The radio announced that heavy snow would continue to fall for the next several hours.

The windshield wipers squeaked at each interval. The sky was darkening quickly, and the falling snow obliterated the visibility. They were traveling no more than fifteen miles per hour. Each time Pablo pressed down on the brake, the car swerved a little and Julia couldn't help but panic. He was being cautious, but she worried about the other drivers around them. She said a quiet prayer as they continued their trudge home.

As Julia watched the cars around them, she could make out a sea of brake lights through the haze. Glancing at the speedometer, she knew they were reaching a near standstill. Some cars had pulled off to the side of the road, their blinking hazards indicating that they had been involved in an accident. She wondered what those people would do. How would they get home?

Pablo was quiet as he concentrated on driving. He was very alert, his attention focused on getting them home. An hour had elapsed from when they had first left KFC, and they were only nearing Roy. They still had over twenty-five miles before they reached Salt Lake.

"You doing okay?" Pablo asked.

She nodded. "Fine. What about you? Does it make you tense to drive in this weather?"

"A little. When I first moved to Utah, it was definitely a new experience. I'm a little more used to it now, but this is the worst I've driven in. It's not your typical storm. It just started off so fast and hasn't let up even a little."

"I know. At this rate, we'll be lucky to make it home by midnight."

Pablo caught her eye. "I'm not sure how far we should keep going. Maybe, we should pull over and wait for the snow to taper off a little."

"But that could be hours."

"I know. I just said maybe. It's so dangerous right now." Pablo shifted in his seat a little. He turned back to the road and kept his eyes fixed on it.

Pablo kept enough space between his car and the car in front of him. Whoever was driving directly in front of them was not the most experienced in the snow. The small Honda frequently fishtailed in front of them, and it took the driver several tries to get the car corrected. Pablo slowed down each time and waited for the car to right itself again.

"These are the times I wish I had a four-wheel drive," Pablo said as his car swerved slightly.

"I know. I would gladly trade my Acura for a Jeep Cherokee right about now."

Pablo laughed. "Well, I would trade this old clunker for just about anything. I'm thinking in about three months I might be able to put some money down on a newer car. I've driven this car since my freshman year at ASU."

"You should get a Subaru Outback. Those have four-wheel drive, but you don't feel like you're driving some huge truck."

"I'll keep that in mind," Pablo said, slowing down again.

The brake lights on the Honda in front of them brightened as the car swerved to the left and then overcorrected. It turned sharply to the right and then veered in the other direction again, causing it to make a hundred and eighty degree turn. Pablo quickly braked and sent his car swerving back and forth. He was able to control it and pulled to a complete stop, only inches away from the Honda that was now facing them.

Julia clutched the dashboard in front of her and turned around. Thankfully, the car behind them had been able to stop, and they came out of the incident unscathed. "Oh my gosh. I can't believe that car is facing us. We could have easily plowed right into them."

"I'm just glad I didn't get hit from behind," he said, looking in his rearview mirror. "I wonder how that guy is going to turn himself around."

Julia watched as the Honda inched forward a little and then backed up in an attempt to clear enough space to turn around. The other cars in the vicinity attempted to make room for it to turn around. The Honda's tires spun and the driver finally turned the car around. When it was facing the direction of traffic, it precariously inched forward and once again joined the endless parade of cars that continued to be bombarded by its white foe.

They continued to listen to the radio, and Julia hoped the broadcaster would announce a possible end to the torturous snow. Instead, there was more bad news.

"A collision involving some twenty-five cars is stalling the already impacted traffic on southbound I-15 just north of Bountiful. Its effects can be felt as far north as Ogden. There is some talk tonight about closing down the freeway, which is somewhat unprecedented. Authorities say it could be hours before the scene is cleared up and the traffic can continue to flow freely. Tonight, authorities are asking motorists to find alternate routes home, or to simply stay off the roads. Please stay tuned for updates every ten minutes."

Julia cringed. They were headed right toward the accident, and she couldn't imagine traffic getting slower than it already was.

Pablo turned the volume on the radio down just as a Whitney Houston song came on. "I don't think we're going to make it home tonight."

"What do you mean?" she asked with alarm no snowstorm could produce.

"We should probably find a place to spend the night."

"What, like a motel?"

"It might be a good idea," Pablo said. "It sounds like they might close the freeway."

"But they said we could find an alternate route."

Pablo shook his head. "Along with everyone else on I-15? The roads are going to be packed, no matter which way we go."

Julia winced at the thought. All she wanted was to get home, crawl into her warm bed, and never feel so helpless again.

"We would have to get separate rooms."

"Of course separate rooms," Pablo said in a way that conveyed he never entertained any other idea.

Julia nodded silently, acknowledging defeat.

Pablo trudged along for another fifteen minutes before reaching an exit. Their car crawled behind a procession of cars that also sought escape from the stalled line of cars on the highway.

The city roads weren't much better, but the plows were already at work. In Layton, it wasn't difficult to find a motel. Pablo pulled into a Best Western and shifted into park. He rolled his head around and grabbed at his neck. He turned to face Julia. "I can go inside and get us some rooms."

"I'll go with you so I can pay for mine."

Pablo smiled. "All right."

They walked through a foot of snow in the parking lot and

reasonable doubt

into the hotel office. Warmth greeted them upon entering, a small introduction of what was to come later in the motel room.

As he had earlier while at the wheel, Pablo once again took charge inside the motel office. "We'd like two rooms please."

The motel attendant looked up from the small TV he'd been watching the snowstorm coverage on. The middle-aged man pushed up his glasses to the bridge of his nose and pulled up the sleeves of his fleece Utah Jazz sweatshirt. "Let me see what I have," he said, moving toward the computer. He hit several keys on the keyboard and studied the monitor. He clicked his tongue and continued to search the screen. "Looks like alls I have left is a queen."

"That's fine. Two rooms, then," Pablo said.

The man looked up from the computer and studied Pablo and Julia in the same fashion he'd been studying the computer screen only moments before. "I just have one room. We're all booked up. Sorry."

Julia pushed her way to the counter. "Surely you have more than just one room."

The clerk peered at her over his glasses, which had slipped slightly down his nose again. "Sorry, ma'am. There's a dairy convention going on in Ogden; a lot of it has spilled over to us down here. Not too many rooms left in town, 'specially with the snow and all. I've had a lot of stranded folks make their way in here tonight. Power's out north of the mall, so a lot of the folks in motels up there are coming down this way."

Julia frowned. This couldn't be the last room left in all of Layton. "Can I borrow your phone book?" she asked the clerk.

He eyed her warily and then shrugged. Reaching under the counter, he placed a worn and ragged, probably outdated, copy of the local yellow pages on it.

Julia quickly turned the pages to the motels section. "You call this page," she said to Pablo, pointing to the right page. "And I'll take this one." She took out her cell phone and spent the next ten minutes calling the neighboring motels. Pablo did the same on the clerk's borrowed phone. All of their efforts were fruitless; there were no vacancies in the immediate area.

Julia frowned and put her cell phone away. There was no way she was sharing a room with Pablo. She turned to him. "I guess we'll just have to try to make it home."

Before Pablo could reply, the clerk butted in. "Wouldn't recommend that, ma'am. The roads are mighty slick."

Pablo nodded. "I think he's right, Julia."

"I do have a rollaway I could throw in, ma'am. You'll be much more comfortable sharing this room than stranded on the road somewhere."

Julia looked at the clerk and then at Pablo. She felt defeated. There was almost no getting out of sharing a motel room with Pablo. She nodded solemnly.

chapter twelve

Julia followed slowly behind Pablo. She pulled her long, wool coat closed with her gloved hands, trying to shield herself from the cold and the heavily falling snow. Pablo used the keycard to open the motel door and held it open for Julia to go inside. She hesitated, frantically trying to think of some other option; but short of sleeping in the car, there wasn't one. She walked into the dimly lit room and stood near the door as Pablo followed behind her. He stomped on the floor, dusting off the snow that covered his shoes and pants. She stepped off to the side, still near the door and still clutching her coat about her.

Pablo slipped his shoes off and left them near the door. He took off his coat and threw it over a chair. Looking at Julia's huddled figure near the door, he watched her. "Are you okay?"

She nodded and then looked away. Julia looked toward the bed and then back at Pablo.

"They're bringing a rollaway. I'll sleep on it. You can have the bed." He paused and the looked away. "I'm sorry about this. You know, we have no other choice. I'm sorry it's making you so uncomfortable."

She shrugged, but didn't move. A heavy knock on the door startled her and she jumped. She hadn't meant to, but her nerves were so frazzled. Clutching her coat around her, she moved slowly away from the door.

Pablo opened the door and helped the motel attendant roll the portable bed inside. Pablo unfolded it and spread the sheets onto it. Julia watched Pablo's movements and wondered if she would be able to endure the whole night. She hadn't been alone with a man in this type of circumstance since Matthew raped her. Julia hadn't allowed herself to be alone, hadn't wanted to put herself in such a vulnerable situation. But here she was in the most vulnerable of situations. She eyed Pablo warily as he finished making up the rollaway bed.

He had done nothing to warrant her suspicions. She didn't feel frightened of him, but the simple fact that she was alone with a man ignited a terrifying anxiety. Pablo sat on his bed and pulled off his suit jacket. After untying his tie, he tossed it onto a nearby table. As his hands reached his collar, Julia's memories collided with present fear. Pablo undid his top button, and she was hit by the vivid recollection of Matthew unbuttoning his shirt as his knees pinned her down. Julia grabbed the doorknob and was tempted to escape into the harrowing blizzard. Pablo was unaware of Julia clutching the doorknob as he reached for his briefcase. He pulled out a small set of scriptures, and as he set his briefcase down, he saw her standing near the door.

"Are you okay?" he asked for the second time.

"Fine. I'm fine," she said, moving away from the door. Julia walked slowly to the bed and sat down. Still wearing her coat, she pulled it around her and lay on top of the bedspread. She couldn't bring herself to take off her shoes or coat. She felt more protected, still wearing them knowing she could make a quick escape if needed. Although she didn't feel in immediate danger being alone with Pablo, she felt better knowing she was ready just in case.

"Mind if I turn on the TV? I want to see what they're saying on the news." He looked around for the remote and then sat on the edge of the rollaway bed.

Julia stared at the TV in a daze as Pablo flipped through the channels. A series of weather advisories and clips of auto accidents caused by the snowstorm flashed on the screen. Julia couldn't focus on any of it.

"Look at that," Pablo said as he watched a pile-up of cars on a stretch of I-15 just north of Salt Lake. "I'm so glad we're out of that."

Julia would almost feel more at ease in the middle of that, rather than trapped in a motel room as she was.

"Do you have anyone you need to call to let them know where you are?"

Julia shook her head, but didn't answer.

Pablo turned to face her. "You're sure you're okay?"

"I already said so."

"Okay," Pablo said, still watching her for a moment. "Would you rather I just turn this off?"

"It doesn't matter."

Pablo turned the television off and then rolled onto his stomach. Opening his scriptures, he lay on the rollaway, silently reading. Julia watched him from her laying position. He was so at peace in the current situation. He'd immediately made himself comfortable and was now immersed in the scriptures. She envied his calm demeanor. She wished she could feel so at ease in the room, but nothing could take away the fact that she was in a vulnerable position.

As she watched Pablo read his scriptures, her nerves began to calm and her fear started to dissipate. Nothing that Pablo had done felt threatening. He had proven himself trustworthy, and Julia was almost at the point where she could trust him. As she observed him reading from the same book that had brought her so much peace and joy, she couldn't help but feel Pablo was a good person.

Julia propped a pillow on the headboard and leaned into it, letting it absorb the day's tensions. Her limbs were weary, and she yawned. Her eyes wandered back to Pablo. His wavy black hair framed his tanned face well, and his facial features were very handsome. Julia stopped her thoughts and mentally scolded herself for allowing her mind to deviate off its course. The last time she'd entertained similar thoughts, she had allowed herself to be charmed by Matthew and had paid a price for it. She wouldn't put herself in that position again.

Getting up from the bed, she walked over to a chair between the door and window. She wanted to be near the door. She pulled her legs up and covered herself with her long coat. Outside, the falling snow had blanketed the ground and had now completely covered the car. She wondered how long they would be stranded tomorrow.

Pablo sat up in the bed and closed his scriptures. "Aren't you going to take your coat off?"

"I'm cold," she said, pulling her coat tightly around her neck.

"Probably because you're still wearing that wet coat. It's covered in snow."

"It's fine," she said, turning to look out the window again. She didn't want to stay here. She wanted to be home. She could sense Pablo watching her, and she wasn't going to give him the satisfaction of knowing that it bothered her. He finally gave up and went into the bathroom. Julia took the opportunity to climb into bed. She pulled the covers completely over her, covering her head. Pulling her knees up toward her chest, she wrapped her arms around them. She could feel the wetness of her coat, but she didn't want to take it off. She hated feeling so vulnerable. She prayed she would be protected and be able to get through the night, but it didn't make her feel any better. Fear hovered in the room, keeping peace from entering. She remembered hearing somewhere that fear didn't come from Heavenly Father. Fear came from the adversary, and she hated that it so easily controlled her.

The bathroom door opened, and Pablo's footsteps came closer. Julia held her breath. His footsteps stopped as he reached the rollaway bed. She could hear the squeaky mattress as Pablo sat down. He didn't say anything, and she kept her mouth shut, not wanting to draw attention to herself. Julia barely moved as she listened for the unsettling sounds that surrounded her. She could hear the muffled sounds of snowplows outside. A television was on in the next room. Pablo's deep breathing several minutes later finally calmed her. He was asleep.

The next morning, she awoke with a start. It took her several seconds to remember where she was. Had she really survived a night in the same room with Pablo? She slowly emerged from the blanket and looked over to where Pablo still lay on the rollaway bed. His body was motionless and she figured he was still sleeping. It was only six o'clock. All was well. She closed her eyes and willed herself back to sleep.

She woke up again, this time to a cascading sound. It was the shower. She sat up and saw that the rollaway Pablo had slept in was empty. The sheets were neatly folded and stacked in the center. The shower stopped, and she figured he would emerge from the bathroom in a few minutes. She pulled the sheets off, swung her legs around, and stood up. Looking down at herself, she didn't recognize the neatly pressed blouse she had picked up from the drycleaners a few days before. It was completely wrinkled and her pants didn't fair any better.

The very least she could do was deal with her unruly mane, which she was certain was full of tangles. She took her brush from her purse and walked over to the mirror. She shrugged. There was very little she could do to improve her appearance. She was a mess! She ran her brush through her hair, starting at the bottom, in an attempt to untangle it. It took several minutes, but she was finally able to tame her hair, and she brushed it into place.

She saw Pablo standing behind her; she hadn't heard him open the door. He watched her for a minute before walking over to her. It wasn't fair; he'd had ample time to freshen up, and after a shower, he looked much better than she did. His hair was still wet, but it was neatly combed. With no razor in the motel, his face was unshaven, but it didn't detract from his attractiveness.

"Morning," he said.

Julia looked away from him. "Hi."

"I hope I didn't wake you."

She shook her head and moved away from the mirror and toward the window. She pulled back the curtains and looked out toward a blanket of whiteness. It had stopped snowing, but every car, building, and tree was a blinding white.

Pablo walked over to stand next to her and looked out the window. "I was just going to get some breakfast. The snowplow hasn't been here yet, so we won't be able to get the car out, but I'll walk to the office to see what they have for breakfast."

Julia looked at Pablo and studied him for a moment. Looking back at her was a different man from the one she had sensed last night. She wasn't sure if it was the brightness of the morning, in contrast to the darkness that had seized her the night before, but something made her look at him differently. Perhaps it was the fact that they had both slept in the same room the night before and she was actually okay. Nothing had happened. The anxiety she felt being trapped in the room with him had slowly dissipated throughout the night. She was no longer panicked; her hands didn't tremble at the thought of having nowhere to go. Pablo posed her no harm. He was safe; he had always been, but she only now realized it.

Pablo looked at her once more before moving and then headed toward the door. "I guess I'll go get us something to eat. You can shower, if you want to. I'll give you some privacy and come back in a half hour or so. Is that okay?"

Julia nodded. "Thanks."

Pablo slipped on his shoes and then pulled on his heavy coat. When he opened the door, a small drift of snow flew in and settled onto the carpet of the motel room. "I guess they haven't had a chance to shovel yet," he said.

Julia peeked out behind his shoulder and saw almost a foot of snow at their door. Pablo braved the elements and took large steps down the outside corridor of the motel toward the office.

Julia looked down at herself again and wished she had a

change of clothes. She hoped they provided an iron, but after checking the room she was out of luck.

In the bathroom, she hung her blouse on the doorknob, hoping the steam would help loosen some of the wrinkles. After letting the water fall for a few minutes, she stepped into the hot water. It felt so good to let the water hit her face, washing away whatever remained of the grueling emotions she had experienced the night before. She squeezed out a small portion of the complimentary shampoo and worked it liberally into her hair.

After the shower, she felt not only refreshed but also renewed. She knew Pablo would be back, once again closing her off from the outside world, but she wasn't afraid. After getting dressed, she walked into the room and sat on the edge of the bed. She toweled off her hair as she watched the morning news. There was ample coverage of the snowstorm, and the anchor was detailing the road conditions.

Pablo knocked and then came in, bringing with him some of the snow that had been the cause of their frustration the night before. His pant legs were completely covered in white up to his knees. His shoes, absolutely not made for hiking in snow, were enveloped in the slushy white stuff. He was carrying an assortment of food, which he promptly deposited on the small table by the door. "I think I've had my exercise for the day," he said, closing the door behind him. He stomped most of the snow off his shoes and then took them off, leaving them by the door.

"You're all wet again," Julia said.

He shrugged. "I'll be okay," he said, wiping the snow off his pants. He took a seat at the table and blew warm air on his hands, rubbing them together. "So, what does the news say?"

"The plows have been working all night. They think the freeways should be fine."

"I think so too," Pablo said. "As soon as they plow the parking lot, we should be able to leave."

Julia turned the television off and came over to sit across from Pablo. "Thanks for getting breakfast. I'm sorry you got snow all over you."

"I'm fine," he said. "There wasn't much choice in the continental breakfast." He arranged his loot, which consisted of two small cartons of orange juice, several muffins, a banana, and an orange.

"Perfect," she said, smiling.

Julia really enjoyed breakfast. It wasn't the food, but the friendship she felt was developing with Pablo. After they had eaten every last bite of the food Pablo had brought, they took a seat at the edge of the bed and watched television. His proximity to her was of no concern; it didn't frighten her.

The news coverage was extensive, and they saw footage of passengers stranded at the airport, cars stalled on the roads, and people digging their cars out of the snow. The program showed clips of dented and banged up cars. They had really been blessed to make it safely to the motel, Julia thought. She looked over at Pablo and could tell he'd been watching her.

"Your hair looks good like that. It looks curly when it's wet."

Julia looked away, self-consciously grabbing her hair. Her spine tingled with the compliment, but her ever-loyal companion, fear, crept in. She turned her face toward him and saw only generosity there. He meant her no harm, she had to keep reminding herself. Finally smiling, she said, "Thank you."

He smiled back and then turned to the TV. They talked about the weather and the inconveniences it had caused around the area. Julia called Sandra and informed her of their predicament. She told her they'd be in the office as soon as they were able to go home and change. They cleaned up what little mess they'd made and went outside. Julia insisted on helping Pablo clean the snow off the car. He turned the car on to help the process along, and they walked in the knee-deep snow as they pushed the snow off the car. It took the two of them working for over twenty minutes to finally uncover his Jetta. By that time, the car was warm, which helped to somewhat dry off their wet clothes.

They drove back to Salt Lake, making casual conversation. Julia felt a gentle comfort within her. Her ubiquitous fear had remained back at the hotel. It ceased to accompany her, and for the first time she could remember, Julia felt calm in her surroundings. She glanced at the man sitting next to her. Pablo's eyes were fixed on the slushy road ahead. His dark brown eyes were gentle and undemanding, just as his demeanor always was. The curve of his mouth was set in a slight smile as he listened to the Beach Boys tune on the radio. Julia was amazed at how different her feelings were from the night before. She'd slept in absolute terror at the thought of Pablo lying only a few feet away from her. Today, she was approaching a feeling of not wanting to be anywhere but sitting by his side.

chapter thirteen

Pablo put on his gloves and pulled up the collar of his navy blue coat. After four years, he still wasn't used to the Utah winters. Sure, the grandeur of the snowcapped mountains was impressive, but on days like this, he really missed Phoenix. Back home, he'd be wearing shorts and sandals. As he walked toward the county jail, he thought back to the soft breeze and mild, cool weather that accompanied the winters back home. The chill in the air hit against his face and reminded him he was still in Utah.

He was going to visit Mick alone. Julia had suggested that Mick might be willing to open up more without her presence. There was more to be learned about Mick and Avery's relationship, and they needed to find out before the trial began.

Before long, Mick sat across from Pablo, looking his usual dejected self. Pablo updated Mick about their interviews in Ogden and the lack of progress in finding out anything more about the pregnancy test.

"Mick, how much do you know about Todd Nielsen, Avery's ex-boyfriend?"

Mick shrugged. "She told me about him, why she broke up

with him. He was really jealous and tried to control her. Avery couldn't take it anymore."

"Was he stalking her?"

"I know he used to follow her around when she still lived in Ogden. She told me that he even came down here a few times. That was before she and I started dating."

"Do you know if he ever tried to hurt her?"

"No. Why?" Mick asked with sudden alarm.

"I'm just asking. Julia and I met with him recently, and I guess I'm trying to decipher whether he would be capable of killing her."

"I don't know, maybe," Mick said. "She never mentioned that he hit her or anything. I think she would have told me, but I guess it's possible. Do you really think he could have done it?"

Pablo shrugged. "I don't know, really. He just seems a bit suspicious. We're having a private investigator look into him. I'll let you know if we find out anything."

Mick nodded.

Pablo put aside his briefcase and clasped his hands together on the table in front of him. He wanted to make this a more informal meeting, to really get to know Mick on a personal level. "Mick, I was hoping you'd tell me about the last few days before Avery was killed. How were things between you two?"

Mick leaned back in his chair and crossed his arms in front of his chest. "She was different the last few weeks. Really depressed. She wouldn't tell me why, said it was nothing, but I could tell there was something. I think she got tired of me asking because she told me to back off. I think that was the first time she ever yelled at me."

Pablo raised his eyebrow in question. "She yelled at you?"

"Yeah, she told me to leave her alone, that I was suffocating her. I didn't know what to do, so I backed off a little, but I could tell she was distressed about something."

"Did anyone see or hear your exchange?"

Mick shook his head. "No, it was at her apartment, but none of her roommates were home."

"So you never found out what was bothering her?"

"No."

Pablo leaned forward. "Some of her friends have also mentioned they thought something was bothering her. One of them said you were pressuring her to move up the wedding and that may have been the reason why."

Mick made a face. "Who said that?"

"It's not important. Were you pressuring her to move the wedding date up?"

Mick wiped his face with his hand and looked away. "I wouldn't use the word *pressure*, but after we realized we wouldn't be able to get married in the temple, I didn't see any reason to wait. We made a mistake; we went too far, but we still loved each other and wanted to get married. I figured the sooner we got married, the sooner we could go to the temple."

Pablo nodded, feeling like some light was being shed on the many questions he still had. "So what was bothering her at the time could have been the disappointment at not being able to marry in the temple, along with the guilt she felt for what you two had done?"

"No," Mick said, shaking his head. "She was like that before it happened. A few weeks before. She'd been depressed for a while when it happened. I think that's why she let it happen. At the time, I told myself that I was trying to comfort her, take her mind off whatever it was that was bothering her." Pausing, he turned away. The look on his face was so far away. "I know now I was just being selfish. I know I was just being a typical guy. I let the natural man take over, and now I'm being punished and rightfully so."

"You think you're being punished for it?" Pablo asked.

Mick looked around the room and made a grand gesture with his hands. "Look where I am. Why else am I here? I'm responsible for what happened between Avery and me. We had sexual relations outside of marriage, broke the law of chastity, and now I'm paying the price for it. She paid a higher price for it though."

Pablo shook his head at Mick's statement. "That's not how it works, Mick. You don't get immediate punishment for your sins like that."

"Well, it seems that way," Mick said, looking up. "I'm the priesthood holder. I was supposed to be strong enough for both of us and not let this happen. I should have been man enough to stop myself, but I wasn't."

"You can't keep blaming yourself for that. Once you've repented of it, you have to move on."

"You're a member of the Church," he said, in more of a statement than a question.

Pablo nodded.

"I could tell the first day I met you. There's just something about you."

"Thanks. I'll take that as a compliment."

"It is," Mick said. "Well, I went through the temple before my mission. I made covenants. I had a greater responsibility to honor those covenants. I shouldn't have let it happen."

Pablo sighed. "You're right, but you can't dwell on that now. You have to focus on the future, on winning this case so you'll have a future."

"I know," Mick said. "I've just been thinking a lot about my mission lately. I was so focused on the gospel, on living righteously. I never thought I'd end up like this."

"You haven't ended up like this. It's a hardship you're facing. Just stay strong. You'll get through this."

"And if I don't? As hard as you're working, you can't guarantee I'm going to walk out of here a free man."

Pablo nodded. "You're right. I can't make any promises. You have to have faith. And pray. Julia and I will do our part."

"I appreciate everything you're doing," Mick said.

"We're not giving up and neither should you," Pablo said. To lighten the mood, he changed the subject. "So, where'd you serve your mission?"

"Honduras."

Pablo smiled. "*Todavia hablas español?*" he asked.

Mick's lips relaxed into a smile. "*Sí, yo hablo español*. Did you grow up speaking Spanish?"

"Yeah," Pablo said. "I spoke Spanish way before I ever learned English. I don't get to speak it very much anymore. My family all lives in Phoenix. Around here, I mostly just speak English."

"Well, I wouldn't mind practicing my Spanish once in a while."

"Anytime."

"Thanks for coming today. I really needed to talk. I don't think I was much help as far as my case goes, but thanks for listening."

"Don't give up, Mick. Hang in there. I know that sounds trivial, but it's all I can say." Pablo rose from his chair. "We'll be in touch. Call us if you can think of anything else."

Mick stood up and shook Pablo's hand. They had to get him off, Pablo thought as he stared into Mick's earnest eyes.

* * *

Thursday evening was so unseasonably warm that it was hard to believe that a snowstorm had engulfed them only days prior. Most of the evidence of that storm had slowly disappeared. After spending most of the day cooped up in the office, Julia was glad to be able to get away from the grueling thought that Mick's case was going nowhere.

An hour spent at judo helped to distract her from the depressing thought that Mick's trial was approaching and none of her defense strategies was good enough to stand against the prosecution's case. As she worked up a good sweat on the gym's mats, she was able to leave behind some of the stress she'd been feeling all week.

At home, Julia scrolled through the messages in the rape forum. Several women she had written to had not responded. She stared at a new posting, afraid to open it and stir the traumatic memories again. Nothing was how it was supposed to be. Her life was not supposed to be like this. Her constant companion was her computer, and even her career was going downhill. If she

reasonable doubt

didn't win Mick's case, it would set her back more than she was prepared for.

She filled the bathtub, and as the warm water passed through her fingers, she wondered if she would always be by herself. Would she ever let down her protective wall and allow someone to care for her? Her thoughts turned to Pablo. He had become more than just her co-counsel. Pablo was now her friend. It felt good to have a friend. He had slowly become someone she could trust, and she was happy about that.

Jim Franco called the next day with interesting news. According to the Ogden police, Avery had applied for a restraining order against Todd Nielsen. The judge had denied her request, apparently because Avery could not show a threat of physical harm. Avery had admitted that Todd had never physically threatened her, and according to the judge, Todd posed no immediate threat of physical danger.

Although the small fragment of new evidence did nothing to exonerate Mick, at the very least it gave them reasonable doubt. By introducing Todd as a witness and entering Avery's application for a restraining order into evidence, Julia could show that there could quite possibly be another suspect. At some point, Avery had feared Todd. It was worth something, and the jury would see that. Julia felt reenergized and vowed to sift through every inch of the expert statements the prosecution had sent that morning.

At four o'clock, Julia put the prosecution's files into a file box and decided to take it home to look through during the weekend. She told Pablo she was calling it a day and would be working at home.

"I think I'm going home too. This has been a long week. If you need a break from all those files, why don't you come over tonight? I'll make you some chicken enchiladas. Second best in the whole wide world."

Julia laughed. She was tempted to accept his offer, and not just because she loved chicken enchiladas. Her austere judgment won over her desire to consent. She just wasn't ready to be alone with any man in his apartment. Memories of the last time she was in such circumstances clung to her mind, and she couldn't shrug them away. It had seemed so innocent to go to Matthew's apartment to study. She knew that it was different with Pablo. He was the first man she'd trusted in so many years, but she couldn't accept his invitation. "I can't, but thanks."

Pablo studied her face. "Is it because you're busy tonight and would rather do it another time, or is it because you would rather not do it at all?"

She couldn't tell him the truth. It would be too hard to explain. Thinking for a minute, she placed the lid on the file box and picked it up. "I'm just going to be swamped going through these files."

"Okay," he said. "Some other time?"

Julia nodded and then proceeded out of the office. "Bye. Have a nice weekend."

"You too," he said. "Don't work too hard."

At six o'clock, Julia had only read through a third of the prosecution's expert witness testimony. She wondered if they had deliberately gone overboard on the testimony just to bog them down with extra work. She dialed China Moon to order her usual, but there was a busy signal. A few minutes later, she was going to try again, but the doorbell rang. Looking through the peephole, she laughed when she saw Pablo standing outside with two oven mitts, holding a casserole dish.

She opened the door and couldn't hide her amused grin. "What are you doing here?"

"I had already bought all the stuff to make these, so I decided to go ahead. I hope you don't mind that I just dropped by. I know you're busy, but I figured you have to eat. I'll just leave these with you and be on my way."

"So, how'd you know where I lived?" she asked, her hand still on the doorknob.

"Arthur pointed it out one day when we drove past here on the way to a golf game. I just circled the parking lot until I saw your car. Good thing your condo number is right on the curb by your spot."

"You really didn't have to do that, but thanks. That was nice."

"Well, I just didn't want you to go on under the false assumption that Mi Ranchito's chicken enchiladas are the best in the world."

Julia laughed. How could she turn him away? "Why don't you come in? You can put it on the table."

Pablo entered her condo, but she didn't feel the anxiety or fear she would have previously associated with it. He looked handsome in jeans and a navy turtleneck sweater, not that he wasn't handsome in his business attire.

Pablo walked through the living room and placed the casserole dish on the counter. "It's still hot, so you should eat it right away."

Julia looked up at him and smiled. "This looks like a lot. Aren't you going to stay and eat with me?"

"Well, I didn't mean to intrude. It looks like you're busy," Pablo said eyeing the files scattered on her coffee table and floor.

"I know it's Friday night and you probably have plans, but if—"

"Julia, I don't have plans. Remember, *I* invited *you* over. I just don't want to intrude on your evening."

"Please stay. You went through all this trouble, and I can't possibly eat all this by myself. Besides, I could use a break from these files."

"Only if you're sure."

"I'm sure. Come on. Let's eat." Julia walked over to her cupboard and pulled out two plates. She grabbed two forks and brought them over to the table. "They smell really good."

"Just wait until you taste them."

After pouring two glasses of water and getting a spatula for Pablo to dish out the enchiladas, Julia sat down next to him. She asked him to offer a blessing. Pablo watched her as she took her first bite. He wanted to see her reaction. She didn't disappoint him there.

"Mmm! These are good. Are you sure you made these yourself?" she asked.

"What, I don't look like a guy who can cook?"

"It's not that. It's just that these are actually better than Mi Ranchito, which I never thought possible. I think you're in the wrong field, Pablo. I bet Mi Ranchito would hire you."

Pablo laughed. "Are you saying that you're getting tired of working with me?"

"No, I'm actually not. But these are really good," Julia said, taking another bite. She didn't mean to pig out in front of him, but how could she resist eating four of them? Pablo also had a hearty appetite and between the two of them, they finished off all the chicken enchiladas.

"I'm glad you liked them," Pablo said, noticing the empty casserole dish.

"You were right. Better than Mi Ranchito."

Pablo grinned, pleased with her response. "Well, in that case, I'm glad I interrupted your work. You needed a break. I can tell by looking at all those files. You sure you couldn't use some help?"

"It is more than I thought, but if you have somewhere to go, it's okay. We can sift through it some more on Monday."

"I don't have anywhere to go. I'd be glad to help as long as it gets me out of dish duty," he said with a smile.

"I'll do the dishes. It's the least I could do after you made that delicious meal." Julia got up and took her plate and glass to the sink. Pablo did the same. "I'll wash these. Why don't you take a look at the file on the couch labeled 'Neely'? He's some expert the prosecution has turned up who is saying that athletes are more prone to violence."

Pablo went into the living room, and Julia quickly washed the dishes. She dried and put them away, leaving his clean casserole dish on the counter. When she came back into the living room, she found Pablo on the couch, reading through the Neely file.

She wondered how much money the prosecution was spending on expert witnesses. She had never seen quite so many experts testifying on one case before. They must really want to win this case. She knew her firm would have to find expert witnesses to counter the prosecution's claims and wondered how much that would cost. Julia took her place across the room from Pablo at her desk. They worked in comfortable silence for over an hour. When she turned around to look at Pablo, he had taken his shoes off and was reading through a different file.

She was thankful for his help and knew she could never handle this case by herself. As she watched him, she was surprised that she didn't feel scared or anxious in the least. "How's it going over there?" she asked.

"I can't believe how much there is to read. It's unbelievable."

"I know. It was a lot more than I was expecting. Thanks for your help."

Pablo smiled. "I don't mind." He picked up the next file and then leaned back on the side of the couch, putting his legs up.

Julia turned around to continue working. It was over an hour later when she finally looked at her watch. She couldn't believe it was past nine o'clock. When she turned in her chair, she saw Pablo asleep on the couch, a file resting on his chest. She walked over to him and knelt down beside him on the floor. Julia couldn't help but watch him. He was so at peace. She watched his even breathing and was so drawn to his handsome face. The stubble on his chin was creeping in, giving him a rugged look. She wondered how he would respond to know that she was watching him sleep. Not wanting to disturb him or wake him up, she turned off the light and went into the kitchen to work. She wondered if he would wake up soon.

At midnight, when she was ready to turn in, Pablo had still not awakened. She didn't have the heart to wake him up. Walking back into the living room, she lifted the file off his chest and laid it on the ground. She took a blanket from a chest behind the couch and covered him with it. Taking one last look at his sleeping figure, she went into her bedroom. How strange it felt to go to bed, knowing that a man was asleep on her couch. Although it felt strange, surprisingly enough, it didn't feel frightening.

The next morning when she woke up, she realized that she had slept well through the night. Sitting up in bed, she wondered if Pablo was still there. It was eight o'clock. Could he still be sleeping on her couch? She took off her pajamas and pulled on a pair of jeans and a sweater. Brushing her hair quickly, she tiptoed into the living room. He wasn't there. The couch was empty. Her blanket was neatly folded on the coffee table. Venturing into the kitchen, Julia noticed the casserole dish was gone. She walked back into the living room and slumped onto the couch. Picking up a throw pillow, she clutched it to her chest. There was no evidence of him having been there at all, expect for the lingering smell of his cologne on the throw pillow and the sudden emptiness in her heart.

chapter fourteen

On Monday morning, Julia entered her office to find Pablo behind her computer. He was very focused on whatever he was doing and didn't even notice her walk in.

"Good morning," she said as she took off her coat and hung it up. "You look awfully busy for first thing in the morning."

Pablo looked up and his face brightened. "Hi, Julia. I've just been doing some research."

She walked around to his side of the desk and took a seat beside him. "What are you looking up?"

"I read through that Neely file the other night and figured we need to find someone to oppose his testimony. There are a couple of people we might be interested in. A professor at UNLV by the name of Frederick Wells published a paper last year. He argues that male athletes are no more likely to commit violent acts than their non-athlete counterparts. He studied many athletes on the collegiate level at UNLV as well as other universities, and his research even includes several professional teams."

"I'm impressed," Julia said, looking at her watch. "It's not even eight o'clock and you've found us a potential expert witness."

"Well, those Neely findings really got to me this weekend. I hope you don't mind that I borrowed the file. I read it through a few times, and I just can't agree with what he has to say. I know a lot of men who were athletes in college, and I don't think any of them have a propensity toward violence, not any more than the average man."

Julia thought about his statement. She couldn't help but think of Matthew. He was no athlete, and he certainly had a proclivity toward violence. She had been on the receiving end of it. "I tend to agree with you. That professor's study definitely warrants a phone call. Do you want to give him a call?"

"Yeah, he's still on staff at UNLV. I have his phone number here, but his office hours don't start until nine, so I'll give him a call then."

Julia was once again grateful for Pablo's involvement with her case. She had to acknowledge that she couldn't do all of this alone. "Thanks. That would be great. I can't believe you worked on this all weekend. Didn't you have anything better to do?" She didn't want to admit it, but she had worked through the weekend as well. There was little else she could have done. She certainly didn't have anyone to spend time with. The only personal time she had given herself the past two days was the few moments she'd allowed her mind to remember the image of Pablo asleep on her couch.

"I didn't have much going on this weekend," he replied. "Work at least keeps me busy. So what else do we have on the agenda for today?"

"I don't even know. I wanted to meet with the coroner or at least call him. I wonder if we can have him check to see whether Avery was pregnant. I don't think they do that sort of test randomly on all victims, especially if they know the cause of death. Let's check with him on that. We need to know for sure if she was pregnant."

Pablo was writing down notes as Julia spoke.

"I hate to say this, but if Avery wasn't buying that pregnancy test for a friend and Mick swears it only happened once just before her death, then there has to be somebody else. Someone that none of her friends knew about or are willing to name. I think there's another man involved."

"I'm afraid you might be right. Maybe we can get her telephone records subpoenaed to see some of her more frequent calls. Whoever this other man is, he might be our guy."

Pablo stared at her. "Are you trying to say that you don't think Mick did this anymore?"

"I don't know. I can't be sure. At first, I really believed he had done it. But lately, I can't be sure. What if he didn't do it?"

"I don't think he killed Avery. I've been pretty sure of that from day one."

Although she couldn't say for certain that Mick was innocent, she was definitely leaning that way. Julia hated the thought of Pablo saying, "I told you so," but he didn't.

"I'll look into the phone records."

"And Jennifer Jensen. Something about her testimony doesn't sit right with me. I keep getting this feeling that I need to talk to her again."

Pablo added it to the list. "Okay, well, I'll take care of these three phone calls. I'll call Professor Wells, the coroner, and then I'll work on Avery's phone records."

"You're going to do all that? What about me?"

"Go find Jennifer. If you're feeling like you have to talk to her again, then you should do it."

"Okay," Julia said, sighing. "I guess I'll go find Jennifer." She got up and walked toward the coat rack.

"Julia," Pablo said, and she turned around to face him. "Sorry I fell asleep on your couch."

She laughed. "That's okay. You looked really tired. What time did you leave?"

"I woke up around five and figured I should probably go home." He paused, fiddling with the pen in his hand. "Thanks for the blanket. That was nice of you. You should have just thrown some water on me and sent me on my way."

"That's okay. I didn't mind. It's the least I could do after you made the second best chicken enchiladas in the world."

Pablo laughed. "I had a good time."

"Me too," she said.

Julia couldn't help smiling all the way to her car. Even the thick chill of the morning couldn't dampen her spirits. As she drove to Jennifer Jensen's place, her mood soured a bit. Jennifer's adamant belief that Mick had killed Avery was the overriding factor in this case. She was the prosecution's key witness.

Jennifer was almost out the door when Julia approached.

Jennifer groaned as she caught sight of Julia. "I'm sorry, Miss Harris. I really don't have much time."

"That's okay. I'll just take a few minutes and then maybe I can set up a better time to come back later."

"Okay," Jennifer said as she walked to car. "You can sit in my car with me while I wait for it to warm up."

Julia obliged and sat down in the front passenger seat. Jennifer was blasting the heat, making the noise level higher than Julia would have liked. "I know you were one of Avery's close friends. You said previously that Mick was pressuring Avery to move up the wedding date. Did she ever tell you why?"

Jennifer shook her head. "No. She didn't say why."

"I hate to ask this, but we are considering the idea that Avery was seeing another man. Do you know anything about that?"

Jennifer made a disgusted look. "No way. Avery is not like that. Is that what Mick is saying?"

"No, Mick is completely against the idea. He would never say that. Certain circumstances are leading me to that theory, but there is no conclusive evidence. So you can't think of anyone else who she might have been seeing?"

"No! Ree was not like that!"

"I'm sorry. I know she was your friend. I'm not trying to denigrate her character; I'm just exploring all options."

"Well, that is not possible. I really have to go now."

"Okay, thanks for your time," Julia said, getting out of the car. As she was about to close the door, something that Jennifer had said caught her attention. "Did you just call her Ree?"

Jennifer nodded. "That was her nickname. Ree is the tail end of her name and sometimes we called her that. We mostly used it on court. I guess none of us really called her that off court. We said it when we wanted to get her attention, when we were open and wanted her to pass the ball, or when we needed her help."

"Oh, okay." Julia thanked her again and then closed the door. As she watched Jennifer drive off, she couldn't get the name out of her mind. Why did that seem familiar? She couldn't remember any of the other girls having called her by that name. Mick never used it. Jennifer had said they only used it while they played basketball. Why had Ree caught her attention?

As she drove back to the office, she kept going over in her mind where she had heard Ree before. She couldn't put her finger on it, but for some reason, it seemed important.

She was deep in thought when she got back to her office and found Pablo on the phone. Sitting in silence beside him, she continued to ponder the name. Pablo finished his phone call and started talking to her, but Julia couldn't pull her mind away from the name Jennifer had called Avery.

"Are you listening to me?" Pablo asked, waving his hand in front of her face.

"Sorry, I was just distracted."

"Well, I was just saying that I spoke to the coroner. Avery was not pregnant. I'm working on the phone records. And Professor Wells is definitely willing to consider testifying. He wants a few more details about the case, and I told him I'd check with Arthur about his proposed fee. How did things go with Jennifer?"

Julia looked at him absently. She'd heard what he said, but her mind was not on it. Suddenly, she froze. Her mind became paralyzed, and she felt the rise of bile in her throat. "What was Avery's number?"

"Her phone number?" Pablo asked.

"No, on her uniform. Her basketball number."

"Twenty-two. Why?"

"I have to go," she said as she came to her feet. "I have to go."

"Is everything okay?" Pablo asked.

"No, I have to go. I don't feel well. I'm going home. I'm sorry. I just have to go. I'll see you tomorrow."

"Julia, are you sure you're okay?"

She shook her head. "No, I have to go."

Pablo stood up and followed her to the door. "Are you going to be okay?"

She nodded. "I'll be at home."

Julia wasn't sure how she made it out to the parking lot or into her car. Her mind was in a whirlwind; her body only going through the motions. She couldn't get the sickening thought out of her mind. Racing home, she ran into the living room and turned on her computer. Willing it to load up faster, she paced the living room floor. She threw her coat off and let it fall to the floor. Once the computer booted up, she immediately logged on to the rape forum. Her head was racing, and her hands couldn't keep up with it as she clicked on the mouse, searching for the message that had permeated her mind.

Searching back several weeks, she finally found the posted message she'd been frantically trying to recall for the past half hour. She reread the message posted by REE22. So many sentences stuck out to her. "I was raped by someone I know almost a month ago. I haven't told anybody. I can't tell anybody."

It was surreal. Could that really be Avery's message, Julia wondered? It was originally posted on February 15, five days before Avery was murdered. Julia had read it and replied to it on March third, more than two weeks after it was posted. Since then, Julia had attempted several times to contact the sender of the message but had never heard back from her. Julia had often wondered how the woman was doing and if she was seeking help. Now, it was obvious that the woman had never replied to Julia's messages because she'd been killed shortly after posting her message. Was it really Avery? Ree was her nickname, and twenty-two was her number.

It all made sense now. Julia grabbed her wall calendar and flipped back several months. In her message, Avery had said that she was raped almost a month ago; that would have been around mid-January. She'd purchased the pregnancy test on February 19, right around the time that she would have reasonably suspected she could be pregnant. That was only a day after she'd been intimate with Mick, so Mick was probably telling the truth about it being their only time.

Everything fell into place. Answers were slowly beginning to make sense. If Avery was indeed REE22, of which Julia was pretty certain, then it was reasonably clear who the murderer was. Whoever raped Avery, somebody she knew, would undoubtedly be a suspect. Julia tried to focus. Avery must have known so many people. Any one of them could be the culprit.

Or could it be like Julia had suspected all along? Could Mick not only be guilty of murder, but of rape as well? Avery had said it was someone she knew. What if Mick had raped her and then killed her later to keep anyone from finding out? Could he be lying about everything? Julia had felt from the beginning that he was guilty. Only recently had she begun to believe that he could be innocent. It was something about the way he talked about Avery that made it doubtful he could have killed her. Maybe it was an act, a ruse that Mick had constructed to get others to believe he was innocent. She just didn't know anymore.

Julia read and reread Avery's message several times. Abruptly, she pulled herself away from the computer and walked to the couch. She clamped her hand over her mouth and cried. She cried for the pain she'd suffered long ago, and she cried for all the hurt Avery experienced during her rape and subsequent death. Julia couldn't put aside the overwhelming feelings of guilt that suddenly assaulted her. Avery had posted her message several days before she died. It had been a cry for help. Julia had been so wrapped up with work that she hadn't checked the forum. If Julia had kept up with the new posts and read Avery's message prior to her death, she could have responded to Avery, encouraging her to come forth and tell someone about the rape.

Julia tried to push aside the feelings of guilt that consumed her. She couldn't think about that now. She had to focus on finding out the truth. Clicking the print button on her computer, she listened to the insufferable noise the printer carriage made as it went back and forth, giving life to the horrible words Avery had written just prior to dying. Julia covered her face and sobbed as she thought about the senseless slaying of a woman who had died too young.

Julia took the paper off the printer and read it again. Following Avery's post were the many messages that had been written in reply. Along with Julia's reply, there were over twenty other messages that had been written by other women in the forum. Julia had communicated with many of the women in the past, and she knew their stories. They had also written kind words of sympathy, along with encouragement and guidance. Julia wondered if Avery had read any of the messages. Had she logged on to the forum after writing her initial message? Would she have read Julia's post had she written it earlier? Would it have made a difference in encouraging Avery to come forward in implicating her rapist?

There were so many questions and not enough answers. Julia did feel optimistic that she was closing in on the truth. If Mick had committed the rape, then it would prove what she had suspected all along. However, if he was innocent of murder and any wrongdoing, then this could be a breakthrough in the case. At the very least, she had reasonable doubt. Perhaps the police would reopen their investigation in search of Avery's rapist. They had to see that the rapist could also be the potential murderer.

Julia could focus on little else as the evening progressed. She kept going over in her mind how to proceed next. She would have to tell Mick about her discovery. She could gauge his reaction. She might be able to tell by his response whether he already knew about and perhaps had committed the rape.

Although if he was truly innocent, Julia might be able to see his genuine surprise and repulsion in finding out that Avery had been raped. If Mick was innocent, he was already in so much pain from Avery's death and over being falsely accused. How could she exacerbate his situation by telling him that Avery had been raped? Julia wondered if the rapist could be someone she had talked to already. The idea made her shudder. Could it have been Todd, someone from Avery's past?

At six o'clock, Julia was grateful to go to judo. She needed something to distract her from the tormenting thoughts that had haunted her for most of the day. She'd already spent hours reliving her own traumatic experience and wondering what Avery had gone through. She couldn't expend any more energy on the negative images playing in her mind. She needed an escape. Tomorrow, she would have to deal with the ramifications of the day's discovery. She would have to show Pablo the printouts, and together they could go see Mick.

As she stuffed the printed sheets into a manila folder and into her briefcase, she knew Pablo and everyone else would wonder how she discovered Avery's message. She would have to find some way to skirt the questions so as not to reveal her own experience. Thinking about her own message printed out on paper, she wondered if anyone would figure out that was her. There was definitely a possibility of everyone finding out, but she would have to risk that in order to find Avery's killer. She also knew some people, especially the prosecution, would argue that it wasn't Avery's message and there was no way to prove it. She was certain that it was Avery. It had to be. Julia knew the website promised confidentiality, but she hoped there was a way to connect the message to Avery. She'd have to figure out a way to investigate that possibility tomorrow. Tomorrow she would think more about it, but tonight she had to let it go. She couldn't carry around the pain and sadness she'd been feeling all day any more. After quickly changing into her workout clothes, she raced to the gym.

chapter fifteen

Pablo sat at Julia's desk, highlighting parts of Professor Wells's paper. It was an extensive report, and there was much information that would be helpful in Mick's defense. Professor Wells made many points that countered the Neely findings, which tried to show that athletes had more violent tendencies. With Professor Wells refuting the prosecution's expert witness, Mick stood a better chance.

Pablo stalled his reading. He couldn't veer his thoughts off Julia. Her behavior had been so erratic when she left earlier that day. She had been in a daze, her mind consumed with something, but she was impossible to read. There was something that transformed her behavior at times, but he wasn't sure what it was. On occasion, he sensed that she was afraid of him or uncomfortable with his presence. The night they'd been forced to sleep at the motel was a prime example.

She had been nervous all night. He remembered she had refused to take off her coat and had even slept in it. He hadn't been comfortable with the situation either, but he'd tried to make the best of it. She had been jumpy and almost panicky from the start. He wondered what caused her to behave like that. Why had she acted so scared?

Last Friday night when he made the enchiladas, he had only planned to drop them off. He had not intended to stay at her place, but she had invited him in. That day, she was more comfortable with his presence and not as nervous. He could tell she was relaxed, and he enjoyed spending the evening with her. He hadn't meant to fall asleep on the couch; he was mortified when he woke up and realized what time it was. But Julia wasn't displeased with him for having fallen asleep. When he woke up, covered by her blanket, it had seemed to him it was her way of saying she wasn't upset; that it was okay.

Even this morning, she was pleased to see him. They had a good talk before she went to see Jennifer. All of that was altered when she came back. What had happened when she talked to Jennifer? What had set her off? Pablo wondered what she was doing now. Was she ill? She said she didn't feel well, but was there more to it than that? Feeling exasperated, he shut the file he'd been reading. It was six thirty and time to go home.

The next morning, thoughts of Julia invaded his mind as he crawled through traffic on the way to work. Pablo marveled at Julia's dedication to her case, her job, and her very livelihood. From what he'd seen of her, Julia lived her career. There she was, on a Friday evening immersed in Mick's case. Mick was lucky to have her. Despite the solid case and the heaps of evidence against Mick, Julia's dedication could likely save him.

It was that dedication that at times confounded Pablo. She had put her life on hold, in a way. She wasn't married, didn't have children, and didn't really have a life outside of her career. Did it make her happy? Is that how she wanted to live her life? That made him think of Christina. They had broken up because she wasn't ready for marriage and children. She sought the elusive career that so many women give up to raise families. Christina was ready to put aside those important aspects of life in order to become a doctor. And she would be a good one. Pablo knew it now that his thoughts were no longer clouded by resentment and hurt pride. Christina was compassionate; she was intelligent; she held so many qualities that were imperative in becoming a doctor. Her patients would love her; he was sure of that. It almost made him smile at the thought of her going to medical school and one day using the qualities he had been so fond of to improve the lives of others.

He was full of regret now for the hurtful words he had used the day they broke up. It was still the right decision; he knew that. They had different goals; their paths were headed in diverse directions. He could have been more understanding, though. He could have taken the time to see her needs. He wished he had acted differently, been more supportive, but at the time, all he could feel was hurt. His pride had been hurt; his direction in life had been derailed.

If he saw her again, he knew he would feel love toward her still and be proud of her success and accomplishments. The love he had for her was not the everlasting kind of love that seeps into your soul. Rather, it was a friendship that he still felt for her and likely always would. If it had been the type of love that is meant to be eternal, he would have been able to see past their obstacles and work with her to combine their distinct goals into a loving marriage. It had not been that kind of love. That kind of love is selfless; each puts the other's needs before their own. He had not been able to do it. If he had loved her in such a way, he would never have let her go. One day he would find that love, and he would put it ahead of any earthly thing.

The world needed doctors like Christina and lawyers like Julia. The men who married those two women would be able to understand that and would find a way to make a marriage and family work in those circumstances. It was possible, but it would take sacrifices on both ends. Pablo wondered if he could be that type of man. With Christina, it hadn't been possible, but if he truly loved a woman, could he do it?

As he pulled into the parking lot, Pablo knew he needed to accomplish a lot today. Yesterday he'd spent most of his time on the Neely and Wells findings. When he walked into the office,

Julia was seated at her desk, reading through a file. She was more relaxed than yesterday, but her face was pale and weary. He'd seen that look on her face before and had been pleased that it wasn't present on Friday night or even Monday morning. Today it was back.

"Good morning," he said as he hung up his coat and took the seat next to hers.

"Hi," she said as she shut the file on the desk in front of her.

"Are you feeling better?"

She nodded. "Sort of."

"Anything I can do?"

Julia shook her head. She fingered the file in front of her, and Pablo wondered how it'd become so tattered. "I'll be fine." She cleared her throat and then continued. "Jennifer said something yesterday that got me thinking. So I spent some time on the Internet." Her fingers continued rubbing the edges of the file folder as she spoke.

She was choosing her words carefully. "What did Jennifer say?"

"It's not important; what is important is that I found this," she said, sliding the file over to him. "It's a message that Avery posted in a forum. It's a rape forum. Read it."

Pablo opened the file and started reading.

"It's this first one," Julia said as she pointed to a message written by REE22. "The others are just replies to her initial message. This was Avery's only post."

Pablo continued reading the brief message. He sighed as he learned that Avery had been raped just before her death. Sadness engulfed him as he realized what she must have suffered in silence. Knowing Mick, Pablo felt he would have been some sort of comfort if she'd had the courage to come forth. There was no sense in dwelling on that thought. The fact remained that Avery was dead, and Pablo could see the significance of Julia's findings. Whoever raped Avery was probably the same person who killed her. Pablo looked up and the pained expression on Julia's face had only deepened.

"I don't know what to say. It's horrible. Are you sure this is her?"

"It has to be. Jennifer said they called her Ree sometimes, and that's her number. It all makes sense now. Her buying the pregnancy test correlates with the date she was raped. And she never posted any messages after this one because she died shortly after."

Pablo blew out a deep breath he hadn't realized he'd been holding in. Julia had asked him what Avery's jersey number was the day before. "How did you find this?"

"I was searching the Internet," she said vaguely.

Pablo felt like there was more to it, but she didn't want to say it. He wasn't going to press the issue. Now wasn't the time. They needed to think about the possibilities. Who did this? "We need to show this to Mick—but it's going to destroy him."

"If he didn't do it himself," she said.

"What?"

"It's possible, isn't it? If Mick raped Avery, then perhaps he killed her later to cover it up."

Pablo shook his head. "Mick didn't rape Avery, and he didn't kill her."

Julia shrugged. "I'm only saying that it's possible. I don't know."

"I believe our client."

"Look, I hope he didn't do it, but I don't know. I'm just saying it's a possibility."

Pablo shook his head. "He didn't do it, and finding out about the rape is going to destroy him."

* * *

At the jail, with Mick across the table from them, neither of them knew what to say. Julia felt Pablo watching her but couldn't react, couldn't say anything. She hoped he would take her silence as his cue to begin.

"Mick, the reason we came to see you is that we've come across some very disturbing news." He sighed and slid the thin file across the table toward Mick. "Julia found this."

Mick reached for the file, a confused look on his face. "What is it?"

"It is a printout of a website that offers help to victims of various types of abuse. In this particular forum, it's rape victims. We believe Avery wrote this first message." Pablo pointed it out to Mick.

Mick quickly looked down at the printed words, shaking his head as he read. "This can't be her."

Julia spoke up for the first time. "Maybe it's not, but I think it is. Jennifer Jensen said they called her Ree sometimes, and her number was twenty-two. The date of the rape coincides with her purchase of the pregnancy test."

Mick looked up, creases formed on his forehead, and he closed his eyes. Disbelief mixed with the gravest fear possible made him incapable of speaking. He shook his head continuously; the action ceased only when his shoulders and head crumbled into a heap on the table. His body shook as he sobbed. He pounded his fist on the table several times, sending vibrations through the room. Julia was at a loss for words. She'd felt the same way many times before. Helplessness and anger were equally debilitating and almost impossible to overcome.

She leaned across the table and placed her hand on Mick's arm. She was not sure why she reached out. Those types of gestures were usually not ones she made. Something about the way he reacted to the news made her want to reach out to him and comfort him, ease his pain. She held her hand on his arm for several minutes until his body stopped trembling.

Slowly, he looked up and wiped his face with his free hand. Shaking his head slightly, he looked up at Julia. "This can't be."

Julia's heart ached. "I'm sorry, but it seems to be what happened."

"But who?" Mick asked.

"We don't know," Julia said.

"It says here it's someone she knew. Who could have done this to her? And why wouldn't she say something?" Mick asked.

Pablo spoke up. "We were hoping you might have an answer to that first question. Can you think of anyone who could have done this to her?"

Mick shook his head. "No."

"I believe whoever raped her is the same person who killed her," Pablo said.

Mick pulled his arm away from Julia's hand. Covering his face with both hands, he bent down and his body started trembling again.

"No, no, no," he repeated.

Julia wasn't sure how to proceed, but she did know one thing. He didn't do it. The message was clear in her mind. Before her sat a man on the verge of desperate pain. The news he'd just been given could push him over the edge. Whatever doubts or questions she had about Mick, she now felt in her heart that he was an innocent man. It was genuine pain and shock Mick was exhibiting.

He needed time to digest the shocking news, but how do you make sense of something so senseless? "Mick," she said.

It took him several minutes to respond or make the least amount of movement. Slowly, he looked up again. His eyes begged for understanding. He looked straight into Julia's eyes, pleading for some kind of understanding. "Why didn't she say anything? Why didn't she tell me?"

His words seized her entire body as she sought to answer his simple question, but there was no simple answer. Julia took her own trembling hands and placed them on her lap, hoping to calm her suddenly shaken body. Why wouldn't she tell anybody? Julia looked down at the floor, hoping to divert Mick's intense and beseeching gaze. "I don't really know, Mick," she said, attempting to regain her voice. "There may be a lot of reasons Avery wouldn't tell anybody. Perhaps she was afraid that nobody would believe her."

"I would have believed her," Mick said in a voice laced with anger and hurt.

Julia looked up at him. "I know you would have, but she probably hardly believed it herself. It's the single most traumatic and life-altering event that can happen to a woman. She wasn't herself anymore. A small part of her died the day she was raped. No matter who she told or what she did, she would never be able to gain that part of herself back."

Julia's words triggered Mick's tears, and he began crying again. "I could have helped her if I'd known. Instead I—" Mick shook his head at the very thought of what he was about to say. "Instead, I let us go too far. She needed me to be supportive and help her through it. We made love after she was raped. She must have thought that all men were the same."

Julia shook her head. "I think you're wrong, Mick. She knew that you loved her. In fact, she probably wanted to tell you but didn't want to hurt you. I'm sure she wouldn't have wanted to see you feeling the pain you're feeling now."

"Then why did she let it happen with us?" Mick asked.

Julia bit her lip. "I don't know exactly. Maybe she wanted to find out for herself that not all sex is violent and ugly. Maybe Avery wanted to replace her hideous memories of physical intimacy with good ones. She wanted to feel that making love could be tender and affectionate, not just gruesome and hurtful. I don't know the reason, Mick."

Mick nodded and pounded the table. "Well, what are they doing to try to find this guy?"

"Well, it's just come to light. In fact, we haven't brought it to the attention of the authorities. We plan to do it soon," Pablo said.

"Then when am I getting out of here? Now that they know I didn't do it, they'll let me go, right? I need to be out there because I will find who did this, and I'll make him pay."

Pablo glanced at Julia, and she turned to Mick. "It's not that easy. There's really no proof. We'll offer this evidence to the D.A. It's my guess that they'll want to proceed to trial despite this revelation."

"I know it doesn't seem fair," Pablo said, "but the D.A. will drag his feet as much as possible."

"I can't just sit here and act like nothing's happened," Mick said.

"It's not going to help your case any if you're out there going for blood," Pablo said. "Saying something like 'you're going to make him pay' will make you look like the bad guy."

Mick stood up. "My fiancée was raped and murdered, and

I'm supposed to just sit here and let some creep get away with it? No way!"

"Mick," Julia said rising to her feet. "We're doing the best we can."

Mick covered his face with his hands. "I think I just need to be alone right now. I'm sorry, but this is too much to take." He uncovered his face and staggered to the door. "I can't talk about this anymore. I have to go."

The guard opened the door and led Mick away. Pablo stood up and walked over to Julia.

"I can't imagine what he's going through right now," he said.

Julia didn't respond. She couldn't imagine what he was going through either, but the recent developments had brought to the forefront memories of what she'd gone through once. She didn't want to think about it anymore.

Despite her silence, Pablo continued. "I guess now's a good a time as any to bring this information to the police. Perhaps they'll reopen their investigation."

Pablo and Julia walked out of the visitor's section of the county jail and across the street to Detective St. Peters's office at the police station.

The detective stood as Julia and Pablo walked into his office. Introductions were made, and he told them they had five minutes. He was already late for a meeting.

Julia started right in and handed him the file. "We have turned up this information. It's a message we believe was written by the victim, Avery Thomas, in a rape forum. In the message, she states that she was raped weeks before her death. In my estimation, the rapist is the most likely culprit in her death and this should be thoroughly investigated."

Detective St. Peters skimmed the file and grunted. "That's hard to say. Really, this is inconclusive."

"Inconclusive? How so?" Julia asked.

"How do we even know this is the victim's message? Even if it were, the rapist isn't necessarily the murderer. Or what if Webber is the rapist? I'm still convinced it was Webber."

Julia stomped her foot and approached the detective. "Are you saying you're not going to look into this possibility at all?"

Detective St. Peters eyed Julia and then looked at Pablo. "Why don't you leave a copy of this with my secretary? I'll take a look at it later. If I do feel that this alleged rape warrants looking into, I'll put a couple guys on it. I can't guarantee anything."

Julia sighed. "Thank you. I promise that this definitely warrants looking into."

"This could be the lead that breaks your case," Pablo said.

"We'll see about that." The detective walked around his desk and toward his door. "Leave a copy with my secretary. I have to go now."

"Thanks for your time," Julia said as she followed him out the door.

They left a copy with the secretary and then went back to their office. Pablo sent a copy of the file via messenger to the District Attorney's Office, while Julia left a message stating that new evidence could quite possibly exonerate their client and was currently on its way. Pablo had also suggested that they send a copy to Jim Franco to see if he could decipher anything from it.

chapter sixteen

Julia was helping Pablo comb through Avery's phone records. Pages and pages of dates, times, and telephone numbers assaulted his mind. All of the numbers started to jumble together, and he could barely keep track of them. He had written a page of several numbers that included Mick, Avery's father, and several of her closest friends. Having already memorized many of those numbers, Pablo crossed them out each time he saw one, leaving behind numbers that he would come back and look through more carefully when he had time.

They spent most of the morning doing the tedious chore and then went to meet with Landon Meyers, the district attorney, regarding a plea bargain he wanted to discuss.

On the way over, they talked about the possibility of Mick accepting any plea. "I don't think that Mick would ever agree to plea guilty for a reduced sentence. I'm almost sure he wouldn't make a deal."

Julia nodded. "We have to at least hear Landon out and present Mick with the proffered deal. But you're right. He won't take a deal."

Julia told him she had argued against Meyers before, and he was a fierce opponent. Pablo wasn't exactly looking forward to the meeting but figured it was time he met the opposition. As they waited outside Landon's office, Julia explained that it was his usual practice to keep his appointments waiting. She was right about that. Twenty minutes after they arrived, Landon sauntered out and led them to a small conference room.

Pablo was expecting an older man, tall and intimidating. Instead, Landon was in his late thirties with dark brown hair and a short stature that wouldn't scare anyone. With his slicked-back hair and wire-rimmed glasses, he looked like a weasel emerging from a marsh.

"You do realize that you don't have much of a defense," Landon said after breezing through introductions. "I'm doing you a big favor by even offering this plea. I'll give you second-degree murder. He'll probably be sentenced to thirty years, could get out after eighteen to twenty. It's a pretty decent offer. Either that or he's looking at death row."

"Following protocol, we will take the offer to our client," Julia said. "But the answer will be no. He didn't do it, and he won't agree to plead guilty."

Landon pushed his glasses up with his forefinger. "I think you should let the client decide that."

Julia nodded. "Oh, we will. Unofficially, the answer is no, but I will get back to you with an official no after we've talked to Mick."

"You know you have no case, right?"

Pablo wanted to intervene and give Landon his two cents, but he resisted. Since Julia was the lead counsel, he decided to let her handle the dealings with Landon.

"Our case is just fine," Julia said. "Otherwise, you wouldn't even be making this offer."

Landon scowled at her. "I would advise your client to accept the plea bargain. It's the only time I will offer it."

"I'm sure that by now you have received the file we messengered over. It's evidence that the victim was raped several weeks prior to her death. It's very probable that the rapist also killed her, quite possibly to keep her from turning him in. We are currently investigating the possibility, as are the police. We're quite confident that the true killer will be found soon."

"If you want to find the true killer, you need not look any further than your own client. He will be found guilty. I'll be sure of that," Landon said, backing away. "And if you're so convinced that the victim was raped, then don't be surprised if we add a count of rape to his charges."

"What?" Julia said. "You're kidding. Mick didn't rape Avery."

"You can only hope. We will be looking into it though. Please advise your client of that."

The D.A. slithered back into his office, and Julia turned to Pablo. She shook her head. "Unbelievable."

"Let's go. Don't let him ruin your day."

Julia followed him to the elevator, and she punched the button with her fist.

In the elevator, Pablo pulled out his Superman Pez dispenser. He pushed several pieces onto his hand and popped them into his mouth, quickly chewing them into oblivion. He held it out for Julia. "Want some?"

Julia held out her hand. "I'll take the rest."

He shook it out over her hand and dropped out the remaining pink candies. "See, don't you feel better already?" he asked after she'd eaten them. "Such a stress reliever."

She shook her head. "You're so weird."

He smiled. "You do feel better."

She rolled her eyes but couldn't suppress a smile.

* * *

Jury selection was scheduled for the following month, and Julia could feel knots tightening in her stomach as she thought about the daunting task. She'd tried dozens of cases, prepared numerous opening statements, and faced countless juries, but this was different. Mick Webber's case was the most important case she'd ever tried. Mick faced the possibility of death if convicted. Julia had never defended someone who faced the death penalty, and the idea that his life was entirely in her hands caused anxiety unlike any she'd experienced in her career.

Julia sat in the passenger seat of Pablo's Volkswagen as he drove to the county jail. Her thoughts in disarray, she tried to focus on what to say to Mick about the D.A.'s offer. In light of the discovery of Avery's rape and the possibility that her true killer was still at large, Julia had hoped Landon would consider dropping the charges against Mick. Of course, that had been the furthest thought from his mind.

Despite his bravado, she suspected Landon was somewhat worried that there could be another suspect. He would want to avoid trial if the reasonable doubts kept mounting. But Landon Meyers was not one to throw in the towel. He still wanted a conviction whether Mick was guilty or not, so he'd offered the deal. That was quite a reduction from the capital murder charges currently pending, which could ultimately lead to the death penalty.

Julia felt that Mick was innocent and was confident she could win the case, but there was always the chance of conviction. Losing the case could mean death for Mick. She couldn't live with that. As she scoured her mind for how to best present Mick with his options, she wondered if she should push him to accept the plea bargain. In the end, it was his decision to make, but she could certainly give her opinion. What was her opinion? Would it be best to forge ahead with an innocent plea, knowing what that could mean for Mick? Or should she encourage him to accept a plea that would guarantee he could be out of prison in his lifetime?

As she watched the cars pass in a blur before her, Julia couldn't imagine making such a decision herself. If she knew Mick at all, she could guess that he would flat out refuse to plead anything but not guilty. Suddenly there was no haze of cars racing past her, and the car she sat in was still. Slowly coming out of her stupor, she focused on her surroundings. They were in the county jail parking lot. Pablo was seated beside her, and he was watching her curiously.

"Are you okay?" he asked.

Julia forced a smile and nodded. "Fine. I'm just thinking about what to tell Mick. I wish I had better news."

Pablo reached out to squeeze her hand, and Julia didn't even think about pulling away from his warm touch. "Do you want me to talk to him?"

Julia thought about it for a moment; but then decided against it. She could take the easy way out and let Pablo handle it, but she was the lead counsel. If she had any hope of winning this case, she had to act like it. "I'll talk to him, but thanks."

Pablo nodded and then opened his door. They walked side by side into the building and sat in the visiting room. Mick came in, dressed in his usual attire. He was less downtrodden than they'd left him, his eyes not as gloomy and his expression not as beaten down. It was possible that he saw the upcoming trial as the beginning of his absolution. Julia only wished that she had as much confidence in herself as Mick had in her.

She couldn't meet his eyes at first. Mick looked at her expectantly, but she stared down at her hands on the table, not sure how to start.

Pablo reached over to cover her hand with his and gave it a gentle squeeze. His gesture encouraged her, and she began to formulate her thoughts to address Mick.

"Mick, the reason we came to see you is because we had a meeting with Landon Meyers. It did not go as expected. We were both hoping he would drop the charges in light of recent findings, but he wants to proceed with the trial. He has offered a deal, but it would include pleading guilty to second degree murder."

Mick shook his head vigorously at the mention of pleading guilty. "No. No way. I'm not taking any deals. I didn't do it, and I won't say that I did."

Julia nodded. "I understand completely, but I am obligated to give you the full details of the deal. Second-degree murder carries a sentence of thirty years with a possibility of parole. I just want you to have all the information before you decide."

"There's nothing to decide. I'm not guilty, and that's how I'll plead until I die, whenever that has to be."

Julia bit down on her lip. There wasn't anything else for her to say. It was obvious Mick had weighed the consequences and had decided to maintain his plea, even if it meant facing death. "All right, Mick. I am absolutely ready to proceed to trial. We have a good case, but there's always the possibility of a conviction. I just want you to know that there are options."

Mick sighed. "I have no options, Julia. The only thing I can do is tell the truth. If I do plead guilty just to get a lighter sentence and possibly avoid—" Mick cleared his throat and looked away, forcing himself to continue, "avoid death, then they'll stop looking for the real killer. People will go on thinking that I killed her. I would be dishonoring Avery and what we shared. I can't do that."

"Okay. I'm glad you're so certain." Julia looked at Pablo and felt his strength through the squeeze of her hand. "We are with you 100 percent. We are going to fight this. There's nothing I want more than to see you walk out of this place a free man. Thanks for your faith in us. We will do everything we can to win your case."

Pablo nodded. "We won't give up. I've never seen anyone work as hard on anything as Julia is working on your case, Mick. If anyone can win it, she can."

Julia looked at Pablo and squeezed his hand, which was still resting on hers. "*We* can."

chapter seventeen

The next day, Pablo took an unusual break from the office when he agreed to meet Adam and Bob for lunch. He had been reluctant to do so primarily because Julia had already accused him of joining their boys' club, and he didn't want to give cause to her accusation. Although he wanted to make an effort to get along with all the attorneys at the firm, he was beginning to like Adam less and less. His arrogance was blooming like a weed, and Pablo despised the way Adam talked to and about Julia. He had zero respect for her, and Pablo had heard just about the last comment he could tolerate. Pablo had been raised to respect women, no matter what, and the way Adam addressed Julia would have been squashed in his house.

At least Bob would be there to absorb some of the negativity that Adam spewed. But Pablo's hope that Bob would act as mediator was obliterated when Adam showed up alone and explained that a verdict had been reached on one of Bob's cases, and he was called away to court. Adam took a seat across from Pablo and perused the Outback Steakhouse menu. The waitress returned with the root beer Pablo had ordered and Adam gave her his drink order. A beer in the middle of the day? How could he go back to the office buzzed?

After their meals were served, they chatted about golf and the new sportscaster on ESPN. Pablo had played a round of golf with Adam the week before, and his opinion had plunged even further. Despite Adam's shameless cheating, Pablo had easily won. Not only was Adam a terrible golfer and an avid cheater, but he was also a sore loser. He could have out-cursed a gangster. When Adam suggested that they play again soon, Pablo played up his busy schedule. Eventually, their conversation turned to work.

"So, how do you like working at the firm?" Adam asked, finishing off the last of his beer.

"It's good so far. I'm learning a lot, and there definitely isn't ever a dull moment."

Adam wiped his mouth and then crumbled his napkin, tossing it onto his empty plate. He leaned back against his seat. "Sorry you have to work with the fire-breathing dragon," Adam said, laughing.

Pablo's face grew crimson. "Don't call her that."

"What?" Adam asked, sitting up.

"I said, don't call her that."

"Come now. Don't tell me you're going to defend her."

"I just don't think it's appropriate to use that epithet to describe Julia. She's not a dragon, and if you took the time to get to know her, you'd know she's hardworking, intelligent, and a compassionate person."

Adam sneered. "Compassionate? Come on, Pablo. Who are you talking about? She's a man-hater. She actually does hate men, you know."

"Have you ever considered the fact that she's not a man-hater? Maybe, she's just an Adam-hater."

Adam shook his head and pushed his plate away. "I can't believe you're going to take her side. She will turn on you; it's just a matter of time."

"What is it exactly that caused you to dislike her so much?"

Adam's mouth gaped open, then he clamped it shut. "It's not

just me. It's everyone. She's not nice; she's a dragon, and soon you will realize it too."

Pablo shook his head. "Stop calling her that. I don't want you to disrespect her in my presence again."

Adam shot to his feet. He dug into his pocket and pulled out several bills, which he carelessly tossed onto the table. "I wouldn't waste my time on her; she would never return the favor, nor is she worth it." Adam turned around and walked toward the door.

Pablo watched Adam hustle away and was tempted to go after him and demand he treat Julia with respect. Better not. No amount of talking would change Adam's adverse opinion and maltreatment of Julia. But he had challenged Adam, made his position clear. He knew Adam would not dare use injurious words against Julia in his presence again.

When Pablo returned to the office, Sandra told him that Julia had left for the day. Pablo was full from lunch and his movements were sluggish. He relaxed into Julia's chair, the soft leather cradling his body. He could see now why Julia hoarded the chair. After five minutes, he pulled himself into a forward sitting position and scanned the files on his desk. He'd already wasted an hour and a half at lunch with Adam. Waste was an understatement when it came to time spent with Adam.

Pablo reached over to grab the file he and Julia had been studying all week. It was a thin file, only five pages, printed off the Internet. It had stunned him to read Avery's account of what had happened to her.

Even now as he reread her words, Pablo shuddered to think what it must have been like for her. He remembered Mick's reaction to the news. Mick had been devastated when they showed him Avery's message.

Pablo leafed through the few pages in the file. Avery's message had been responded to by several women in the forum, taking up more than four pages of encouraging words and advice. Pablo had quickly read through the other pages when Julia had first brought the file in, but he hadn't examined them closely. He wondered how Julia came across the information. He had asked her, and she had been vague with her response. Not wanting to make an issue of it, he had accepted her evasive answer and had decided to bring it up another time.

The people who posted in the forum were anonymous, with usernames much like Avery's. She had used REE22, and that name was typical of most of the other ones Pablo saw. Pablo read through the first three responses to Avery's post. They were short but very sympathetic and encouraging. The fourth response was longer and really struck Pablo. As he read what IVYLG wrote, each word hit him with increasing apprehension. "I was a sophomore at Harvard when I was raped," and "I kept the ugly secret to myself and never sought help." Julia? Doubting his intuition, Pablo read it again. He mentally articulated each word. Then he shut his eyes and covered them with his hands. He finally understood so much: how Julia had found Avery's message, Julia's aloofness, why she detached herself from other people.

Julia was IVYLG.

She had gone to Harvard, and Pablo surmised that her username was an abbreviated form of Ivy League. As he formulated his conclusions, anger mixed with revulsion inside of him. He felt sickened, close to losing the meal he'd just had. The feeling of powerlessness overwhelmed him as he realized what Julia had suffered long before he knew her. Ghastly images of what could have occurred infiltrated his mind, leaving him with a bomb of anger that could not easily be diffused. He opened his eyes to expel the vicious thoughts. He was infuriated that men could use their strength to divest women of their right to choose, and the thought was only made worse by finding out that it had happened to a woman he was beginning to care deeply about.

* * *

At home that evening, Pablo was looking forward to relaxing in front of the TV for the rest of the night. The Phoenix Suns were playing the Jazz on TBS, and Pablo was glad he finally had time to watch the Suns play. Their games weren't televised very often, so it was something he'd been looking forward to. Half an hour into the game, he was regretting having chosen satellite over cable. The reception was inconsistent due to the impending thunderstorms. The picture was coming in and out, and as Pablo heard thunder strike again, he knew that he wouldn't be watching the Suns play after all. He unplugged the satellite and waited five minutes. Plugging it back in, he still couldn't get a picture. As he turned the television off, he asked himself why he'd gotten satellite in the first place. He shook his head and threw himself on the couch.

He started thinking about Julia. He was almost certain that she was IVYLG. That was the only way to explain how she'd found Avery's post. There was almost no other way to explain it. The more he thought back on the time he'd spent with Julia, the more it made sense. As Pablo heard the thunder strike again, he remembered what Julia had written in her reply to Avery. Even now, thunderstorms frightened her. He wondered how she was doing at that moment.

Pablo decided to check on Julia. He knew it wasn't her first thunderstorm, nor would it be her last. She was tough and could take care of herself, but for some reason, he felt the overriding need to go to her. He wanted to comfort her. Pablo realized those were Julia's words in Avery's post. From the instant of realization, he'd wanted to take Julia in his arms and hold her until her pain went away. He knew it wasn't his place, and there wasn't anything he could do to take away her pain, but he wanted to at least try.

The rain was falling slowly when Pablo went out to his car. The conditions would probably worsen, but he wanted to see Julia. As he arrived at her place, the rain was blasting from the skies. He ran the short distance to her door and avoided getting drenched. As he stood outside her door, he wondered what he would say. He hesitated for several minutes before he rang her doorbell.

Julia opened the door. She was wearing a cream colored oversized sweater and jeans. Her eyes were a little puffy, and Pablo wondered if she had been crying. She looked at him expectantly, and Pablo was at a loss for words.

"Hi," Julia said. A clap of thunder struck and she jumped.

"Sorry to just drop by," Pablo apologized, "but I wanted to see how you were doing."

"I'm okay," she said.

"Well, good. That's good. I was just wondering."

"Do you want to come in?"

Pablo went inside. He wasn't sure what to say, but he felt like he needed to be there. "I hope I'm not interrupting anything."

Julia shook her head and took a seat on the couch. "No. I wasn't really doing anything. You can have a seat if you want."

Pablo sat on the couch next to her. "I know you don't like thunderstorms, so I just thought I'd check on you."

Julia looked away. "I'm fine."

"I'm glad. If you want me to leave, I will."

"No. It looks like the storm's getting worse; you should probably just wait it out."

Pablo looked out the window. "You're right."

Julia brought her legs up on the couch and rested her chin on her knees. "You're an intelligent person. I knew it wouldn't take you long to figure it out."

Pablo suspected he knew what she was talking about, but he didn't want to come out and say it. "I just want you to know that I'm here for you if you want to talk about it or need anything."

She turned her head toward him, resting it on her knees. "Thanks."

They sat in uncomfortable silence for several minutes. He wasn't sure what else to say. He couldn't take his gaze off Julia. She was contemplating what she wanted to say to him. He kept quiet, giving her time. She still didn't say anything.

Julia lifted her head and turned to look away from him. "It happened a long time ago. There really isn't any reason to talk about it now."

He sensed there were still lingering effects, feelings unresolved. Perhaps he wasn't the appropriate person to help her confront her trauma, but he wanted her to know he would do anything to help her. "You don't have to say anything, Julia. I just want you to know that I'm your friend, and I care about you."

"Thanks," she said looking in his direction again.

"Mick was really upset finding out that it happened to Avery," Pablo said in an attempt to change the subject.

"Yeah, I hated to be the one to give him the news. He's already going through so much."

"It must be so frustrating to love someone and know that it happened to her and not be able to do anything about it."

Julia nodded.

"Why do you suppose she never told him? Never told anyone?"

Julia looked away again and stared out the window. She watched the rain fall for several minutes. "She was probably ashamed, thought it was somehow her fault."

"Her fault? How could it be her fault?"

"She didn't protest enough. She allowed herself to be in the situation. She was too weak to fight back."

Pablo wasn't sure if Julia was talking about Avery or herself. He figured the feelings that she was describing probably fit both women. "It's never the woman's fault if she is raped."

"I know that!" Julia snapped. "I know that in here." Her voice softened as she pointed to her head and then placed her hand on heart. "But in here there are always doubts. Did I do or say anything to give him the wrong idea? I shouldn't have gone to his apartment; maybe that's why he expected it."

Pablo wanted to put his arm around her to comfort her, but he felt like part of her was still shutting him out. "It kills me to know what you went through. I know there isn't anything I can do or say, but I want you to know that I'm here for you." Pablo reached over and placed his hand on her back.

She recoiled, and he removed his hand. "I hate that I do that when you touch me. I don't mean to. I don't want to."

"It's okay," Pablo said as he rested his hand on the back of the couch.

"It's not okay, Pablo. I don't want to be like that. For a long time now, I've been uncomfortable around men. The fact that I'm sitting here on this couch next to you and not running for that door is quite a step for me."

"Well, that's a start then."

Julia nodded and then leaned back on the couch. Finding Pablo's arm there, she took it and wrapped it around her. She turned to face the other way but leaned back against him. It was a big step for her, but she was comfortable with it.

"I was an undergrad at Harvard, and Matthew was in my political science class. He was so good looking, and very intelligent, the smartest guy in the class. I was doing really well in that class, and the professor was often impressed with my insights. I guess Matthew was used to being the favorite student, and I sensed that he sort of resented me at first. A few weeks into the semester, he asked me if I wanted to study together. I figured it was his way of showing me there were no hard feelings. We got together a few times at the library to study. Then we went out a couple of times. So when he asked me to go over to his apartment to study for an exam, I didn't think anything of it. I was excited. I thought he really liked me. Well, his mind was not on studying. After I explained my standards to him, he just got so mad. He said that I thought I was too good for him and that I liked showing him up in class. Well"—she paused—"he was so angry at me. It was like he wanted to put me in my place, show me that he was superior and stronger."

Pablo pulled Julia a little closer, and she didn't draw away. He whispered softly in her ear. "I'm so sorry that happened to you. I hate thinking he did that to you."

"I dropped that class. I could never face him after that. For the most part, I knew that it wasn't my fault, but on some level, I felt like if I hadn't made him angry, he wouldn't have done it."

"Nothing you did could ever warrant him raping you." She leaned back against him comfortably, and he found that he enjoyed having her in his arms.

"I remember right after it happened, the first thing I wanted to do was take a shower, wash any trace of him off of me. I thought, if I could only get out and get cleaned off, it would all go away. I thought the next day when I woke up, the pain would all be gone. The physical pain eventually wore off, but I live with the emotional pain every day. I don't know if it will ever go away."

Pablo wasn't sure what to say. How could he comfort her? "It must be really hard for you."

"I guess I just haven't had any closure. Maybe if I had gone to the police, had him prosecuted. It's ironic that the first thing most rape victims want to do is to shower, to wash it away, but we also wash away any evidence we would have to convict them. It would have been my word against his. He was well liked by everyone. He came from a wealthy local family. No one would have believed me."

"I think talking about it now will give you some sense of closure. In your comment to Avery, you said you never told anyone."

"You're the first person I've ever said it out loud to. The first time I've done it face to face—well, sort of," she said referring to the fact that she was still leaning against him, but facing away from him. "Other than writing about it on the website, cowering behind my computer, I've never told anyone I know."

"Then this is a start," he said, gently squeezing her shoulder.

"Yeah, but it was so hard. I don't know if I can do it again."

"It might help to talk to someone who can help you work through it more."

"Like a shrink?" she said, laughing.

"Yeah. It's not such a bad idea," Pablo said.

"I probably should have done it a long time ago."

"Well, it's not too late to start." Pablo put his other arm around her and pulled her even closer. She was so at ease leaning against him. It was definitely a world of difference from the aloof person he'd first met.

Julia leaned back against him and held his arm close to her. She sighed. "Maybe someday I will. I can't really think about it right now. The thought of saying what happened to me out loud is suffocating."

"You've taken a big step by coming forward with the messages. When you're ready for the next step, you'll know."

Julia nodded and rested her head on his arm. "Thanks for coming over and for listening."

Pablo was glad he'd followed his instinct and come to her. Sharing her nightmare with him had been difficult, but now that it was in the open, maybe she could stop carrying around so much of the hurt. As she reclined against him, Pablo thought about how much he wanted to wipe away her pain. He couldn't do it; she would have to work through it herself. He wondered if she would ever find herself in a better place. Would she one day be able to remove the pain from her heart and allow herself to truly care for someone? As he held her in his arms, he hoped he would be around when that happened. He couldn't think of anywhere else he would rather be than in Julia's life.

chapter eighteen

Julia stared at the computer screen. She couldn't get past the first line. Jury questions were her forte, but today her mind couldn't focus on anything. She took a bite of her bagel, hoping it would get her motor running. Nothing worked that morning; feelings for Pablo dominated her mind.

She closed her eyes and remembered how it felt to have his arms wrapped around her the night before. She couldn't ever remember feeling anything so gentle, so loving. But it wasn't just his actions that had soothed wounds from long ago; it was also the unspoken way he could almost feel her pain. It seemed unimaginable, really. Could he care about her in such a way that it hurt him to know what happened to her? Somehow, she thought so.

She heard a noise and opened her eyes to see the image in her mind manifest itself before her. Pablo walked in, and as she smiled, she wondered how she could have ever felt anything but kindness toward this man.

He smiled. "How are you doing today?"

"Good, thanks." *Thanks to you*, she wanted to say but didn't.

He walked around the desk and sat down next to her. "I hope

you know you can call me any time you need me."

Need him. She liked the sound of that. She couldn't remember the last time she needed anybody. Everyone needs someone eventually, and she wanted him to be it for her. "Thanks."

"So, what's on the agenda for today?"

Oh, that's right. They were at work. She had a case. Why was she letting thoughts of Pablo cloud her ability to concentrate? "I think we need to talk to Mick again. We need to ask him about any male friend of Avery's that he can think of."

Pablo agreed and they left to visit Mick. Sitting beside Pablo in the car, she felt her stomach tumble with nervous energy. Things were so different than the first ride she'd taken with him. When Arthur had initially assigned Pablo to work with her, she had wished him far away from her, and now she didn't want him anywhere but at her side. She wondered if he felt the same way.

When he parked the car, he turned to face her. "I really think it's going to be okay. I don't know why, but I know we'll find a way to get Mick off."

She smiled, but she wasn't so sure. At this point, nothing about the case was sure. The only thing she was certain about was that she didn't want the man seated next to her to ever go away. When he placed his hand on hers, she wondered if he could read her thoughts. The smile his touch elicited was simply a reflex caused by the tiny surges of electricity that coursed through her body.

They walked into the county jail and waited as usual. Although the motions were all the same as past visits, the feelings were altogether new. She felt unified with Pablo as never before. Part of it was that they were working in unison to help free an innocent man, and part of it was that they had somehow become connected in the process. They were connected in a way she could not explain. Clarifying that matter would have to wait until their first task was completed.

Even Mick sensed that something was different. "*Que está pasando con ustedes?*" Mick spoke the words to Pablo in Spanish. Julia didn't understand any of it, but the grin on Mick's face and his lighthearted tone did plenty to illuminate his subject matter.

Pablo's lips relaxed into a smile at Mick's words. "*Es muy bonita, no?*"

Mick's smiling eyes met Julia's, and he nodded. "*Sí. La quieres?*"

Pablo turned to Julia, and his warm smile directed itself at her. "*Sí*," he said.

Julia listened, understanding nothing. She knew they were talking about her. She wished she had taken Spanish in high school. What were they saying?

"Stop it, you two," she said, waving her pen. "You're being rude."

Mick smirked and Pablo tucked his hands into his pockets.

"Anyway, Mick, we're here to talk a little more about the possible rape suspect. We're trying to narrow it down."

"Okay," Mick said.

Pablo pulled out a file folder. "According to Avery's post, she was raped by someone she knew. A friend, she says, who started showing interest in her."

"Do you have any idea who this could be?" Julia asked.

Mick's humor from moments ago evaporated as they talked about Avery, and Julia was sorry that she had ruined the moment.

Mick shook his head "I can't think of anyone who would call himself a friend who could do this."

Pablo spoke up next. "The next question is if you can think of anyone that might have been showing interest in Avery before she died."

Mick gritted his teeth. "I can't believe she wouldn't tell me that someone was bothering her. Why would she keep it from me?"

"I don't know," Julia said. "She was probably trying to handle it herself."

Mick nodded. "She probably knew I would have leveled the guy. I still will when I find out who he is."

"Why don't we just concentrate on coming up with possibilities?" Pablo said.

"Can you think of anyone who was hanging out with her more than usual?" Julia asked.

Mick shook his head.

"How about anyone who she shied away from, didn't want to be around?" Julie continued. She had to make him think. Whoever the rapist was, he probably was someone Mick had seen before, maybe even had met.

"Was her old boyfriend hanging around or anything?" Pablo asked.

"If he had been, I would have taken care of him," Mick said.

"Well, I truly believe whoever raped Avery is the same person who killed her," Julia said. "You have to really think, Mick. Go back in your mind to those days before her death. What did she do? Where did she go? What was she afraid of?"

"Let's give you the night to think about it, and we can touch base tomorrow. How does that sound?" Pablo asked.

"I'll try. It's hard, though, to think about that time, to think about what I could have done differently, how I could have prevented this."

"There isn't anything more you could have done, Mick. The only way you're going to be able to get through this is to stop blaming yourself." Pablo laid a hand on Mick's shoulder as he stood up.

"I can't," Mick replied.

"You have to," Julia said as she got up.

They had to find the answer now more than ever. If Mick never found out who had committed this crime, he would live forever in grief and pain.

When they got back to the office, Julia slumped into her chair. She leaned back against its softness and felt as though a weight had been lifted off her shoulders. The trial loomed like a hurricane, but she suddenly felt as though she wasn't alone. She had Pablo, and his support and confidence had bolstered her faltering spirit. He was on her side, and together they could win this case. The hesitancy and doubts that had accompanied her all morning vanished the moment he rested his hand on hers. She honestly felt that working jointly, they could accomplish anything.

When Pablo returned to the office, Julia said, "What were you and Mick saying in Spanish?"

His smile broadened, and he looked away momentarily. "Uh, well, I suppose you know we were talking about you."

"Yes, and what were you saying?"

"I'm not telling."

Julia narrowed her eyes at him. "Come on. You can't just talk about someone right in front of her and then not tell her what you were saying."

He sat back in his chair and smiled. "Yes, I can. The whole purpose of talking in Spanish was so you wouldn't know what we were saying. So why would I tell you now?"

"Come on. What did you say?"

"I'm changing the subject now," he said as he sat up straight. "So, I found a place in Provo that has the third best chicken enchiladas in the world. Third only to mine and my mom's."

Julia shook her head at his lame effort to change the subject.

"Maybe next weekend if you're not busy, you'll let me take you?"

She half shrugged.

"You are, after all, the chicken enchilada expert. I'd really like to get your opinion."

Julia smiled again. It was becoming quite a habit in Pablo's presence. The usual nervousness that accompanied such moments was absent. Why refuse his offer? She didn't want to. "I'd really like that."

Pablo's anxious face relaxed into a smile. "Good. Maybe on Saturday?"

"Saturday would be fine."

"Okay, then."

chapter nineteen

Julia brushed her long tresses, smoothing her hair down with her hand. It was the third time she'd brushed her hair in the last fifteen minutes. Pablo was picking her up in ten minutes, but it felt like an eternity. Time had never moved more slowly. She glanced at her watch again and then walked into the living room. She looked down at her outfit. She was wearing casual black pants and a charcoal gray cashmere sweater. Patting down her pants, she walked into the bedroom to check her makeup. She looked at her watch and noticed only a minute had elapsed since the last time she'd checked. Julia scolded herself for allowing her eagerness to overcome her rational demeanor.

It had been years since she'd been on a date. Taking this step, going out with Pablo today, was something she had never envisioned herself doing. Julia sensed the knock on the door almost before she heard it. The acceleration of her heart was instantaneous. She didn't think her heart could beat any faster, but as she opened the door and caught a glance of Pablo, her excited nervousness soared.

He wore beige Dockers and a navy sweater. His cologne

was a bit overpowering, but she breathed it in. Her senses were appeased by what she saw and smelled. His gentle smile and kind eyes dispelled her fears.

Pablo presented her with a small arrangement of tulips. "You look nice," he said as he handed her the flowers.

"Thank you," Julia said. "Come in. I'll put these in some water." She walked into the kitchen and fumbled around for a vase, which she filled with water. Her hands were shaking as she placed the pink tulips into the vase. It wasn't fear; she was sure of that. It was something she'd never quite felt before. It was anticipation. It was exhilaration. It was the firm knowledge that something good, something really good, awaited her. It was the awareness that her feelings for the man in the next room were more than just friendship. That was something she'd never felt before, something she never believed would be possible. And now here it was. It was the manifestation that not only was love viable for her, but it had completely engulfed her and overrun her senses. She smiled at the realization that her nervousness was due to the possibility that she was in love.

Julia walked back into the living room, afraid her feelings would give themselves away in her look, her words, or her actions. As she caught Pablo's eye, she saw a near-reflection of her own feelings. Was it possible he felt the same way she was feeling? He smiled at her and held out his hand for her to take. Julia took his hand and walked alongside him down the stairs to his car.

As they drove to Provo, Julia and Pablo talked about a range of subjects that did not include their case. The date was to be spent on more pleasant thoughts and conversation. There was a dark cloud looming over them. Not far from their thoughts was the reality that a man's life was held in their hands, but neither of them wanted to talk about it today.

Pablo talked about his family and how he grew up. His family struggled financially during his childhood, which was quite different from her own upbringing. Despite his family's lack of money, Pablo's description of his childhood was so positive and happy.

reasonable doubt

His parents worked hard and encouraged their children to do the same. Education was of utmost importance, and Pablo had been pushed to excel in school. His parents were immigrants who had come to the U.S. in search of a better life. Pablo explained how he felt that he couldn't disappoint them because they had sacrificed so much for him. They wanted all their children to be college graduates. And their dream came true the day he graduated. His older brothers had also graduated from ASU; one was now a high school principal and the other was an accountant.

"They must be really proud of you," Julia said.

Pablo nodded. "They are. 'Our three returned missionary college graduates.' That's what my mom always says anytime we're all together."

"So are you and your brothers close?"

"We are now. It wasn't always that way. I was the baby, so my brothers didn't want me around to mess up what they were playing. I was always right behind them, whatever they were doing. I tried to impress them, so they would want me around."

"Like how?"

Pablo thought a moment, and then shook his head at the memory. "Once, they dared me to skip two bars on the monkey bars at the park. I fell down and broke my arm. They felt so guilty about it that they would bring me snacks, do my chores, and change the channels on the TV for me."

"So everything was better after that?"

"Just for a little while, until I got my cast off, and then it was back to normal. They would tease me, try to keep me out of the room, and gang up on me."

"When did that all change?" she asked. Not having any brothers or sisters, she loved to hear about sibling dynamics and had always wished for a bigger family.

"Once I turned twelve, it was different. They'd let me hang out with them more. I guess they thought I was old enough to do cool stuff then." Pablo turned to her and smiled. "What about your family?"

"It's just me. My father died when I was five. My grandparents took care of us, and I always had whatever I wanted, but I think what I wanted most was a brother or sister. I think my mom never had the heart to try again. My dad was the one for her."

"Where is she now?"

"She travels a lot; she spends a lot of time in Asia, working with different charities. I see her once a year, maybe."

"That must be hard."

Julia shrugged. "It is, but I guess I'm used to it. We email a lot and talk on the phone."

The drive to Provo went fast as she asked Pablo more questions about how he grew up. When they reached the restaurant in downtown Provo, Julia was almost disappointed that they had arrived at their destination. All trace of disappointment dissolved as they entered the small restaurant and she got a hint of the delicious aroma.

She'd sat across the dinner table from him before. They'd shared many meals together in varying places and circumstances, but this was different. Everything was different. The food was the same. Chips, salsa, chicken enchiladas, but the steady racing of her heart had never been present before. The thin layer of moisture on her palms was new too. Something hidden deep within her, a feeling she had suppressed for too long, was infiltrating her system. She'd worked to keep it buried, away from reach, but now it was involuntarily breaking through the deep layers of dirt she'd thrown over it. Like the first blossom of spring, it was pushing its way to the surface, dying for sunlight, aching to be seen. And for the first time, Julia wasn't fighting it. She was welcoming it, reveling in the feeling of attraction, longing, and love.

Pablo smiled at her, and Julia's heart danced. "I'm glad we did this," he said.

"Me too."

"I know you've been hurt before. I would never want to hurt you. I hope you know that."

Julia forced a smile. She didn't really want to talk about it.

"I hope you trust me," he said.

"I do. I haven't trusted anyone in so long. I feel safe with you."

Pablo reached across the table and took her hand. He squeezed it, sending an array of electric shocks coursing though her body. "You'll always be safe with me."

She wondered if he'd felt it too. She eased her hand out of his, but smiled. "I know that, but I have a lot of issues. You shouldn't have to deal with them."

"I know your issues. I've stuck around this long. I'm not going anywhere. I don't want to. I'm not saying I can solve your issues. No one can do that except you, but I'm willing to stand by you as you work on them. I want to do anything you let me do to help. I don't know the depths of your pain. I know I'll never understand, but I'll listen. I'll be there for as long as you let me."

Julia wasn't sure how to respond. His sincerity reached her very core. She smiled and nodded, reaching now for his hand. He'd opened the door to her inner soul and had seen the darkness that had plagued her for years, but he didn't mind. He knew things about her that she'd never shared with anyone. He'd seen her at the height of her fear, a trembling being at the mercy of her self-made prison in a hotel room on a cold, escapeless night. It didn't matter to him. None of it mattered. She could sense it, not only in his words but also in the love she saw in his eyes and felt through his touch.

Dinner never tasted so good. True, the enchiladas weren't as good as Pablo's, but Julia was full of something else. A sense of knowing that she didn't have to live in fear, in bleakness, in consuming and oppressing darkness that blocked out the tiniest ray of light. Pablo said he couldn't solve her issues, and she knew that. She would have to do it herself, but for the first time, she really wanted to, or felt she could work through the dreadful memories and constant fear. Peace could be hers one day, and she was ready to embrace it.

They walked hand in hand out of the restaurant and toward his car. Pablo started the car and turned to face her. "So, it's the moment of truth."

Julia raised an eyebrow and waited for him to continue.

"How did you rate the enchiladas?"

"Not as good, but tolerable considering the company was excellent."

"Well, maybe one day you'll come down to Phoenix with me and taste the originals."

Her smile couldn't be wider. "That would be nice."

"Do you want to drive over to the temple and walk around?"

They spent an hour lingering around the temple grounds and talking, creating an idyllic aura that Julia had never imagined she could be a part of. Automatically, her thoughts turned to the wonderful edifice before her and the idea of temple marriage. She wondered if that would happen for her. Holding Pablo's hand as she walked around the temple made her think it was possible. Beautiful, brown-eyed children could be in her future, and she couldn't think of anything she wanted more.

The ride back to Salt Lake was like a blissful carriage ride. She felt this was only the beginning of her happiness. Pablo kept his hand on Julia's for most of the drive, steadying the steering wheel with only one hand. They passed the Point of the Mountain, and Julia's heart sank. They would be home in ten minutes.

Julia would return to her condo, a place shrouded in loneliness and fear. It had been her haven from reality and life. So many memories of lonely nights and moments of wrestling with painful thoughts were housed within the four walls of her condo. She didn't want it to be like that anymore. Tonight, she'd tasted of true happiness, of love for someone who might be able to return that love. That was the direction in which she wanted her life to go. She wouldn't dwell on unhappiness anymore. She didn't have to.

Pablo pulled up in front of her condo and turned to her. He shrugged. "You're home now." Leisurely, they made their way to her door.

They walked with slow steps to her door. She unlocked the door and opened it, and he leaned against the doorframe.

"I had a really good time. Thanks for dinner," Julia said.

"I hope we can do it again."

"Me too."

Pablo pulled himself away from the doorframe and stood up straight. He didn't leave, just searched her eyes. She didn't flinch, didn't retreat or back away from him.

He leaned in closer and waited an instant. Slowly, he moved toward her. She was surprised by her reaction, or rather non-reaction. She stood still, waiting, anticipating. He gently pressed his lips to hers and kissed her tenderly in a way that was unfathomable to Julia. A simple and soft kiss that didn't demand anything in return. It asked no question, posed no threat, made no claim. It was a gentle sign of affection, a reassurance and a promise of further joy.

* * *

Monday morning's drive to work was an unprecedented one. Never before had anticipation awakened so many butterflies in Julia's stomach. She would be seeing Pablo in only a few moments, and remembering his kiss from Saturday night only heightened her anxiousness. She parked next to Pablo's Volkswagen. He was there already. She took a deep breath before going inside.

Turning the corner toward the office, she felt like a little girl coming down the staircase on Christmas morning. As she opened the door, she wasn't disappointed. Pablo smiled as she walked in, but it wasn't just his lips smiling. It was his eyes. It was his voice, in the way he said good morning. It was in the way his gaze followed her as she walked across the room and sat down next to him.

"Hi," she said.

"How are you this morning?"

Strained small talk, a sure sign that he was nervous too, she thought. "Good."

"Do you want to have lunch today?"

"That would be nice," she said.

"Okay, good."

Their weak attempt to bypass their nervousness through

casual conversation was interrupted by Sandra's announcement that Detective St. Peters was on the phone.

The detective was terse. The police were dropping the investigation into Avery's alleged rape.

Julia slammed the phone down. "The police are dropping the investigation. They still think Mick's their guy, and they're not going to look for other suspects. St. Peters said he's had his best two guys on it for several weeks and they haven't turned up any evidence that would implicate anyone other than Mick."

Pablo sighed. "So, what next?"

"I owe Jim a visit to see if he's turned anything up."

"I can talk to Mick and try to figure out what she was doing around those few days. Maybe she kept a day planner. I'll try to get her class schedule. Maybe it was someone in one of her classes."

As Julia drove to Jim's office, she mentally dissected her morning encounter with Pablo. It had been a bit awkward at first, but his kind smile had put her at ease. They'd instantly reverted to talking about the case, which remained the focal point of their time spent together. Julia looked forward to the date when they could look back at the Mick Webber case with only vague memories. Hopefully at that time, Mick would be a free man and Julia and Pablo would be more than just co-counsel on a case.

Jim was behind his desk when his secretary led Julia into his office. Jim signaled for her to come in as he finished up a phone call.

"I'm glad you came. I was going to pay you a visit. Have a seat."

"What's up?"

Jim pulled out a thin manila folder. "I have a copy of a work order dated February 2. It's for the east door of the women's locker room at the Huntsman Center. According to the maintenance schedule, the emergency alarm had failed two consecutive tests. It did not sound off automatically as it is programmed to do when opened. A scheduled maintenance on February 18 was not completed due to an emergency cleanup of a flood in one of the upstairs restrooms. Maintenance was redirected to take care of that. It was rescheduled, but the work order was misplaced and only recently turned up when I went over there to shake things up."

Julia took the file and skimmed it. "So this means the alarm was malfunctioning at the time of Avery's murder?"

"Was not working at all. Anyone could leave the locker room through the emergency door at any time with no alarm sounding."

"This is just what I need. This shows that anyone could have come into the locker room, killed Avery, and sneaked out the emergency exit before Mick even entered."

Jim smiled broadly. "I figured you'd be pleased."

"You're a genius."

"Oh, and one other thing. I checked the alibi on the ex-boyfriend. Airtight. He was at work the day of Avery's murder. He clocked in and everything. He's not your guy."

Julia sighed. "Oh well, I guess I can't have everything. But this will help," she said holding up the file he'd just given her.

Julia thanked Jim, and with file in hand, almost skipped on the way to her car. How could her day get any better? It did get better, though, when she met Pablo for lunch. He was pleased with the news, and they shared a pleasant lunch together. Reasonable doubt was within reach.

chapter twenty

Pablo had met with Mick earlier in the morning to go over Avery's schedule. He asked Mick detailed questions about some of the men she would have come in contact with on a daily basis. When he returned to the office, Julia asked him how it had gone with Mick.

"Okay, I guess. He mentioned a few guys she knew from an American lit study group. And I guess she took a basketball officiating class with Mick and some of his teammates."

"You think it might be one of his teammates?"

Pablo shrugged. "Could be. Mick doesn't seem to think so."

Julia opened up a new document on her computer and typed out the words "Reasonable Doubts" in large bold letters. "Okay, what do we have so far?"

"A malfunctioning alarm allows for someone to sneak out the emergency door just before Mick walks in."

Julia continued typing as he spoke.

"Avery's post of having been raped by someone she knows leaves the possibility open for a different culprit."

Julia nodded. "No history of altercation between Mick and

reasonable doubt

Avery. Everyone says they had a good relationship."

Pablo looked over her shoulder as she typed. "That's a good start. Why don't we start a list of possible suspects, starting with Avery's ex-boyfriend?"

Julia shook her head as she typed "Possible Suspects" just below their list of reasonable doubts. "Jim says he's got an airtight alibi."

"Okay, who else then?"

"Avery's coach," Julia said as she typed.

"Are we still on that?"

Julia nodded. "It is possible. We have to write everyone possible."

"Okay, then. Let's write Mick's teammates," Pablo said as he started naming the ones in her class. "There's also this Paul guy from her American Lit study group."

Pablo finished reading the screen and then took the seat next to her. "I mentioned to Mick the good news about the malfunctioning emergency exit in the women's locker room. That seemed to buoy his spirits."

Julia saved the document and then sighed. "I feel like we're still back at square one."

"I guess it's not really up to us to solve the case. We just have to go with the doubts and make sure we emphasize them for the jury. They can't convict Mick without being absolutely sure, and this list of doubts brings his culpability into question."

Julia printed out the document and shook her head.

"It's a good list, Julia," he said taking it off the printer. "You can make this case. I know you can." He put his hand on her shoulder and she leaned her cheek on it.

* * *

They worked late and walked out into the darkness. They stood still in the chilly evening. She wasn't too eager to leave his presence, and she could sense that he felt the same way.

"I hope you're not feeling too stressed," Pablo said as he lifted a hand up to her cheek and caressed it.

Her spine tingled at his touch. What was it about this man's touch that had the opposite effect of any other? The warmth in his fingertips reached her heart, and in an instant she knew she could not live her life without feeling that touch every day. She looked up to meet Pablo's eyes and wished she could see into their depths and understand the sentiments of his heart. She pushed the thought away; Mick's case took priority. She needed to think about reality and leave fairy tales for another day. Happily ever after would never be obtained if Mick were executed.

"I'll be okay," she said.

"I think we have a really good case," Pablo said. "No jury will convict Mick with so little evidence and so much doubt."

"I hope so." Julia pressed her hand on Pablo's, which had moved, from her cheek to her shoulder.

Pablo slowly pulled her into an embrace, and she welcomed it. She wrapped her arms around him and held on tight. She didn't want to let him go, not ever, not after she'd finally found the one thing she had thought would forever be out of her reach.

He smoothed her hair down with his hand. "Julia, don't carry the weight of the world on your shoulders. Please let me help you."

"I'm trying to. I want that."

He kissed her forehead and pulled away. "Go get some rest. We'll think about the case tomorrow."

She smiled. Actually, there was only one thing she wanted to think about that night as she went to bed. She wanted to close her eyes and forget about the case, to think only about the dreams that would be made sweet by a pair of dark brown eyes and the kiss that would be felt long after its trace was gone from her forehead.

"Okay, I promise," she said. "I won't think about the case tonight. Tomorrow."

"Bright and early," he said, smiling. "Tomorrow, in the light of day, we'll be able to see how good a case it is. All they have is fingerprints, Julia. That's all they have."

Julia wished it were true. It sounded good, so she would go

with it. Pablo opened her car door, and she raced home to begin her peaceful dreams of dark brown eyes and the lovely man that accompanied them.

At home, she sat down to watch the news. She took bites of her chocolate chip cookie dough ice cream. All thoughts turned to Pablo, and she paid little attention to the happenings on the television. Maybe it was the frivolity of ice cream that lightened her mood or thoughts of his gentle lips on her forehead earlier that evening, but she couldn't even concentrate on the news. Her brain felt as mushy as the remains of the ice cream in her bowl.

Her attention was quickly caught by a live shot of protesters standing outside of the main Webber Sporting Goods store. It wasn't anything new. Every couple of days the news covered the ongoing dilemma of James Webber, whose stores were being boycotted by outraged citizens who believed his son was guilty of murder. The Webbers had already closed down several stores, and their business was suffering desperately. Perhaps exoneration for Mick would also mean a resurrected business for his father.

There wasn't much difference in this segment, but Julia watched closely as a camera crew followed Mr. Webber from the store to his car. The reporter kept a microphone close as he asked Mr. Webber what he planned to do if business continued to dwindle. He largely ignored the reporter as he bypassed a small crowd.

The reporter asked him another question, this one about how he dealt with living in a city where he and his family were hated by much of the population. Mr. Webber stopped outside his car and turned around to face the reporter and mob.

"My family may be hated now, but that will all change when my son is completely exonerated of any wrongdoing."

"Do you really think this is going to happen?" the reporter asked.

"Certainly. In light of some recent findings and new evidence, we feel sure Mick will be acquitted. The private investigator who is working for Mick's attorney has found almost conclusive evidence that Mick did not commit this crime. Of course, all the evidence hasn't been released, but it will be soon. The people of this city will see that my son is innocent beyond a shadow of a doubt."

The reporter on the news kept after Mr. Webber. "What evidence?"

Mr. Webber looked around the crowd. "I can't really say, but it is conclusive evidence that someone else committed this crime."

"Conclusive evidence?" Julia dropped her spoon and stood up. "What is he talking about? What are you talking about?" she yelled at the television.

"I have no further comment," Mr. Webber said as he entered his car and the camera panned back to the reporter.

The reporter continued his reporting. "You heard it here first. James Webber, father of accused Mick Webber, has stated there is conclusive evidence that his son did not commit this crime. We will continue to follow this story and delve into this possibility."

"There is no conclusive evidence," Julia yelled at the reporter. What had provoked him to make such a declaration?

She called Pablo to see if he had seen the segment.

"What was he thinking?" Pablo asked.

"I don't know. He was desperate. We'll have to make a statement to the press. Explain the misunderstanding."

"I can start on it in the morning," Pablo offered.

"The D.A.'s going to be livid. I can't wait to get that call tomorrow."

"Don't worry about it, Julia. It wasn't anything that you did."

"I know. I'd better call Mr. Webber and tell him to keep his mouth shut."

"Don't let this get you down. We'll clean it up in the morning."

"You're right. Thanks."

"Good night, Julia."

Julia hung up the phone, feeling grateful that she had someone to call. She felt that Pablo was the kind of person she could call at any time; it was nice to have someone like that in her life.

chapter twenty-one

Julia tried to call Mr. Webber to admonish him about making any type of statements, but she couldn't get through to him. She also left a message for Jim, apologizing in advance for the barrage of phone calls he would receive tomorrow from the media, asking for a statement. As she sat down to finish her ice cream, she heard a knock on the door.

She checked the peephole; it was Mick's teammate, Brian McKay. As she opened the door, she wondered what he was doing here.

"Hi, Brian. What can I help you with?"

"Well, you said if I thought I could help with anything to contact you."

"Yes, but I meant at my office. How did you know where to find me?"

"Your secretary gave me the address."

Sandra would never do that. He was lying. Julia planted her feet firmly at her doorway and gripped the doorknob. "What information do you have?"

Brian fidgeted with his backpack, which he carried on one

shoulder. "Well, I heard on the news that you have a lead on who did this."

"I can't really talk about the case," Julia said.

"But you have proof he didn't do it?"

Julia hesitated. "I wouldn't say proof."

"Well, what is it then?"

She put her hand on her hip. "I really can't say."

"Well, why not?"

"Because it's confidential. It isn't something we're ready to release."

"Well, you know who did it, right?"

"I wouldn't say that, no."

Brian sighed and shifted his weight from one foot to the other. "Look Miss Harris, Mick is my best friend. I just need to know if he's going to be released."

Julia gripped the doorknob. "We're doing everything we can to get him exonerated."

"But how do they know he didn't do it? Is it because they know who really did it?"

"I know you're trying to help your friend, Brian, but I can't give you any information. I don't know everything."

"Well, can you please call me once you know more?" Brian asked.

Julia sighed. "I guess so," she said, since that was the only way to get rid of him.

"I have a new phone number. Let me write it down." Brian took a small notebook out of his backpack.

Julia waited as he wrote.

Brian wrote his name down next to the phone number. "It's just that he's my best friend, and I don't want to see him going through this. Every time I visit him, it's just so hard; you know, to see him like that locked up and everything."

Julia nodded her understanding. "I know it's painful to see your friend in jail." It was difficult for her as well to see Mick in jail, to know that he didn't belong there. She watched Brian's urgent face. He wanted information about his friend right now.

"He's just such a good friend, you know. I have huge love for him."

Why did that sound so familiar? Avery. Her post. Huge love. Rational or irrational, it didn't matter. She'd learned long ago that fear shouldn't be questioned. She stood frozen, hand still on the doorknob with the whites of her knuckles screaming for him to finish. He went to tear the page out of the notebook.

Just take it and shut the door, she said to herself. She extended a trembling hand to take the paper, but she couldn't look up to meet his eyes. If only time weren't going so slow. Her hand dangled in the air as she prayed for him to hurry. Brian held the paper too long and didn't give it to her right away. She could feel his stare, but she couldn't look up.

His voice turned icy; her entire body felt the chill. "What's wrong, Miss Harris?"

"Nothing," she said, finally looking up. "I'm just tired."

Fear had paralyzed her body and her face betrayed her.

"What's the matter, Miss Harris? You look scared."

Fear was coursing through her veins, but she couldn't let him see that. "No." She shook her head. "I'm fine, just tired. It's been a long day."

Brian put his hand up and thrust it against the door, holding it open. "You're lying. You know something." He looked down both corridors and then came in closer. "Now, tell me," he said in deliberately enunciated words.

"Brian, I already told you. We don't know anything. Mr. Webber was shooting his mouth off. There is no conclusive evidence." Julia looked at Brian's hand, which he still held firmly against the door. There was no way she'd be able to close the door against his strength. Still, she kept her grip on the doorknob.

"What do you know?" Brian demanded.

"Nothing. The only new evidence we found was that the emergency door of the woman's locker room was malfunctioning the night of the murder. That's all we know," Julia said, turning to look at Brian's hand still on the door. How could she get him to leave? Was he the one? She quivered, and he caught her look. She'd given herself away; she'd let him see the fear.

With one swift and powerful movement, he hit his palm against the door, sending her backward a few steps. He cursed and then swung the door violently behind him. As he entered the condo, he walked toward her.

Julia felt herself paralyze. He was a formidable opponent, but she'd thrown down heartier men on a judo mat. For some reason, all those years of self-defense vanished from her memory almost as if they'd never occurred. Her body weakened, and she felt as though she was literally shrinking, becoming that young girl who was hurt so many years before.

Brian stood in front of her, his figure towering over her shrunken being. "What do you know?" he asked through gritted teeth.

Julia shook her head. Words escaped her.

Brian grabbed her shoulders and jolted her body slightly. "Tell me."

Shaking her head, she fought to regain her voice. "Noth— Nothing. Look, we're just trying to get Mick off. We don't know who did it. It doesn't even matter as long as we get Mick off."

Brian released her and turned to the side. "You're lying!" he said as he brought his hand down and slapped her face.

Julia grabbed her face and stepped back, trying to focus on the present. She was not eighteen years old, this was not Matthew, and she would not be a victim again. Not ever again. "You need to leave. Now," she said.

"Why are you scared, Julia?"

"Why did you hit me?"

"Because you're lying. I can see the fear in your eyes. You're scared of me." Brian took a step toward Julia and grabbed her hair near the nape of her neck.

Julia held Brian's wrist, trying to pry his fingers from the agonizing hold he had on her hair.

"Why are you scared?" he repeated, this time more angrily.

"Because you're hurting me."

He shook her head. "Don't play with me. Why were you scared before?"

Julia closed her eyes to shut out the pain, but equally painful memories flooded into her mind. Matthew's angry face, along with his ferocious blows ran through her mind. *This isn't Matthew and you are not weak,* she said to herself. But the words didn't translate to reality. "Let me go."

Brian continued his cruel hold on her hair and brought her head up toward his. He looked right into her eyes. "You know, don't you? Why don't you just say it?"

Julia screamed. Surely someone would hear her. The condo walls were thin; she could always hear her neighbor blasting U2. Her scream was obliterated by Brian's pronounced fist hitting her jaw. She grabbed her face just as he let go of her hair. Julia took a step back, holding her jaw with both her hands. She hadn't felt that sort of pain for many years, but she remembered it well. It was that pain that had forced her to submit to a vicious man's attack so many years before, but not today. Today she would die before she allowed it to happen again.

"Why'd you do it, Brian?" she asked with newfound courage. Or perhaps it wasn't courage at all, but the fearless thought that it didn't matter what she said. She was almost certainly facing death.

"She would have loved me if it wasn't for him," he said.

He didn't come after her. He didn't hit her again. "Is that why you killed her?"

"Shut up! You don't know anything."

Julia backed away from him. If she could just make it to the door, she might be able to run for it. She took a tiny step backward, her hand still holding her now throbbing jaw.

"This was all Mick's fault. He had to have everything!" Brian ran a frantic hand over his forehead.

A tiny step toward the door had Julia's heart beating faster. She was almost there, and from what she could see he didn't have a weapon. She took another small step.

"Where are you going?" he growled as he grabbed her hair with one hand and jerked her toward him.

Julia yelled as she felt a rush of pain in her head. He didn't need a weapon; a single hand forced her into submission. He held his fist tightly around the length of her hair, and Julia bent forward to relieve the pain from her scalp.

"I don't want to hurt you, Julia, but you're making me do it. Just like Avery. I loved her. I didn't want to hurt her, but she left me no choice."

Julia scanned her memory for the lesson learned long ago about what to do in such a situation. Something about using your body as leverage. Julia couldn't remember what any of her self-defense instructors had said. She should know; she should remember. She had vowed long ago to never be in such a situation again.

Brian released his grip on her hair but then grabbed her wrist. "Don't do this, Julia. Don't make me do this."

"I can help you, Brian. I'm a great lawyer. We can get you out of this."

"You're lying. Why would you help me?"

"If you let me go . . ."

Brian held her wrist tightly and shook his head. "No, Mick's going down for this. It's all his fault. He's the one who ruined everything."

Julia grimaced against the pain.

"I deserved the starting spot on the team. I deserved to have Avery. She was too good for him. I told her that. We used to have such good talks, but then he proposed, and it was like I didn't exist anymore. She told me to leave her alone, that she thought we should only be friends. But I convinced her she was wrong. I convinced her we should make love, and when we did she became mine."

"You raped her!" Julia said, pulling her wrist out of his grip.

"No. I convinced her!"

"That's not convincing. That's rape, you freak!"

"It's her fault. She's the one who belittled what we shared when she slept with Mick."

"She told me to leave her alone, or she was going to tell Mick what I did. She told me Mick wanted them to move the wedding up, and she was going to agree. They were going to talk to their bishop that day and that Mick was probably waiting for her outside. She didn't want to tell me why they were moving the date up, not until I showed her my knife. I was only going to scare her into telling me, but she made me do it. She said she had slept with Mick and couldn't wait to marry him. That's when I knew she would have to pay. And she paid."

During his moment of enraged reminiscing, Julia made a run for the door and almost had it opened when she felt Brian throw her against the door from behind.

He flipped her around and pinned her against the door. He brought both hands up to her neck and squeezed. "Do you really want to know what happened to Avery?" he asked. "Well, you're about to find out."

Julia shut her eyes as she felt Brian squeeze harder. When she opened them again, his wild eyes showed that he meant what he'd said. With what little force she could muster against his debilitating hold, she pressed her fists against his chest. She brought her knee up with a sharp thrust toward his groin. It caused him to release his hold on her neck as he grabbed himself. She brought her knee up again and kicked him in the chest, throwing her whole body into it.

Although he was a large man, it jarred him back a few steps and gave her time to open the door and run out. Julia ran wildly down the corridor screaming for anyone to help. She could see Brian running after her and she quickened her pace down the stairs until she reached the parking lot. There was a couple coming toward her and she ran right into them.

"Help me," she screamed as she grabbed hold of them. Just as she stopped, she turned around to see Brian run in the opposite direction toward the street. "Call the police," she said out of breath.

The woman pulled her cell phone out of her purse and dialed quickly. The man took off after Brian, only to come back and report that he had jumped into a car and fled down the street.

The woman handed the phone to the man and then put her arm around Julia. "Are you okay?"

Julia nodded numbly. "I will be. Thanks for being here."

"They're on their way," the man reported as he gave the phone back to the woman.

"Why don't you come into our place and we can wait for the police there?" the woman asked.

Julia followed the couple up the steps to their condo. "Can I use your phone?"

The woman gave it to her and Julia stepped away to dial Pablo's number. When he answered, all she could do was cry. Sobs that had been building up within her swelled to excess and erupted.

"What's the matter, Julia?" he asked.

"I need you" was all she could say amidst her tears.

"I'll be right there. Are you home?"

She nodded, but of course Pablo couldn't see that. The sobbing started again, along with involuntary shaking. The woman who was just behind her took the phone and recounted what she had seen, along with her condo number.

The woman took Julia in her arms and held her until she could control the sobbing and shaking. Julia nodded her thanks but couldn't speak.

chapter twenty-two

Pablo parked in the empty spot at an angle and raced toward the line of condos, searching for the number the woman had given him over the phone. Several uniformed police officers were in the corridor, and he jogged toward them. He entered the condo and spotted Julia on a couch, talking to an officer.

She saw him walk in and quickly stood up. He'd never seen her like that, tear-streaked face and arms hugging herself tightly. He walked past an officer and she hurried to him. Julia melted into his arms amidst sobs of terror, like she'd been holding them in and saving them for him. He didn't ask her any questions; she couldn't talk. He tightened his embrace and caressed her hair as she cried in gasps. Pablo didn't care that all eyes in the room were on them. He only worried about the fragile woman in his arms. Fragility was not a word usually associated with this stalwart woman, but at the moment that was the only way to describe her. It was also the way he felt inside. He didn't know what had happened, only that she'd been in danger. Something, someone, had penetrated Julia's usual steel exterior and had left her petrified. He didn't like the way it made him feel—vulnerable, afraid, out of his mind. What if something had happened to her? What if she'd been hurt? The thought of losing her scared him, and he squeezed her harder. Her sobbing subsided, but her grip around his waist remained.

He kissed the top of her head and wondered how he'd live if she weren't right here, right now, in his arms. He couldn't bear the thought and kissed her again.

An officer approached. "Mr. Torres?"

Pablo nodded. "What happened?"

At his question, Julia pulled slightly away and looked up at him, a little composed.

"It was Brian," she said before the police officer could speak.

"Brian?" Pablo asked looking down at Julia who was still in his embrace.

"Brian McKay, Mick's friend. He's the one who killed Avery."

Pablo let out a breath. "So is he in custody?" he asked the officer.

"No. The suspect fled the scene before we arrived. There's an APB out on him, and we have several units scouring the neighborhood. We have a description of the vehicle and are working on the plates."

Pablo nodded. "Are you okay?" he asked, turning to Julia.

Julia straightened up from her slumped position in his arms. She pulled slightly away, now only his arm rested around her shoulder. "I will be. Thank you for coming."

"Miss Harris, we'll need you to come down to the station tomorrow to sign your statement. We'll keep you posted on any developments." He pulled out a card and gave it to Julia. "Call me if you need anything. We'll place a car outside the complex to keep an eye on the place, in case he comes back."

Julia nodded. "Thank you."

The officer explained that they would take a few moments to survey her condo since it was the crime scene. Julia thanked the couple whose condo they were in and then followed the officers down to her place.

The officers lifted fingerprints, took pictures, and made notes. Pablo knew Julia had been at crime scenes before; it was part of her job. The invasion of her home by the officers was part of their job, but he felt like they were trampling her privacy. Intimate details of her life were on display and they took their time in withdrawing minute fragments of what was hers.

There was a bowl of the melted remains of uneaten ice cream on her desk. A few scattered files lay on the carpet near her chair. There was a backpack near the door. One of the officers picked it up with a gloved hand and placed it in a large plastic bag, which he sealed. He wasn't sure how long they stayed, but the interminable moments in which he watched them rifle through Julia's living room were tolerable only because she was right by his side and his arm was safely around her.

The police officers left, and Pablo stayed with Julia in her condo. He didn't know exactly what had happened here, but he could feel the ominous presence in the room.

Julia walked to the couch and, pulling her legs up, hugged her knees toward herself. Pablo took the seat next to hers.

"Are you sure you're okay?"

"I will be," she said, forcing a smile.

"You want to talk about it?" Pablo knew what Brian was capable of.

"I haven't been that scared in a long time."

Pablo reached over and squeezed her shoulder, leaving his arm there. "Did he hurt you?"

Julia rubbed her face tenderly. "He hit me twice. They're physical marks; they'll heal."

Pablo moved closer to Julia and pulled her gently toward him. Brian had hurt her. Pablo's hand involuntarily formed into a fist. "Tell me what happened."

Julia used few words to recount what had occurred, beginning with Brian's knock on the door and ending with her knee in his groin.

"You're very brave, Julia."

She scoffed. "I don't feel brave. Besides, I let him get away."

"You were protecting yourself. It's what you had to do." Pablo took her hand.

Julia shook her head. "I just let him go. He's getting away with it again. I let him get away with it again. Don't you see that?"

"He's not getting away with anything. As soon as they find him, he will pay for everything."

"He's going to get away with it again," Julia said, almost trancelike, almost as if she hadn't heard a word he'd said.

Julia was so much like a lost little girl, compared to the confident, if sometimes arrogant, woman he knew. How he wished for her arrogance to reemerge at that precise moment. Was she referring to Brian when she said, "He's getting away with it again," or was she thinking back to Matthew? "Julia," he said quietly.

"I could have done something, but he just went on with his life, almost as if he hadn't done anything to me. I'm the one who's been in prison all these years paying for his crime, and he's heaven-knows-where, living his life like an innocent man! I hate him!"

"Julia," Pablo said, placing a hand on her shaking figure. "This wasn't Matthew. This is Brian, and he's not going to get away with anything. He will pay. They'll find him."

"What if they don't?"

"They will."

Julia sat up and pulled away. "But what if they don't?"

"You think he'll come back?"

Julia nodded as tears threatened to emerge, and her lower lip quivered. She looked away.

Pablo took her hand again and whispered in her ear. "I won't let him come within a mile of you, even if I have to spend every waking moment at your side and every sleeping moment on your couch."

"You'll sleep on my couch?" she asked, turning toward him.

Pablo smiled at her. "I think I remember this couch being particularly comfortable, and there was a very soft blanket around here somewhere," he said, looking around.

Julia smiled back. "You're sure you don't mind sleeping on my couch?"

"Only if you're comfortable with it," Pablo said, remembering a time when she most certainly wouldn't have been.

"I don't think I'll sleep tonight, knowing he's still out there, but it will help if you stay. I know there will be an officer outside, but I want you to stay, if you will."

Pablo kissed her hand. "I'm so glad you're okay. I don't know what . . . I don't know; I'm just glad you're okay."

Julia smiled and nodded. She sniffled and wiped a stray tear away. "We need to tell Mick."

"Mick," Pablo said. He'd almost forgotten that this involved their case. It'd become too personal for him today, but yes, there was still Mick's case.

"What will he say when he finds out it was Brian?"

Pablo shook his head. "I don't know. They were friends. It's going to be hard for Mick."

They decided to wait until the next day to give Mick the news. By then, perhaps Brian would be in custody.

Pablo looked at his watch. It was almost past ten. Julia sat on the couch, staring at the door. He wondered how far today's incident would set Julia back. She'd come a long way in trusting people since he'd first met her. She was a different Julia.

He reached over and pulled her close. She didn't pull away or hesitate. Instead, Julia buried her face in his chest and clung to him. Pablo sighed, relieved that his nearness didn't evoke fear or repulsion as once it had. Now that she was close to him, he didn't want her to ever be out of reach—physically or emotionally. He needed her, and he would spend every waking moment from this point forth proving to her that she needed him too.

"Are you tired? Are you going to go to bed?" he asked.

"Not yet. I like it right here."

"I'm glad you're okay," he said for probably the tenth time that night. It was only a fraction of the times he'd thought it, though. "I can't tell you what I was feeling driving over here and not knowing what had happened." He stroked her hair.

"Thank you for coming. You were the first person I thought of calling."

Pablo squeezed her shoulder and kissed her forehead. They sat together on the couch, quietly savoring the moment. He wanted to hold her this way until he could dispel the helplessness he'd felt since she called him. After a while, Julia said she would try to go to bed. A half hour later, Pablo tiptoed to Julia's door. It was ajar. He watched her sleeping for only a moment, grateful for her safety. He never wanted to be too far away from Julia.

chapter twenty-three

Julia sat upright upon awakening. The dream had come again, and she instinctively looked out the window, but it wasn't raining. The thunderous sounds had only seemed real in her sleep, but the coldness that enveloped her was authentic. She rubbed her arms and tried to focus on reality, leaving behind the nightmare that would revisit her slumber another night.

Brian. She remembered now. A momentary panic caused her to take a better look out the window to check if the police car was still there. It was. She relaxed for an instant and then remembered that Pablo had spent the night on her couch. Julia walked over to her dresser and looked at herself in the mirror. A purple hue spread across her cheek. A quick glance caused her to recoil, and then she remembered the pain. She gingerly fingered her bruises, not knowing which was worse: how she looked or how she felt. Anger seeped into her core; she would make Brian pay. Fear would not impact her decision to bring Brian to justice. If not for herself, then for Avery. She ran a brush through her hair and went into the living room. Pablo was in the kitchen. He was chopping green peppers.

He turned around as she walked in. "How are you feeling?"

"Okay." She subconsciously touched the bruises on her face.

His eyes went immediately to where her fingers stroked her cheek. "I thought food would help you feel better. How about an omelet?"

"You sure do know me."

Pablo beat the eggs with a small whisk and then poured the mixture onto a hot pan. It sizzled, and he spent the next few minutes expertly tending to it. Julia watched Pablo's hands as he easily folded the omelet. His movements were graceful and flawless, and she was impressed by the finesse with which he cooked. He flipped the omelet onto a plate and brought it over to the table where she sat. He smiled and sat down beside her.

"Aren't you going to eat?" she asked.

"You start. I'll make myself one in a few minutes."

She took a bite and savored it, not just for its delectable taste, but also because of the one who'd prepared it. Pablo cared for her, and it showed in how he'd offered to stay the night, in how he ministered to her this morning, but more than anything in how he'd looked at her last night. He'd been frightened that Brian had hurt her, and it felt good to matter to someone. Especially someone like Pablo.

She ate quickly and then went to shower. The warm water soothed her aching muscles. Her body was feeling the full effect of Brian's anger from the night before. She rubbed the tender spots from the injuries he'd inflicted. Physical pain made way for emotional anguish of reopened wounds from long ago. Yesterday's attack had brought back vivid memories that she'd spent more than a decade burying. Memories and pain that had never been dealt with were now forcing their way back to the surface.

Tears mixed with cleansing water from the showerhead. The pulsating water drowned out her sobbing, and she cried as painful memories resurfaced and mingled with her present ache. She let the water wash away the still lingering tears and hoped the torment would go down the drain, but pain was inevitable and would likely reemerge one day. For now, she hoped it would give her some semblance of peace, if only for one day.

They went to the county jail to see Mick. Julia had forgotten what she looked like until she saw Mick's expression.

"Julia, what happened?"

She felt Pablo's warm hand on her shoulder. "We have some good news," he said.

"What kind of good news comes from this?" Mick asked, signaling to her face.

"I had a run-in with Avery's killer."

"A run-in? Who?"

"It was Brian," Pablo said.

"McKay." Mick exhaled, like he'd been holding his breath in for an immeasurable amount of time.

"Brian came to my condo last night. I think he was worried that we had some evidence linking him to the crime. Your father's impromptu press conference had him anxious."

Mick nodded, taking in the life-saving words. He'd probably imagined how this moment would be. Vindication. It had come at last.

"His actions were suspicious, and then it just made sense." Julia told him what had happened. Saying the words solidified the events, almost in a tangible form that she could pack away. Recounting what had happened helped soothe the still-painful wounds, and she hoped one day she could put them to rest.

Mick nodded as she told her story, as if he was putting together the pieces of a jigsaw puzzle and would delay reaction until it was complete. Julia finished her account by informing him that Brian was still at large.

Mick slammed the table in front of him. Then he slammed it again. He looked up at them, his jaw set, his eyes wild with anger. "When can I get out of here? I'll find him." He clenched his fists, his knuckles white like fire. "When can I get out of here?" he yelled.

Julia jumped at his sudden rise in tone. Pablo put a calming hand on Mick's clenched fist, and he immediately pushed it off.

"Mick. Mick, you cannot do this. The D.A. will nail Brian. You can count on it."

Mick looked at Pablo. He opened his mouth to say something, but then he bent forward on the table and pounded it with his fist. The rhythm of his sobbing accompanied the heavy pounding.

There wasn't anything they could do for him. She looked at Pablo for help. He frowned, but said nothing.

They gave him a few minutes to recuperate, but how do you recuperate from finding out that your friend raped and killed your fiancée?

Julia walked over to Mick and placed her hand on his trembling back. She leaned down and whispered in his ear. "I'm so sorry, Mick. You can't let this destroy you. She wouldn't want it."

His weeping continued at the mention of Avery. He stopped the pounding and moved his hands to his face, and the sobbing continued.

"You can spend the rest of your days hating him and hiding from your life, or you can use the life God gave you. Use it, Mick. It does no good to hate; you only end up hating yourself for letting life pass you by."

Mick shook his head. He didn't want to hear those words. Julia hoped she didn't sound trite, but she knew what hate was. When you dwell on it, it makes way for self-loathing, and happiness can never find you. She'd realized it almost too late, but another chance was looming. Maybe one day Mick would embrace that chance.

Mick pleaded for them to go, and he was led back to his cell. It was the place where he'd suffered since the day Avery died.

They left the room. It was probably the last time she would visit Mick there. Pablo put his arm around her shoulder, and she pulled him closer.

"You okay?" he asked as they walked down the corridor.

She nodded.

"We should go so you can sign your statement from last night."

"That's right." Julia had almost forgotten about the night before. One day Matthew would completely depart from her daily thoughts, and she would be able to focus on the present.

As she read over the statement, the events from the night before came alive again. Pablo was beside her, and she was grateful for his incalculable support. But Brian was still out there, and fear of him remained.

* * *

Pablo left Julia at the office and went home to shower and change. Julia was safe at the office, with a police car parked outside. He'd been hesitant about leaving her, but Brian wouldn't go there. He was a coward. He attacked his victims when they were alone and vulnerable. In the presence of others, he ran from his prey. But he would emerge soon; he couldn't stay hidden forever. They would find him. The system didn't always work, but this time it would.

He couldn't believe this journey was coming to an end. Mick's case: it had been what he and Julia subsisted on for the past few months. It had been what drove them, the impetus of every working hour. Mick's case is what had bound him to Julia, what had allowed their lives to be woven together. And during those arduous hours of piecing together Mick's defense, moments of intense feelings had seeped into their lives.

The previous night's near tragedy had created feelings that were too real. He witnessed Julia's vulnerability, saw the bruises inflicted by a madman, and knew that past memories were haunting her anew. He wanted to erase her pain, to obliterate the wounds that tortured her, but he couldn't. All he could do was be there, feel for her.

Julia's inhibitions drew him. He wanted to show her that the world could be a good place where one's life could be blessed by sharing it with others. She wanted it too; he knew that. At moments, she'd allowed him to see that there was a light and love inside her, screaming to come out. She wanted to share that sacred part of her but was afraid. He wanted to be the one to show her it was possible to open up to someone without being hurt, to love someone and be loved in return.

Did he love Julia? The intense fear of losing her last night solidified it. He did love her. He wanted to join his life with hers just as they had joined together in Mick's defense, but would it work? Did she even want a relationship? Work accompanied her home at nights and on weekends. She ate most meals in front of the computer. He had ended his relationship with Christina because she wanted to go to medical school, to set aside family to focus on a career. Julia's career drove her life; would there be room for him? Did she want children? Her goal was to become a partner in the law firm. Would she sacrifice that for a family? Could he ask her to?

He was supposed to take care of his family, provide for them. His father's callused hands were evidence of a life devoted to hard work so he could provide for his family. Pablo had known that since childhood. It was why he'd worked tirelessly to excel in school. He wanted to be a good provider; it's what men in his family did. Julia didn't need that from him.

As he pulled on a crisp white shirt and buttoned it, he looked at himself in the mirror. He'd let Christina go because she didn't fit into the picture. She didn't allow herself be molded into the final piece that would complete his life. With Julia, the mere thought that she would wander out of his life was devastating. He wondered if fitting into the plan he'd created for himself mattered anymore.

He tightened the knot on his tie and then combed his still-wet hair. He hurried back to the office; he needed to know how Julia was.

Back in the office, Julia stood trembling in front of the TV. He peered over her shoulder and saw that it was a live feed of the news.

"What are you watching?" Pablo asked as he came to stand by Julia's side, his hand reaching for her shoulder.

"They found him," she said.

Pablo watched the TV. A helicopter was following a car as it sped down a stretch of highway. "Where?"

"Just outside of Wendover."

Brian's red Jeep was speeding on I-80 with two police cruisers in pursuit. The helicopter followed them in the air. That stretch of highway was never congested, so Brian passed only an occasional car. The police cars kept up the speed, but Brian made no attempt to stop.

The newscaster recounted that a truck driver had recognized the car and license plate number from the news coverage earlier that morning. The truck driver had called the police and alerted several news organizations.

Pablo and Julia watched in silence as the police continued the high-speed pursuit. Julia chewed on a fingernail and Pablo kept his arm around her.

Bob and Adam came into the office, followed by Sandra. They gathered around the TV next to where he and Julia stood.

"I can't believe this guy's trying to outrun the police," Adam said. He snickered and shook his head.

Bob stood next to Julia. "They'll get him," he said to her.

"I'm calling Arthur," Sandra said, picking up Julia's extension.

They stood transfixed in front of the TV for several minutes as the Jeep veered around cars in the next lane. The police cruisers continued behind it.

"He's got to be going close to a hundred," Adam said. He sat on the corner of Julia's desk. He shook his head and laughed, like he was watching someone play a video game. His intense gaze went beyond curiosity; it bordered on a morbid delight of danger.

"Arthur's watching at home," Sandra announced after she hung up the phone. She came to stand closer to the TV.

Brian passed a slower-moving semitruck, and as he pulled in front of it, his Jeep swerved. The brake lights indicated that Brian was trying to slow down. Then he overcorrected. The Jeep skidded across the highway and rolled over onto the shoulder. The camera focused in on Brian's now-still Jeep, which lay on its side. The police cars came to a stop nearby.

"Oh, man!" Adam yelled out as he clapped his hands. "What an idiot."

The police officers approached the Jeep with guns drawn. The door opened and Brian jumped out with arms in the air. They rushed toward him and quickly placed him in handcuffs.

"I can't believe he just stepped right out," Bob said.

The live coverage ended and the news anchor took over, summing up what had occurred.

Julia let out a long breath that she'd apparently been holding in. She looked around her office as if she just now noticed that everyone was there.

"I'm sure they'll call us as soon as they hear anything," Pablo said.

Julia nodded. "They'll have to bring him back to Salt Lake. It will probably be hours before we hear anything."

Sandra squeezed Julia's arm and then, at the sound of the phone ringing in the front, left the room. Bob's cell phone rang, and he followed Sandra out.

Adam got up from where he sat on the corner of Julia's desk. "Well, I've got to hand it to you, Julia. You keep things interesting. You couldn't just go to trial; you had to go and solve the case too. I guess you really do want to be partner."

"Adam," Pablo said in warning.

Julia walked past Adam and toward her chair. "Don't you have any work to do?"

Adam slid his hands into his pockets and started to walk out. Then, he turned around to face Julia, who was now seated. "Seriously, I'm glad you're okay."

Julia stared at Adam. Without anything further, he walked out.

"Was that really Adam?" Pablo asked, equally surprised at his parting words.

Julia nodded. "I think so."

"How do you feel?"

"I don't know. Relieved, I guess. But I don't know what to do now. Mick's case is solved, but he's still in jail. I don't have any other cases. I'm sort of in limbo."

"Why don't we work on the motion to have Mick's case dismissed? Maybe in a few hours we'll hear from the police. Once Brian is back in Salt Lake, they'll question him about Avery's murder. We might have some answers then."

That's what Julia needed to hear. She opened a document on her computer and began typing the words that would ask the judge to dismiss Mick's case.

That afternoon, Pablo filed the motion, and they waited to hear back from the court. Finally, Detective St. Peters called. Pablo and Julia listened on speakerphone as he spoke.

"I questioned McKay myself. He was in denial for several hours. He finally confessed to killing Miss Thomas. Said he only intended to scare her, wanted her to break up with Webber. He said he'd sneaked into the women's locker room during practice and waited for her in the shower. After all the other players had left, he confronted her. He admits to leaving via the emergency exit and had been surprised when the alarm didn't go off. He also confessed to the rape. He claims he thought it would bind her to him."

"Sounds like a good confession," Pablo said.

"Very clean. His attorney was present and everything. It sounds like he wants to cop a plea, doesn't want to go to trial and risk capital murder charges."

"So what are the charges going to be?" Julia asked.

"It's up to the D.A. I'm hoping he'll add assault charges for what he did to you."

"He'd better," Julia said into the speakerphone.

Pablo placed a hand on her shoulder and squeezed. She might finally see some justice on her behalf.

"I'll keep you posted," the detective said before hanging up.

Julia looked up at Pablo and smiled. "I guess we'd better go get our client's case dismissed. You ready?"

"Ready."

* * *

They took their appointed places inside the courtroom and waited for the bailiff to bring Mick in. It was the first time she'd seen him out of the standard issue jumpsuit. He was wearing a black suit with a red tie. His usual pallor had gained a rosy tint and his brown eyes had lost their dullness. He was escorted to Julia's side, and she squeezed his hand. The action surprised her; she'd never done that with a client. But Mick wasn't just a client. He'd become so much more.

He symbolized the culmination of various aspects of her life. It was her greatest success as an attorney despite not having gone to trial. She'd had a small part in saving his life and in his vindication. He'd probably sealed her fate as partner of the law firm. Most importantly, he'd been the galvanizing force in her relationship with Pablo. If it weren't for Mick's case, she would not have had the daily interaction with Pablo that made it possible for her to fall in love with him. For all those reasons, she looked at Mick as someone who had forever changed her life.

The bailiff called for those in attendance to stand as Judge Walters entered the courtroom and motioned for Julia to proceed.

"Your Honor, the defense would like to bring forth a motion to have this case dismissed. Brian McKay has confessed to the murder."

The judge read through the file in his hand and then took off his reading glasses. He looked at Julia. "Is this what he did to you?"

"Yes, your Honor. In light of the new testimony and because there is no real evidence that my client committed the crime, I move that all charges be dropped. There is neither motive nor eyewitness. All the state has is fingerprints on the murder weapon that occurred when my client removed it from the victim's body."

"And you, Mr. Meyers. Any objections?"

Landon Meyers glared at Julia and then turned to the Judge. "Your Honor, the prosecution would leave it to the discretion of the court."

"Very well, the court accepts the defense's motion. This case is dismissed. All charges are dropped. The defendant is free to go."

Mick embraced Julia and Pablo collectively and then turned to his parents seated behind him. Julia looked to Pablo and melted into his arms. He held her and she felt safe in his strong arms. It was a place she'd dreamt of for so long and she didn't want to leave her newfound haven. He released her, and Mick and his parents approached them.

"Thank you so much," Mick said, hugging them again.

His parents expressed gratitude amidst tears. Julia watched Mick's reunion with his family and got caught up in the emotion. Arthur was seated in the last row. He gave her a thumbs-up. She walked toward him and greeted him.

"Arthur, you're here."

He stood up. "I had to come see you win your case."

"I didn't exactly win. The case was dismissed."

"You won."

Julia beamed. "It's so good to see you."

"I guess I should tell Sandra to order the new letterhead. Stanley and Torres. How's that sound?"

"What? He's only been here for a month."

Arthur laughed and brought a hand to his chest. "Oh, Julia. There was never any question; you must know that. Who else would I choose as my partner? Of course it's you. Stanley and Torres," he repeated.

"Arthur, you aren't making any sense."

"In the five years I've known you, I've never seen you embrace a man in the manner you did Pablo. There's something there. I can see it in the way you look at each other. Hang on to him, Julia. He's a good man. You couldn't find a better husband, and I don't think he could find a better wife."

Julia bit her lip and looked away. She tried to dispel the sudden warmth and coloring that came to her cheeks.

"I'll tell Sandra to hold off on the letterhead. You let me know what you decide. Julia Torres. I like the sound of that."

Julia looked back at Arthur, unable to hide a smile. "I'll let you know."

"Congratulations, partner." Arthur extended his hand and Julia shook it.

"Thank you." Julia's smile widened. Partnership—it had driven her for so long. Was it possible that it would be enhanced by marriage?

Arthur walked over to where Pablo stood with Mick. After shaking Pablo's hand, he moved over to Mick. Pablo caught her eye and he walked toward her.

"Arthur offered me the partnership."

Pablo smiled and took her hand. "Congratulations. You deserve it. I never had any doubt."

"Thanks."

"You must be on cloud nine."

"You can't even imagine."

He interlaced his fingers with hers. "I think I can. So what else did Arthur say?"

"I'm not telling."

He guided her toward the door, and they exited the courtroom. Ahead of them stood a group of reporters who had coalesced to await a statement. Pablo and Julia paused a moment before addressing them.

"You'll do great," he said as he let go of her hand.

She nodded and then turned toward the crowd, but he took hold of her arm and stopped her. "Tell me this is only the beginning."

"It's only the beginning."

Pablo looked at the crowd of reporters and then back at Julia. "They can wait, but this can't. I love you, and I worry that once this case is behind us, everything will be different between us."

"It will be different. Good different." Julia looked away, not at the reporters, not at anything. She'd never said it before. She looked back at him. "I love you."

He smiled and then slowly unclasped her arm.

Julia took a step in the direction of the crowd and then

paused. She leaned toward Pablo. "Arthur said he might order letterhead that reads 'Stanley and Torres' for the law firm. I told him I'd let him know."

Pablo furrowed his eyebrows and then his lips relaxed into a smile. "I like the sound of that. Tell him it gets my vote."

Julia smiled and turned toward the reporters.

"Is that a yes then?" Pablo whispered to her as they approached the throng of microphones.

"Yes," she whispered back and then leaned in toward the microphones.

Marcia Argueta Mickelson was born in Guatemala but grew up mostly in New Jersey. In high school, she started writing her first novel, which she didn't finish until ten years later. She graduated from BYU with a degree in American studies. There, she met her husband, Nolan. Upon graduating, she worked for a nonprofit organization in Salt Lake City, running a foster care program.

When Nolan graduated, Marcia convinced him to move to New Jersey, where they started a family and lived for five years. They now live in San Antonio, Texas, with their three sons: Omar, Diego, and Ruben.

Marcia stays busy by substitute teaching in local elementary schools and writing. She enjoys reading, watching movies, scrapbooking, and playing with her boys.

She is the author of *Star Shining Brightly*, also published by Cedar Fort. For more information about Marcia and her books, go to www.marciamickelson.com.